THE NIGHT HAG

THE LAMIA SEQUEL

STEVEN G. JACKSON

King Family Press
Shanghai
San Francisco

Book Cover and Interior Design by Monkey C Media
Edited by Sandra Homicz
Author Photo by Ryan C. Jackson

First Edition
Printed in the United States of America

ISBN: 978-1-7355528-2-8 (Trade Paperback)
ISBN: 978-1-7355528-3-5 (Ebook)

Library of Congress Control Number: 2020923145

This is dedicated to Sean, Ryan, Melody, and Tiffany, who are the best examples of young adults imaginable. I hope all of your dreams come true.

CHAPTER 1

Vatican City State

Snared inside a vampire bat's dead body. Locked within a silver-lined box. Buried deep in the Vatican's library vaults, the demon Lilith seethed.

Within the silver prison, the demon had no access to the outside world. Lilith thrashed, knocking the bat's lifeless, useless body against the metal walls. *Trapped for eternity in this dead bat. A damning vexation! I am meant for greatness. Not this penal state.*

And yet, the entombment remained a gruesome reality. Continuous attempts to escape had failed. Every time she abandoned the bat, she ended up in an eternal darkness, spiraling toward an undeserved hell, with nowhere to turn but back into her decaying host, the rotting bat.

Lilith shrieked. *Unable to complete my mission. Unable to transfer to another host. Incapable of possessing and turning young girls into lamias. Caged, while humans pretend this world is theirs.*

Lilith flashed back to the Awà and Father Chancho exorcising her from the Taylor girl. There in the Bribri village high in the mountains of Costa Rica she fled into the nearest unholy body, a vampire bat. The very one that now encaged her.

A trap I didn't see coming. I underestimated Morgan. I named him The Arrogant Loser, but my confidence cost me everything. After thousands of years, I should have known better.

And the girl. *My Taylor.* Unfinished business, that one.

Without warning, Lilith's silver cell rattled. Lilith shook like a bucking bronco, deep within the bat's rotting carcass.

Then, a noise. Like metal being cut. Followed by the screeching sound of silver against silver.

The lid opened, exposing a wrinkled man with shriveled hands in a burgundy robe and a pointed hat. Lilith recognized the garb from centuries earlier.

Despite the holy uniform, Lilith sensed unholiness welcoming her. *I'm free!* Seconds before possessing her new victim Lilith detected someone else. *Siren-like. Bewitching.*

A teenage girl, blindfolded and weeping, stood next to the man.

"Don't worry, my child," Lilith whispered into the girl's mind. "I will make you invincible."

Lilith swooped into the young woman.

CHAPTER 2

Salem, Oregon

Dr. Richard Morgan sat with his arm around his daughter Taylor watching TV in his living room, with Linda Copeland sprawled next to him, each wearing casual sweats. His yellow lab Bear slept at his feet. On the evening news, a CDC rep explained the Salem quarantine was over, and the Hantavirus, carried by local rodents, had been contained and eradicated.

So that's how they explain the unexplainable.

"I didn't expect them to tell the truth," Linda said, "but Hantavirus?"

Morgan lowered his voice and did his best Jack Nicholson impression. "They can't handle the truth."

Taylor squirmed. "Why would they lie? Is that what I had?"

Morgan's insides clenched. *Can Taylor handle the truth?* He clutched her tighter. "You picked up a different virus in Costa Rica. Nothing to worry about." He thought about the demon, Lilith, eternally trapped inside the silver box. "You're okay now, and that's all that matters."

He felt the warmth of Linda nestled into him. A blaze fired his face. *I'm finally turning the corner on my relationships. This one feels so right.* Gray streaked the long locks at her temples, much like what he'd seen in his own reflection, although his brown hair helped camouflage it more than her black. *Too much stress. Losing her daughter and facing the demon.* He kissed her cheek, grateful she was interested in him after all they'd been through. *Probably* because *of all we've been through.*

A text message buzzed. "Sorry," Linda said. "Forgot to turn my phone off."

"That's another dollar in the fine jar," Morgan kidded.

She smiled and reached for the phone, then stopped. Morgan felt her muscles tense.

She sat up with a wild look. "It's Cardinal Vitelli at the Vatican. The one who gave me access to the scrolls with the instructions to capture Lilith. What do you think he wants?"

A chill ran the gamut of Morgan's bones. And his stomach grumbled like it had when the lamia-hunter Margarita threatened Taylor in the Bribri Village. *Taylor's still in danger.* He held his breath, unable to peel his eyes away from Linda's phone.

Linda opened the message, and Morgan gasped.

Lilith loose. Help!

Blinding flashes crossed Morgan's vision. He leapt to his feet, sending Bear scampering to the corner looking apologetic and puzzled. White-hot pain ran up and down his arms, and he struggled to inhale. *Do you think? How? No!*

"Dad?" Taylor shrieked. "What's wrong?"

Linda took his arms. "Richard, look at me. Breathe."

Morgan slowed his breath and steadied himself. Equilibrium returned. The tightness in his chest eased, and his heart rate slowed. "That has to be a mistake, right? Some hacker trying to mess with us? The Vatican would never release Lilith."

"Who's Lilith?" Taylor asked, helping her father onto the couch.

"I'll call Cardinal Vitelli," Linda said. Her eyes shifted to Taylor, reminding him Taylor was paying close attention. "You two wait here."

Morgan gulped and sat next to Taylor. Linda hurried off. He waved Bear over. "It's okay, buddy. Good boy." Bear came closer to receive his usual petting.

"What's going on, Dad?"

"Nothing to worry about, Sweetie." *But what if it's true? What would that mean for us? For Taylor?*

Calm down. The demonic possession is over. Taylor's safe.

Before having to explain further, Linda reappeared, a pained expression telling Morgan all he needed to know.

It's true. Lilith escaped.

Linda's typical rosy expression was a washed-out yellow. Her eyes, usually radiant, looked dull and lifeless.

"How did this happen?" Morgan asked.

Linda sat next to him. She gave Taylor a concerned glance, then focused on Morgan. "Cardinal Vitelli says someone let Lilith out."

"Who's Lilith?" Taylor repeated.

The bright lights spun. *How do I even begin to explain this?* "A bad person." Then, to Linda, "Someone broke into the Vatican vaults?"

"Access is controlled by the Swiss Guard. He suspects another cardinal."

"A cardinal?" Morgan said, dumbfounded. "But why?"

Linda teetered on the edge of the couch. "Cardinal Vitelli says this other cardinal, Roman Drakul, has been behaving strangely ever since Lilith arrived in the silver box."

Morgan rose again, agitated. This time, Bear ran toward Morgan's bedroom. "Did Cardinal Vitelli confront him?"

"Drakul's disappeared." Linda seized his hand. "There's more. A girl on a tour of the museums also vanished. Last seen talking with Drakul."

Morgan collapsed back onto the sofa. "You don't think Drakul is doing Lilith's bidding?"

"I don't know what to think," Linda said. "But, if Lilith was released, a young girl is exactly what Lilith wants."

Morgan flinched. *And turning them into lamias.*

"Does this Lilith hurt girls?" Taylor asked. "Is she the one who hurt my friends?"

Morgan hugged Taylor. *Sure. That's a good explanation.* "She had a contagious disease, sweetie, and your friends caught it. But she's gone, and so is the disease. Nothing to worry about." *I'm glad Javi isn't here to witness me lying to my daughter. Even Catholic priests must have limits on the whole forgiveness deal.*

He turned to Linda. "So, Cardinal Vitelli wanted to give you a heads-up?"

"Not just that. I have expertise he needs. He wants to fly me, and anyone else I need, to Rome to help as a consultant. To explain everything to the Swiss Guard. Tell them how to capture Lilith."

Well, that's not happening. No way we go near that demon again. "We can explain all that without flying halfway around the world. The Vatican have something against phones? Skype?"

"He wants me there in person," Linda said. "He might need to make a quick decision, and he's afraid we'll lose precious time if I'm not right there."

"Rome?" Taylor said. "Sounds way cool. Can I come?"

Morgan stiffened. "Not this time, Taylor." Regarding Linda, he said, "He doesn't want *you* going after it, does he?"

"No," Linda said. "He promised I'll be protected inside the Vatican. The Swiss Guard will do the actual capture."

"They've got the finest security on the planet," Morgan said. "And the ancient scrolls you read to figure it out. They can handle it without you."

"He says we're the only ones who've been able to capture it in centuries. That if I don't help, it could threaten us all." Linda kissed Morgan's hand. "I hate to admit it, but he might be right."

"Why do you keep calling her *it*?" Taylor asked.

Morgan eyeballed Taylor. "Just a figure of speech." He lowered his voice and spoke to Linda. "I don't like this. You know you shouldn't go anywhere near it."

Linda teared up. "After it killed my daughter, I promised myself I would destroy it. I thought we had. I thought we could move on. Maybe even together." She blushed. "But that's all changed now. I have to make sure it can't hurt any more girls."

"This Lilith *killed* your daughter?" Taylor asked.

Linda lowered her head. "It did."

"That sucks!" Taylor shivered. "Did she try to kill my friends?" Then a new thought flashed in her eyes. "Did she try to kill *me*? Is that why you're after her."

Morgan hugged her. "Taylor, I told you, she was spreading a contagious disease. But it's over. Now, I need a moment alone with Linda. Okay?"

Taylor pulled away and stared into her father's eyes. She pursed her lips. After several seconds she shrugged and smiled at him. "Okay." Her grin widened. "You two gonna make out?" Taylor's smirk made it clear, unlike his ex-fiancee Azra, she was okay with Linda.

That's a good sign. She's getting over her mother's traumatic drowning. Accepting I should move on. "I wish, but right now, Linda and I need to talk over a few things."

Taylor moved past them to her room. "Call me when you two kiss. I want to post it on Instagram."

After she closed her bedroom door, Morgan sighed. "Fifteen, going on twenty."

"She's terrific. You're handling the possession and her exorcism quite well."

"I don't know about that." Morgan took Linda's hand. "But let's talk about Rome. I don't want you to go."

"I have to."

A blast of wind gust against the house. The windows rattled and the front door creaked.

Shit. She's really going to do this. Can I let her go by herself? And if I go, what do I do with Taylor? "I don't feel right letting you go alone."

He peeked toward Taylor's room. "And I can't leave Taylor here by herself."

"I get it. I could never ask you to leave Taylor after all you've been through." She exhaled. "I would feel safer with you protecting me. And I know Father Garcia would watch Taylor. But I also know you can't leave her now."

"I'm sure Javi would watch her, but what if I'm halfway around the world and Lilith comes for Taylor?"

Tears spilled down Linda's cheeks. "Then you have to stay."

Morgan's internal conflict crushed his soul. "I could bring her."

She squeezed his hand. "Take her *toward* Lilith? If you're worried Lilith will come after her, that would be riskier. It's okay. Really."

Morgan wiped Linda's tears away. "I don't feel good about you facing this without me. What if something happens?"

"I'll be surrounded by holy men and their security force. Nothing will happen. Taylor has to come first. She must be protected. I won't be gone long."

"Unless you meet some Italian lover and I never see you again," Morgan joked, eyebrows raised.

Linda pecked Morgan's cheek. "Smart ass. I better go. Need to book a trip for tomorrow morning."

"I can't talk you out of this?"

She nuzzled him. "Stop worrying. I'm a big girl."

And Lilith is a powerful demon with evil intentions.

CHAPTER 3

After walking Linda to her car and watching her wave goodbye, Morgan's cell chimed. He closed the front door to block the freezing winter gale. "Yeah?"

Father Garcia responded. "Pennywise! You busy?"

Oh jeez. How to tell Javi about this? "Hi Javi. I was about to call you."

"Why's that? Wedding planning?"

Hilarious. "Slow down, cowpoke. We just started dating. She needs time to recognize how lame I am at this relationship stuff."

"So, what's on your mind?"

Several seconds elapsed before Morgan could get himself to talk. "Lilith escaped."

After another delay, Garcia whispered. "What do you mean, escaped?"

"The Vatican thinks someone let it out. Linda's flying there in the morning to tell them how we captured it. Hoping it hasn't disappeared out of their reach."

Silence.

"Say something," Morgan pleaded.

"Taylor okay?" Garcia asked.

"Sure. Lilith's nowhere near here."

More silence. Somehow louder.

"I feel guilty not going with her, but I won't leave Taylor alone, and I'm sure as hell not taking Taylor anywhere near Rome with Lilith on the loose. A girl already went missing. Lilith probably has a new host."

"Another girl? Pennywise, this demon must be stopped. We've seen how fast the plague spreads. Forget the personal hell we went through exorcising it from Taylor. We have a responsibility to society, and to God, to put an end to Lilith."

Morgan's stomach churned. He thought back to the exorcism. The lamia. The attacks of bats and wolves. Taylor's heart stopping, then the Awà bringing her back to life. "I hear you, brother, but the Vatican has an elite security staff and exorcists up the wazoo. They can handle it."

"Can they? Could our police?"

"Either way, I won't put Taylor in jeopardy. Listen, I need to check onTaylor. Sorry for the disturbing news."

"Tell Linda to call me if she has questions about my end of the exorcism."

"Will do. Night, Javi."

Morgan hung up and stared at the phone. *The Vatican can handle this, right? Linda will be safe. She's too old to be a target.* His mind wandered to a scene when he'd explained that to her, with poor results. *Probably best not to mention her age again.*

Bear wandered back in and nudged his nose against Morgan's leg. Morgan rubbed Bear's shiny white fur. "No worries, Bear. Taylor's safe here."

But Bear whined and peed on the floor.

Morgan recognized Bear's behavior and shuddered. *That's how he acted when Taylor was possessed.* A chill ran from his neck to his feet, and back to the top of his head. *But Lilith is on another continent.*

Then terror replaced logic as Morgan heard Taylor screaming. He dropped the phone and raced to her. "Taylor! What's wrong?"

He barged into her bedroom and froze, his knees barely able to sustain his weight.

Taylor's bed was vibrating six feet away from the wall, with Taylor perched on top, her face distorted in fear. "Dad?"

CHAPTER 4

Taylor's bed quivered, and Morgan's quaking body moved in sync. *Like it's alive.* Morgan swept Taylor up and carried her into the hallway.

"What *is* that?" Taylor cried. "The bed's moving all by itself!"

They gawked at it until the pulsating stopped.

"Probably an earthquake." *Bullshit. Lilith's sending a message. Taylor's in real danger. What do I do now?*

"In Oregon?"

Morgan retreated to the living room and settled Taylor on the couch. "It happens. Listen, I need to talk with Linda."

"Don't leave me!"

He clutched her. "I'm not going anywhere."

"Is the earthquake over?"

That's the million dollar question, isn't it? "I don't feel anything. Must be."

Taylor yawned. "I feel super tired." She closed her eyes.

Before Morgan could call Linda, Taylor's face turned crimson.

"Dad, I don't feel so good."

"Stomach?"

"No." Taylor felt around her jaw. "My teeth."

Time stopped. The grandfather clock stopped ticking. Crickets stopped chirping. Morgan stopped breathing.

Morgan thought back to Javi's warning, after the successful exorcism. *Once you see the darkness like that, there's no way to escape it. It will follow you everywhere.*

"They hurt," Taylor continued.

Morgan dry-swallowed. "Your jaw? On the outside?"

"My teeth and gums. Like I just had a cavity filled, and they forgot to give me Novocain."

Morgan steeled himself. *If her incisors are growing, I don't know what I'll do.* "Let me see."

Taylor opened wide. Morgan moved her head to face the light. *Teeth look normal. But her gums around the incisors. Are they inflamed? Like when the demon began turning her into a lamia?* He shook the thought off and kissed her forehead. "Looks okay. Probably nerves about the earthquake."

"I don't feel nervous."

For the record, I'm nervous enough for both of us. "Just rest now."

"Dad?"

"Yeah?"

"Do you know where my crucifix is? The one I got for Confirmation when I turned thirteen? I stopped wearing it when Mom drowned. I'd like to wear it again." She shrugged. "I feel like it's important."

"I think it's in your closet. I'll get it."

When he returned, he found Taylor sound asleep. He slipped the crucifix chain over her head. *I'm glad you want to wear this again.* He took a deep breath. *It can't hurt.*

He knew he needed to warn Linda and pushed her number on his cell. "Linda, there's been a development."

"What happened?"

"Taylor's bed got thrown across the room."

After a moment of dead air, Linda stuttered. "You mean?"

"Yeah. And her teeth are hurting. Her gums are inflamed. We're coming with you."

"Are you sure?" Linda asked. "Like you said, we'd be taking her straight to Lilith."

Morgan wasn't sure about anything. But staying in Salem, alone, waiting for another attack, scared him more than going. "After what just happened, the distance isn't relevant. We have to end this. It's the only way."

"Okay. I'll book you on my nine o'clock flight. I'll pick you up at five."

"Thanks."

"We'll get through this, Richard. Try to get some rest."

"That's a good thought, but I don't see much sleep in my immediate future."

* * *

As predicted, Morgan stayed awake all night. He set Taylor in his bed and watched her from a chair. Bear refused to sleep in his normal spot next to Morgan's bed, instead pacing in the hallway for hours.

With each twitch, with each grunt, with each sigh from Taylor, Morgan relived the horror of the past weeks. Half expecting Taylor's incisors to emerge elongated from her mouth, he waited for Linda, and the uncertainty of Rome.

Linda let herself in at 5 a.m., before Taylor awoke. Bear followed her to Morgan's bedroom door, but no farther. "How's Taylor doing?"

"Okay, I guess. No sign of her incisors growing. Bear's freaking out, though. Just like before." Morgan licked his dry lips. "I think that's the scariest part of all. Dogs can sense stuff."

"You still want to go to Rome?"

Morgan approached his sleeping daughter and stroked her unruly black hair. "I wouldn't say *want*, but I don't see a choice." Morgan broached a subject he'd been pondering all night. "Do you think the Vatican will need to hear from Javi and Valverde, since they exorcised the demon? Javi already offered to help via phone. But there's no way to reach Valverde."

"The *Bribri Awá*? I hadn't even considered that. But the Vatican will have several exorcists on site."

"But none with experience like Javi and Valverde."

"True, but like you said, there's no way to reach Valverde."

"Yeah." Morgan gazed upon Linda's angelic face and felt the need of her. He pulled Linda to him and kissed her. "You taste good."

"Down, boy. We have a flight to catch."

Morgan smiled and released her. "Right." A fresh thought bounded into his head. "Do you think Lilith will try to get back to Costa Rica?"

"Not clear. Her origins are along the Mediterranean. She might consider that home. Besides, the *Bribris* are on to her, and defeated her. Europe might be an easier mark." Linda pulled the blanket off Taylor's legs. "Time to get her up. Did you tell her?"

"Not yet. She'll be stoked. She turns sixteen next week, and she's always wanted to see Europe, so we'll couch it as a birthday trip. And she gets to skip a few days of school. Double win for her."

Linda thought a moment. "That's good."

Morgan tapped her nose. "I figure it'll take at most a few hours to tell your Cardinal what he needs. Then we get the hell out of Rome and go somewhere where Lilith can't find Taylor."

"Isn't it safer to come home?"

"Lilith's in this new girl now." Morgan scratched his head, feeling a sweaty mess. "They said she was a tourist. We don't know where that girl is from, or where she's going, but she's probably back with her parents now, continuing their vacation."

Linda nodded. "So you think Taylor will be safe."

"Short of a chance meeting, I don't see how Lilith can transfer to Taylor. I don't want to stay in Rome, since that's the one place we know she might be, but everywhere else is kinda the same. And Lilith knows where we live, so if it has any influence on where the girl goes, it might come looking for Taylor here."

"And you're okay traveling?" Linda asked.

"It's better than sitting around here. Might as well celebrate Taylor's birthday in style. Find something fun to do. After we tell the Swiss Guard how to capture Lilith."

Linda snuggled up to him. "I've always wanted to hike Pulpit Rock in Norway."

"Then that's what we'll do."

She shoved him playfully. "You sure? It's a challenging hike."

"Are you calling me old? At forty?"

She tapped his exaggerated belly. "Not old."

"Fat?"

"You haven't been exercising much since I arrived. Just saying."

I don't know about that. Some exercise is more fun than others. Especially with you. "You just worry about yourself. And try not to slow *me* down."

Linda kissed him on the lips. "That blur you see on the trail will be me and Taylor blowing by you."

Morgan took in a hesitant breath. *This will be good for Taylor. The safety of the Vatican, then disappear where Lilith can't find us. It'll be fine.*

But Bear whined, and Morgan's skin turned icy.

CHAPTER 5

Vatican City State

Morgan gawked at the marble statues, and the words carved above the Vatican Museum's exit, MVSEI VATICANI, on the fifty-foot-high wall off of Viale Vaticano. "It's magnificent," he said to Linda and Taylor.

Taylor clicked photos on her phone. "It's way cooler than I expected."

"It gets even better," Linda said. "The majesty and serenity blew my socks off when I was here last. Makes you feel like you shouldn't speak." She waved at someone inside. "There's our escort. Name's Romanoff. Nice guy."

"Russian?" Morgan asked.

"I think so," Linda answered. "Vatican City employs people from all over. It's not just Italians, even though we're surrounded by Rome. They require everyone to speak English, French, German, and Italian."

A young man with a linebacker's body and a tailored black suit opened the door and motioned them in through the exit, bypassing the long line of tourists. Two members of the Pontifical Swiss Guard, each uniformed in the Medici colors of red, yellow, and blue checked their bags and persons to make sure they weren't carrying anything forbidden into Vatican City.

"Doctor Copeland," Romanoff said to Linda. "Nice to see you again. Cardinal Vitelli is expecting you." His English was passable, his accent Russian. Morgan looked at his own blue blazer and gray slacks, wrinkled from the flight. *Am I underdressed?*

"*Grazie, Signore* Romanoff," Linda replied in a flawless Italian accent, shaking his hand. "Allow me to introduce Doctor Richard Morgan, and his daughter Taylor."

After handshakes, Romanoff pointed south. "This way, please. We take a shortcut through the museum." They bypassed the crowds and walked the 600 feet to the Palazzo Apostolico. Halfway through the museum they passed signs for the Biblioteca Apostolica Vaticana.

"That the library?" Morgan asked Linda.

"Yes. It's where Father Garcia deposited Lilith inside the silver box."

Morgan glanced at Taylor. "Lot of good that did." But he couldn't help admire the purity of the surroundings. The walls were spotless, a combination of light gray and gold. "Back before I sort of lost my faith, I wanted to come here so badly. I can feel the power of this place." He reached out and took Linda's hand. "I'm glad we're seeing it together."

"It's super cool, Dad," Taylor said. "This vacation rocks."

Vacation. Right.

"I've never met a Cardinal before," Morgan whispered. "Javi's as high as it gets for me. I'm kind of nervous."

"Well," Linda said, "whatever you do don't treat him like Father Garcia. No chest bumps."

Taylor joined them in a good chuckle.

After climbing two flights of stairs they arrived at Cardinal Vitelli's office. Two life-size paintings depicted Christ battling with Satan, and His crucifixion. Marble statues flanked the Cardinal's desk. *Forget Occupy Wall Street. This is where the real wealth is.*

The pale, wrinkled face of the elderly Cardinal contrasted with his black wool cassock, scarlet silk rabat, black stockings, and black shoes. A pectoral cross hung from a gold chain around his thin neck. Linda, looking professional in a deep blue pantsuit, approached reverently and shook his outstretched, shriveled hand.

"Thank you for coming," the Cardinal said to Linda. "These are trying times for the Church."

"We're happy to help. These are the friends I told you about."

The old man's powerful grip surprised Morgan. After shaking Morgan's hand, the Cardinal moved aside to Taylor, who rocked a flowery, pink dress. "Welcome, young lady. It's not often I have someone of such blessed notoriety in my chambers."

Taylor looked perplexed. "Blessed notoriety?"

Oh, shit. Didn't Linda tell him she doesn't remember any of it? Morgan coughed. "Cardinal Vitelli, perhaps we can get to it. Is there somewhere Taylor and I can rest while you and Linda discuss your business? It was a long flight."

The Cardinal smiled. "Of course. Romanoff will escort you."

"Oh, no reason to waste his time," Morgan said. "Just point us toward some chairs and we're good."

"Visitors are never alone in the Vatican." Vitelli pointed at a camera lodged by the ceiling. "The Pontifical Swiss Guard oversee everyone. And God watches us all."

Tension gripped Morgan's stomach when he thought of leaving Linda alone in the Cardinal's office. *Relax, dude. The Vatican's the safest place on the planet. Linda will be fine. And Taylor and I will be with Cardinal Vitelli's guy.*

Romanoff escorted Morgan and Taylor to an uber-decadent sitting area, with a view of Saint Peter's Square, crowded with tourists and vendors. After seating Morgan and Taylor on a luxurious scarlet couch, Romanoff stood by the window, staring outward.

"How you feel?" Morgan asked Taylor.

"Good. A little tired. But excited to see the sights."

"Your mouth any sorer?"

"About the same."

Thank God for that. Being in closer proximity to Lilith hasn't triggered more symptoms.

"Why did he say 'blessed notoriety'?" Taylor asked.

Morgan squirmed. "Not sure, sweetie. He probably gets a steady stream of guests and confused you with someone else." He relaxed when she nodded. *I think she bought that.*

"Does it have to do with this Lilith you and Linda keep talking about?"

Well, so much for her buying it. "That's why we're here. To talk to him about Lilith. But it's nothing you need to worry about. We'll be out of here soon."

Taylor shrugged and sat back in the overstuffed couch. "I'm not worried. But you and Linda seem to be. Maybe *you* need to chill."

Indeed.

Taylor closed her eyes, and Morgan followed suit. *C'mon, God, show us the way to that little girl. Then the Swiss Guard can do their thing. With Linda's input, and all the exorcists here, should be a piece of cake.*

Morgan heard the sound of soft shoes approaching. Morgan perked up when he saw Linda with a second escort. "Done?"

"Richard," Linda said, "it's worse than we thought. You need to come."

Morgan checked on Taylor, who had fallen asleep. *I don't want her to hear this.* "Can you watch Taylor?" he asked Romanoff, now at his side.

"Of course, sir."

Morgan rose, watched Taylor for a moment, gave Romanoff another once-over, then followed Linda and her escort back to the Cardinal's office.

Vitelli sat at his ornate desk, slouched and disheveled. *Jesus. He looks bad. Defeated.* The Cardinal signaled for the escort to leave them, then motioned for Morgan and Linda to sit. "Linda tells me your daughter doesn't recall any of it."

"I'd like to keep it that way. So, what's going on?"

Vitelli glanced at the door, then pointed a crooked finger at Morgan and spoke in a hushed tone. "Evil has infiltrated the Vatican."

Morgan squirmed. "Linda said you referred to a Cardinal Drakul in your call for help. Is he involved?"

"I fear Cardinal Drakul is leading a secret society within the Church," Vitelli said. "One determined to see the prophecies of the Book of Revelation occur in our lifetime."

Morgan looked back and forth between Linda and Vitelli. "That's why he set Lilith free? Is Lilith part of their plan?"

"I'm afraid so," Vitelli said.

"So, have the Swiss Guard round them up," Morgan said.

"Drakul has disappeared," Linda said.

Vitelli squirmed. "I have no evidence. The Guard will defend the Pope, but they won't go after something external unless it directly threatens the State. They'll leave that to local authorities."

"I'm pretty sure they'll do what the Pope tells them to," Morgan said. "Does he know about Lilith?"

"No." Vitelli rubbed his eyes. "I thought it best if I was the only one who knew about the box. It's hidden in a part of the archives where no one ever goes. Strictly forbidden and guarded. With a note from the Pontiff to never open the box."

"But someone got in there!" Morgan stared at the Cardinal, who looked flustered. *Was it a mistake to trust this guy?* "You better tell the Pope about Lilith and your suspicions."

"Perhaps I made a mistake," Vitelli said. "I will tell him as soon as I can get an audience. But it won't do any good now."

"It's not too late!" Morgan said. "He can order the Guard to find Drakul, and the demon. What other choice is there?"

"Actually, there is only one good option. You two must go stop Lilith."

Morgan put his hands up. "Oh, no. That's not the deal. We came to *consult*. Nothing more."

The Cardinal turned to Linda. "Please. The soul of every human may be at stake." He pulled a thin envelope from his robe and handed it to Morgan. "Take this. It is where you will find Cardinal Drakul and his followers. And the financial means to track him without being followed."

"You're not listening," Morgan shouted. "We're not going anywhere near that demon. Understand?"

"I can trust no one else." Vitelli pushed the envelope on Morgan. "And neither can you. Drakul's people could be anywhere inside the Vatican."

Morgan took the envelope, stuffed it in his pocket, then rose while he mulled over the last statement. *Taylor!* "What about Taylor's escort? Could he be with Drakul?"

Vitelli's face lost all shades of color.

Morgan's body convulsed. Then he raced through hushed hallways to reach Taylor, and found no one there.

CHAPTER 6

Morgan rushed to the window overlooking the Piazza San Pietro. He no longer noticed the beauty, nor the pageantry, nor the magnificent surroundings. Terror masked his perception.

"Taylor!" Morgan screamed. Blood drained from his face, and his vision blurred. *I left her alone. What was I thinking?*

Linda caught up. "Where is she?"

Morgan wiped his eyes and scanned the plaza, trying to search the sea of color, expecting to find Romanoff abducting her. *Trust no one else. Drakul's people could be anywhere inside the Vatican.* "We need the Vatican sealed off. No one in or out. Tell Vitelli to alert the Guard."

Linda's face washed out. "You think they're taking her to Lilith?"

"That's exactly what I'm afraid of."

Morgan dialed Taylor's cell phone. "She's not picking up." He scanned the ceiling in the sitting area. "No cameras in here."

Vitelli caught up to them. His expression filled with panic. He dialed his cell. "I am calling Romanoff."

"You need to lock down the Vatican!" Morgan turned on Vitelli. "Now!"

Vitelli lowered the phone, puzzled. "No answer. He always answers."

"Did you hear me?" Morgan said. "Lock it down!" He reverted his attention to the plaza. "Every second we waste is a second Taylor gets closer to Lilith." *To demonic possession. To becoming a lamia.*

"I will call the Guard." Vitelli dialed. "They will secure the grounds."

"There can't be that many fifteen-year-olds in a pink dress out there," Linda said.

Morgan's world spun. *Once they get to Saint Peter's Square, with all those people, it won't be hard to get her out.*

Vitelli spoke on the phone in Italian. Morgan stepped away from the window and joined Linda.

After some back-and-forth, Vitelli hung up. "They're alerting everyone. The Guard will watch the exits and do a search. If she's in Vatican City, they'll find her. There are cameras everywhere."

"You warned us not to trust anyone," Morgan said. "How do you know we can trust the Swiss Guard?"

"It is unlikely they have been infiltrated," Vitelli said.

Unlikely. Great.

"They are sending someone here to speak with you," Vitelli continued.

"Forget that," Morgan said. "We need to do our own search. What's the fastest way out?"

The Cardinal considered for a moment. "To get into Piazza San Pietro, I'd go down the back hallway, and through the Poste Vaticane. They make sure no one enters the Palazzo Apostolico from the post office, but going out is routine."

"Show us!" Morgan said.

Vitelli pointed east. "Down the stairs through those double doors. You'll see the Guard at the entrance to the Poste. Give them code word 'Constantine' and tell them I sent you. Go. I will only slow you."

Morgan needed no additional prompting. He secured Linda's hand and the two of them bolted through the double doors, down the stairs, and into a narrow, poorly lit hallway. Ahead, two Swiss Guard stood at attention on each side of a door marked "Emergency Exit."

As they approached, the guards unholstered their pistols. "Stop! You are not allowed here."

Morgan and Linda froze. "Vitelli said to tell you 'Constantine.'" Morgan put his hands up and pleaded, "I'm looking for my daughter. She disappeared with an escort named Romanoff. Did they go through here? My daughter's fifteen, in a pink floral dress."

The guard on the right showed his recognition. "Romanoff left a few minutes ago, with a girl."

"I'm her father. He's trying to abduct her. You have to let us through."

The other guard scoffed. "We don't know you. We *do* know Romanoff."

"But they have the code," the first guard pointed out. "I better call Cardinal Vitelli."

"There's no time!" Morgan screamed. But the guard's guns kept him in place.

"Did you get the alert to lock down the Vatican?" Linda asked. "The girl's the reason."

The walkie-talkie at both guard's sides crackled. "*Stare all'erta!*" came a static-filled voice. "*Tutti solvate della Guardia Suisse, stiamo cercando di signorina, probabilmente con Romanoff. Detenere e portare loro in Centrale.*"

"We need to hurry!" Morgan shouted. "We haven't much time."

The guard on the right sprung into action. He opened the door into the rear of the Poste Vaticane. "Follow me." The other guard remained at his post.

Once through the crowd in the post office, Morgan. Linda, and the guard emerged in the Piazza San Pietro, where throngs of people milled about. Most were strolling toward Saint Peter's Basilica, away from the outlets to Rome.

"They'll go for the exit," Morgan said.

Pin-balling through the maze of tourists in the direction of the Piazza's main opening, they passed dozens of souvenir stands. Taxis parked near the exit. *He's heard the alarm. If he gets her to a taxi, we'll never find her.*

"Do you see her?" Linda asked.

"No," Morgan said. He judged the distance to the gate at fifty yards. His legs wobbled. Then, at the margin of his vision, he saw her pink dress. Thirty feet ahead. "There!"

She stood next to the escort, Romanoff, neither of them moving. Only fifteen feet to a taxi. Morgan screamed for her, but knew he couldn't be heard in the flock. *But why aren't they moving?*

He saw why. Romanoff was staring at the guards who had assembled at the departure gate, stopping all traffic.

He can't get out!

With an adrenaline rush, Morgan pushed past the guard and reached Taylor first. She licked a chocolate ice cream cone. "Taylor!" He separated her from Romanoff. "Thank God you're here."

She looked at him with a puzzled expression. "Where else would I be?"

The guard caught up and grabbed the escort's arm. "*Signore* Romanoff, you must come with me, please."

Romanoff tried to extricate his arm, but the guard held firm. "What is this?"

Morgan turned Taylor over to Linda and faced Romanoff. "You son-of-a-bitch. You tried to kidnap my daughter."

Romanoff's eyes bugged out. "What are you talking about? She asked to see the Piazza. I didn't see the harm. I showed her the Pontiff's balcony and bought her an ice cream."

"He did," Taylor said. "This place is way cool."

"I called, and you didn't pick up," Morgan said. "You've got to answer me."

She pulled her phone out. "Sorry. It was really loud once we got outside."

The Swiss Guard tugged on Romanoff. "We'll straighten this out inside. Come with me. All of you."

* * *

Inside security headquarters, with the Commander of the Swiss Guard presiding, Vitelli joined them. Portraits of every pope, going back to the founding of the Church, adorned the walls. Linda took Taylor to another room. Morgan sat across from the Cardinal in chairs nicer than in Salem's finest residence.

"I did nothing wrong," Romanoff said to Vitelli.

"Why did you not answer my call?" Vitelli asked.

"I never heard it," Romanoff said. "Like the girl said, it was too loud in the Piazza."

"That's bullshit," Morgan said. He blushed, realizing where he was. "Sorry."

The guard, wearing a badge identifying himself as Commandanté Berger, gaped at Romanoff. "You did not have permission to take her outside. You violated your duty as an aide to the Cardinal."

Romanoff looked down. "I am sorry for the trouble I have caused." He looked at Morgan. "Please accept my apology."

Morgan narrowed his eyes. "You're not fooling me. If the guards hadn't arrived at the gate, you'd have hopped in a taxi and driven her right out."

Vitelli sighed, a deep sadness in his eyes. He whispered something to Berger, who nodded.

"*Signore* Romanoff," Berger began, "you are relieved of all duties in Vatican City. One of my guards will escort you from the state."

Romanoff jumped to his feet. "All because a tourist accuses me? You can't do this." He turned to Vitelli. "I have served you for years. How can you allow this?"

The Cardinal stared at the floor.

"It's done," Berger said. "Consider yourself fortunate we don't have enough to prosecute you."

"What do you mean?" Morgan said. "He kidnapped my daughter."

"This is all I can do," Berger said.

Romanoff shifted his attention to Morgan. "You. I hope you can live with yourself. I have a family. My entire life is dedicated to the Church."

Morgan felt neither remorse nor uncertainty. "You bastard. Who are you working for?"

Then Morgan saw it. A twinkle in Romanoff's eyes. A silent message, directed at Morgan. *He knows I know. And he's telling me he'll keep trying, until he reunites Taylor with Lilith.*

CHAPTER 7

Through hallways of ornate statues and religiously themed paintings dating back centuries, Vitelli escorted them to his chambers. Morgan kept a tight grip on Taylor's hand. *She needs to understand she's in danger. I need to tell her everything.* He winced. *It will destroy whatever innocence remains in my little girl.* A crushing pressure gripped his chest. They separated into chairs facing Vitelli's desk.

As petrified as Morgan felt, Linda looked worse. Beads of sweat lay across her face, and her skin tone matched the statues. Only Taylor looked unaffected.

But once I tell her, she'll never be the same.

Linda dabbed her eyes, which made Morgan's insides cry out. He stood and crossed to her. "You okay?"

"Just tired. Probably jet lag."

"You've been through too much," Morgan said. "Come on. Let's get out of here."

"And go where?" Linda asked. "There's nowhere to hide."

"Somewhere safe." He regretted the phrase immediately.

Linda's eyes opened wide. "Safe? Explain how *that* works."

"Hide from who?" Taylor asked. "The Lilith lady?"

Morgan winced. *This isn't the time, or the place, to tell her everything. We just need to get away from here.* "Yes, Taylor. But, like I said, you have nothing to worry about. I just need to think."

"I'm afraid Linda is right," Vitelli said. "You can not hide from this evil. Even if you try, it will find you."

Linda pulled away from Morgan. "We need to go after Lilith."

"Hell, no!" Morgan said.

The Cardinal coughed, a rattling affair with a big, wheezing finish. "She is right. You must."

"You keep quiet," Morgan said to the Cardinal, his voice climbing. "As if Lilith wasn't enough to worry about, you invited us here, knowing it's got allies *in the Vatican*. You've put Taylor in enough danger."

Taylor cringed, her chocolate skin showing an amber finish. She held onto the crucifix around her neck. "Why is Lilith after *me*?"

Morgan kneeled in front of her and took her hand. "It's complicated, sweetie. I'll tell you, once we're safe."

As Morgan stared into her eyes, they changed. The irises turned darker, then lighter, then stabilized to her typical brown. Her skin cooled, and her face turned gray.

Morgan came close to throwing up. "Taylor?"

"What's happening?" Vitelli asked.

Taylor growled.

"No!" Morgan screamed. He shook Taylor and stared toward the heavens. "You can't let it have her!"

Taylor drew in a rush of air, then fell limp into Morgan. He leaned her back in her chair and her skin returned to its normal shade.

"The demon?" Vitelli asked.

"A warning shot, I think," Morgan said. "Showing us it still has influence, even if it isn't in possession of her."

"Richard," Linda said, "none of us will be safe until we destroy Lilith. As frightening as it is, we have to go after the demon. What's the alternative? Spend the rest of our lives in fear, wondering when it will show up?"

"I have to protect Taylor. At any cost."

"*How?*" Linda asked. "After what you saw in Taylor's room, what you just saw here? You know we can't hide. Even if we could, the plague will spread. We can't sit back and ignore it."

Morgan lowered his head. *What do I do?*

Vitelli startled him with a hand on his shoulder. "Dr. Morgan, have faith. God is with you. The power of Christ is with you. Just as He saw you through your ordeal in Costa Rica, He will see you through this."

"But it wasn't just us," Morgan said. "We had a priest. A Bribri shaman. They did the heavy lifting."

Vitelli pointed to a painting of the tortured Christ on the cross. "No, my son. It was Christ doing *all* the lifting. And He can use you as his vessel, just as He used the priest and the shaman. But you must have faith. Faith powers everything."

Faith. After all that's happened? That's a big ask.

"Dad?" Taylor said.

Morgan almost toppled over at the sound of her voice. *She's awake. And herself.* "Yes, sweetie."

"I don't understand all this, but I do have faith. In you."

Morgan's eyes filled with tears. He hugged her. "That means a lot."

"And," Taylor continued, "I'm not afraid to go after this Lilith lady. Don't worry about me. Okay? She needs to be stopped, and it sounds like we're the ones to do it."

Morgan studied Taylor. *No fear. And perhaps a little excitement. Great. She thinks it's an adventure.*

Hands on hips, Linda said, "Either way, I will find it, Richard. I will kill it."

Morgan extricated himself from Taylor and Vitelli and kneeled next to Linda. "All right. We'll do it together."

She kissed him hard. "Thank you."

Morgan winked at her. "I warned you I wouldn't be easy to get rid of." He stood and faced the Cardinal. "I don't suppose you know where we should look."

"The envelope," Vitelli said. "Don't be distracted by the demon. Cardinal Drakul is the head of the snake."

Before Morgan could ask what's in the envelope, or why Drakul's more important than Lilith, the sound of shattering glass and a shrill noise stopped him. The Cardinal's body spasmed, then collapsed into Morgan.

"Your Eminence? You okay?"

Vitelli's dead weight sagged against Morgan. Morgan eased him to the ground. When Morgan held up his hands, blood smeared both palms.

CHAPTER 8

For a moment, Morgan stared at his red palms, confused, then realized what had happened and how vulnerable they were. "Get down!" They all dropped to the floor.

Morgan checked the Cardinal's pulse, found a slight one, then looked at a fist-sized hole in the window. *Oh, shit.* He rushed to Taylor. "You two okay?"

"I'm fine," Taylor said. The look on her face said otherwise.

"Me, too." Linda looked over Morgan's shoulder toward the Cardinal. "What happened?"

"The Cardinal's been shot."

"Shot?" Taylor cried. "*In the Vatican?*"

A member of the Swiss Guard rushed in, saw the Cardinal on the floor, and pulled his pistol. "*Fermo!*"

Morgan sat up and pointed to the Cardinal. "He's been shot!"

The guard raised the pistol up. "*Mani in alto!*"

Morgan didn't know what that meant, but raised his hands. Blood dripped from them.

The guard's eyes widened. "*Lei. Cosa hai fatto?*"

Morgan looked at Linda for an explanation, but she shrugged.

Taylor came to the rescue. "He asked what you did."

Morgan gulped. "When did you learn Italian?"

"On the flight over. While you were snoring. Just the basics."

"I'll take the basics," Morgan said. "Tell him I didn't do anything. He was shot. Through the window."

Taylor gave Morgan a frustrated glance. "Jeez, Dad, I said basics."

Morgan turned to the guard. "You speak English?"

The guard ignored him and approached the Cardinal. He checked for a pulse. He then pulled out a radio, keeping his aim directed at Morgan. "*Cardinale Vitelli bisogno visita medica.*"

"He was shot," Morgan tried to explain.

The guard ignored him. "*Persona sospetta in detenzione preventiva. Mandare sostituto. Fretta!*"

Morgan wiped his brow. *Sospetta? Detenzione? That doesn't sound good.*

Taylor scurried closer to Morgan. "He said you're a suspect."

"Yeah. I got the gist." Morgan noticed for the first time the lack of blood on the Cardinal's chest. *No exit wound. The bullet must still be in there.* He pointed at the window, with a spiderweb of cracks emanating from the hole. "Check the window. Someone shot him."

"*Silenzio!*"

"Is he alive?" Linda asked.

The guard's face gave away his concern.

Morgan shifted his attention back to Taylor. He moved in to cradle her, but she put her hand on his chest. "Gross, Dad. You'll ruin my dress."

Morgan remembered his bloody hands. "Sorry. Just worried about you."

"Who would do this?" Linda said.

Morgan considered the Cardinal's conspiracy theory. "Cardinal Vitelli discovered something evil within the Church. They're protecting their secret."

"It all has to be connected," Linda said.

"*Te l'avevo detto silenzio!*" the guard yelled, his face turning redder.

All the screaming in a language he didn't understand was giving Morgan a headache. Then, an ear-piercing alarm flooded Morgan's ears. Morgan winced at the jarring noise.

Two medics arrived with a gurney covered in black bags. One cleared the gurney and opened the bags. The other attended to Vitelli. "His breathing is weak. We need to get him to the infirmary."

Morgan let out a breath. "Thank God. English. You'll find the entry wound in his back."

Two more guards arrived with Commander Berger. Berger pointed to a guard with a radio in his hand. "Shut that alarm off!" The guard complied, and the alarm stopped instantly.

Berger approached Morgan cautiously, his eyes focused on Morgan's bloody hands. "What happened?"

"Someone shot him in the back from outside, through that window," Morgan said. "I caught him, and he bled on me."

Berger glanced at the window, then turned to the medics. They lifted the Cardinal to the gurney. "How is he?"

"Too soon to say." The medic tore open the Cardinal's shirt and checked his back. "Looks like a stabbing with a sharp, round weapon." They positioned him on the gurney.

"No," Morgan said. "I'm telling you someone shot him. Look at the window!"

But the medics were on the move. Berger motioned to the guards to bring Morgan, Linda, and Taylor with them.

"*Il prigione?*" one guard asked.

Morgan tensed, his calm short-lived. *Prigione?* "What does that mean? It sounds like prison."

Berger shook his head. "For now, I'm taking you to the Vatican infirmary." He turned to a guard. "And get an investigative unit up here."

* * *

Morgan held Linda's and Taylor's hands in the sterile infirmary waiting room. They sat in subdued silence, the only sound the clinking of medical instruments. *What have we gotten ourselves mixed up in?*

After a tortuous ten minutes, Commander Berger barged in, followed by the two armed guards posted outside.

"Is the Cardinal going to make it?" Linda asked.

Berger stayed erect. "He is in critical condition. Our doctors are working on him. They are the best in the world. If he can be saved, they will find a way."

"Did you find the bullet?" Morgan asked.

Berger's face darkened. "There is no sign of a bullet at the crime scene. They will X-ray the body when it is safe to do so."

Morgan let go of Linda's and Taylor's hands, leaning toward Berger. "We heard it spit through the glass. The window has a hole in it. I was standing with him when it struck. There's no other explanation."

Palms up, Berger said, "My crime scene investigator reports the wound could be from a stabbing, like with a letter opener." His eyes bore into Morgan's. "We discovered the Cardinal's letter opener is not in his desk." He let that sink in. "And my investigator says someone broke the glass from the inside. Consistent with someone stabbing him and throwing the weapon out the window. And you have blood on your hands."

Morgan felt the red drain from his face. "You can't think I attacked him."

Taylor looked back and forth between her father and Berger. "What are you saying?"

Berger pulled handcuffs out. "I am saying, your father was very upset with Cardinal Vitelli when you were taken by Romanoff. Perhaps he snapped. Please turn around and place your hands behind your back."

"This is absurd." Linda put her arms around Morgan. "We all saw it. Richard didn't do this."

The room spun, and Morgan's skin temperature dove. *This guy's serious. Is Berger in on it? No, he helped free Taylor earlier. It must be someone else involved in the investigation.*

Morgan turned around. "This is a mistake. Someone inside Vatican City shot him and is framing me. Because Cardinal Vitelli, and now we, are seen as a threat."

"Dad?" Taylor said.

"It's okay, sweetie," Morgan said. "Just a misunderstanding."

Berger trapped Morgan's wrists in the cuffs. "You will come with me."

"What about us?" Linda asked.

"You follow."

Berger dragged Morgan into the hallway by his wrists. Pain shot up Morgan's arms to his shoulders. "Take it easy, will you?"

Berger grunted.

As they dragged Morgan down the hall, Linda and Taylor trailed, escorted by the two guards. They moved toward a door marked "*Operatorio Stanza Uno.*" When he reached the entrance, Berger turned to the guards following them. "Stay here! I want to talk to the doctors."

"We can watch them," a guard said.

"No," Berger said. "I'm not letting these three out of my sight."

The guards glared at Morgan, but shrugged their acceptance of the order.

Berger opened the door and the guards shoved Morgan into a small room. Medical supplies lined the walls, and a stainless steel sink sat under a large window which provided a view of the operating room itself. Two doctors and a nurse in sterile gowns and masks worked on the Cardinal.

With Morgan, Linda, and Taylor jammed beside him, Berger called to the doctors via an intercom. "Did you find a bullet?"

"X-rays came back negative," one of the doctors answered. "No exit wound, and no metal in the chest cavity."

Berger raised an eyebrow and jostled Morgan's handcuffs. "No bullet. No gunshot. How do you explain that?"

Morgan's mind raced. *I heard it. It has to be there.* "I can't. But I know what I heard, and what I saw. Most importantly, I know I didn't do it, so a gunshot is the only explanation."

Berger grunted. He faced Linda. "And you? You corroborate his story?"

"I do," Linda said.

"Me, too," Taylor said, stepping up to Berger as best she could in the cramped conditions. "My Dad would never hurt anybody."

"We came to help Cardinal Vitelli," Linda said. "At his request. Why would we want him dead?"

Berger pursed his lips. "I don't like this one bit. First Romanoff, now this. My nose tells me something is wrong. And my nose is never mistaken."

"Commandanté!" a doctor called. "Your nose, it may be right again."

Berger tapped the side of his nose. "Tell me why."

The doctor approached the window with a silver plate. It held a tiny puddle of water in the middle. "See this?"

"What is it?" Berger asked.

"The remains of an ice bullet. Designed to melt in the body and destroy the evidence. If we'd been a minute later, we'd have missed it."

Morgan whistled. "I thought ice bullets weren't a real thing. I saw this episode of 'MythBusters' once." He stopped at the lack of recognition surrounding him. "Never mind. American television. Can't believe everything they tell you."

"It is a tricky technology," Berger said. "Most who try can not succeed. The ice must be processed just so, and the weapon is very specialized. And to go through thick glass and keep on its target, very hard to do. An engineering feat only the best experts can accomplish."

"So, we're dealing with highly skilled specialists," Morgan said. "Like military special forces."

"And every member of the Swiss Guard," Berger said, his tone somber. "We all have special forces training. We are *the* elite military force."

"I'm surprised Cardinal Vitelli's office doesn't have bulletproof glass," Linda said. "I expected it to be everywhere here."

Berger exhaled. "When this Pope removed it from his transport, many inside the Vatican followed his lead." He shook his head. "It makes my job that much harder."

Morgan shivered. "There's one thing I don't understand. Your investigator said I shattered the glass from the inside. He lied?"

Berger's face turned to stone. "Yes. Clearly, I have a problem inside my ranks. After today, I wonder how deep this problem goes."

Morgan gazed through the glass at the Cardinal. "Is he going to make it?"

"We think so," the doctor replied. "The bullet missed his heart by millimeters."

Berger undid Morgan's handcuffs and pointed to the sink. "Clean up."

Morgan washed his hands. As soon as they were unstained, Taylor hugged him.

"What now?" Morgan asked Berger.

"The envelope," Linda said. "We follow the trail."

"So we just walk out of here?" Morgan looked at Taylor. "What if the shooter is still out there? What if one of your men is involved?"

"I will arrange for a transport to take you out," Berger said. "My story will be that Rome has a warrant out for your arrest on another murder charge, and you're being transferred there while we sort it all out. I will drive the transport myself, make sure you are safe."

* * *

An hour later, the sun set on the outskirts of Rome. What should have been a postcard sunset, with dreams of romance and fine dining in a setting made for the gods, was instead a scene filled with tension and anxiety.

Morgan, Linda, and Taylor stepped off the back of a Swiss Guard transport van. Morgan walked up to the driver's window, where Berger held an automatic rifle in the driver's seat. "Thanks."

"Be safe," Berger whispered to Morgan. He handed Morgan a photo. "This is Drakul. Follow the clues Cardinal Vitelli provided you. And stay in the shadows. Whoever is responsible for the Cardinal's shooting and the attempted abduction of your daughter is still out there."

"Roger that." Morgan perused the picture. An Eastern European stared back at him with piercing black eyes.

"Leave your cell phones. You can't afford to be tracked."

"Right." Morgan motioned for Linda and Taylor to hand theirs over.

"Seriously?" Taylor said. But she complied.

Morgan tossed all three phones inside the van. He turned to go.

Before Morgan could move away the driver's window shattered just off his ear. The sting of exploding glass against his steamy cheek followed. When he looked up, Berger's forehead had a quarter-sized red hole, dead center.

Morgan knew enough from his army training to recognize a sniper shot. He yelled toward Taylor and Linda at the back of the van. "Sniper! Get down!"

He dove on the pavement just in time. Another shot, this time above his head, tore into the van's metal side.

He crawled on forearms and knees to the rear of the van, grabbed Linda's arm and Taylor's hand, and ran.

CHAPTER 9

Salem, Oregon

Within the muted, pine-scented refuge of his side of the confessional, Garcia speed-dialed Morgan's cell phone for the third time. Still, no answer. His throat tightened. *Where are you, man?* He squeezed the cross on his chest tighter.

The other side of the confessional creaked open, sounding like a coffin lid in a horror movie. Garcia pocketed his phone and prepared to perform his duty.

The slider in the thatched window between them scratched open, and Garcia heard a woman's familiar Pakistani dialect. "Javier, can we get out of this infernal contraption?"

Azra Khan! In my church. Didn't see that coming. "Have you come to confess?" He could hear the edge in his own voice.

"Get real." Azra's razor-sharp tone matched Garcia's, adding to the tension. "You need to talk sense into Richard."

Garcia kept his face forward despite his temptation to face her. "I'm sure whatever you have to say to Pennywise, you can say yourself."

"He won't take my calls."

Well, you fought us on Taylor's exorcism. If not trapped here by duty, I wouldn't talk to you either. Maybe if I ignore you, you'll go away.

That didn't work.

"It was all a stupid misunderstanding," Azra continued. "If I can just talk to him, without that bitch Copeland around to poison our relationship, he'll see we belong together."

Misunderstanding? Bitch? I wonder what the required tolerance for a priest is during confession.

"He's not home," Azra said. "Or at his office. You know where he is."

The dark paneled walls closed in, and Garcia's energy drained. "It's not my place to speak of this."

Through the confessional window his peripheral vision picked up Azra's harsh movement. She stood, climbed out, and slammed the door. Her high heels clicked on the marble, fading in proportion with his anxiety.

"But I *don't* know where Pennywise is," he whispered to a wall used to hearing the darkest secrets. "Don't know why, but that scares the shit out of me." He cringed at his word choice. "Bless me, Heavenly Father, for I have sinned."

A gruff voice in front of the confessional guffawed. "Tell me about it, padre."

Garcia swung the door open and found Lieutenant Smokey standing there in his trademark off-white trench coat, an unlit cigar in his mouth. Garcia didn't wait for an invitation, rather he lunged toward Smokey and gave him a bear hug, almost knocking Smokey's hat with the "Grandpa" stitching off. "Man, am I glad to see you."

Smokey reset his hat and held Garcia at arm's length. "What's up, padre? I ran into Dr. Khan on the way in."

Looking through the front entrance, Garcia admired the rarest of Salem sights. Bright sunshine, and no wind. "She's looking for Pennywise."

"Humph. Did I hear you say you're afraid?"

"Pennywise isn't answering his phone. Neither is Linda, nor Taylor. Something's *wrong*."

Smokey twirled his cigar. "They flew halfway around the world to go after a demon which just escaped because of a crooked Cardinal in the Vatican." He let that sink in. "What could go wrong?"

Garcia didn't join Smokey in smiling. "It's not a joke. And Azra's trouble."

"Sorry. I know how serious this is. What kind of trouble can Azra possibly cause?"

"She's too into Pennywise. She won't let him go without a fight."

Smokey rubbed his nose. "Is that priest code for batshit crazy?"

Garcia flinched. "Didn't say that." *And I'd prefer we leave the bat references alone.*

"Look, I've worked with her for a long time. Always professional. She'll get over the Doc."

Garcia flinched an eyebrow. "Possibly. Something about her seems unhinged right now."

"Let's get back to our real problem. The Doc."

Garcia paced around the floor, then sat in the last pew. "I don't know how to explain this horrible feeling." A sharp pain in his stomach emphasized the point. "Like he's in terrible danger. I've never felt anything like this. And, the more I pray for him, the stronger the feeling gets."

"You think someone's trying to tell you something?"

"*Sí.*"

Smokey's face curled up. "Then we better go get him."

Garcia couldn't hide his confusion, nor his relief. "We?"

"You bet." Smokey laughed. "The dynamic duo rides again."

"Can you just up and leave?"

Smokey chuckled. "One of the many perks of being retired as chief of detectives. I'll still have my consulting gig with them when I return. After saving the city from vampiric extinction, I have a long leash. What about you?"

"Don't know. Have to ask the Bishop for a sub."

"You do that, pronto. If your gut is right, there's no time to waste."

"But where will we go?"

"Wherever he is. Don't worry your holy little head. I'm a detective, remember. We'll find him. We'll start at the Vatican. And this time, we don't trust the demon with anyone else. We find it and kill it. And I mean extinction, forever."

CHAPTER 10

Rome, Italy

An hour after Berger's demise, after random turns through a maze of high-rise apartments with cafés, coffeehouses, and gelato shops lining the first floors, Morgan led Linda and Taylor into a dark alley. The moon peered over the rooftop of a five-story apartment, providing the only light. But it was the windows staring down that unnerved him. As if they were tracking his every move with lifeless eyes. He expected a sniper shot at any moment.

A trash can lid clanged, and he froze. His stomach dropped to his knees.

"What's that?" Taylor whispered, her hand firmly grasping her crucifix hanging from a necklace.

Morgan sighed. "Someone taking the trash out. Not to worry."

A nearby door hinge squeaked.

Morgan held his breath until the door slammed shut, and silence hung over them.

"Safe?" Taylor asked. Anxiety gripped her voice in a choke hold.

Morgan lied by nodding.

"Hang on." Linda held on to Morgan as she removed her high-heels and held them by the heel straps. "I can't run in these. What about you, Taylor?"

"I'm okay. Where are we going?"

Morgan looked at his dress shoes and recalled a previous bout with plantar fasciitis. *Maybe I shouldn't run in these either. But barefoot's no better on these uneven cobblestones.*

"Dad?"

"Far away." He pulled out the envelope Vitelli had given him and opened it. A sheet of paper and a black credit card fell out.

Two messages were on the paper. The first read: *Untraceable and unlimited credit for travel.*

The second: *Patmos.*

He handed it to Linda. "Looks like the cardinal is paying for our search. And one word, in Italian. I don't know what it means."

Taylor checked the page. "Not Italian. It's the Greek island where John wrote the Book of Revelation."

Morgan snapped his fingers. "Of course. In the Aegean Sea, near Turkey. Javi went there on a pilgrimage. He took a ferry from Athens."

"You think Lilith is on Patmos?" Linda asked, putting the paper in her purse. "Seems too remote for what it's trying to do."

"Agreed," Morgan said. "Perhaps it's where we find this Cardinal Drakul and his organization. He should be able to lead us to Lilith." He looked up at the moon. "I wish Javi were here. His experience on Patmos could sure help."

A sudden noise silenced him, this time approaching footsteps. Morgan turned back the way they'd come. Two shadows entered the alley. His skin burned.

"Take this." He handed Linda the Vatican credit card. "Run! I'll slow them down." *With a bullet to the chest? Yeah, that'll slow them.*

Linda and Taylor hesitated, but he shoved them. "Go! Don't stop until you get to the US Embassy in Athens."

"Athens?" Linda said. "How are we going to get to Athens?"

The two shadows ran toward him. "*Alt!*"

Morgan didn't need a translator for that. Fifty yards separated them, and the gap was closing fast.

I should have taken Berger's gun. "Go now!" Morgan told Linda.

She took Taylor by the hand and they ran.

The figures moved into the moonlight at breakneck speed. One wore a police uniform, the other, a much younger man, perhaps even a boy, sported street clothes. They hadn't pulled a weapon.

"*Alt!*" the policeman repeated. "*Vieni con me!*"

As the pair moved closer, Linda and Taylor disappeared around the corner. *At least* they *got away. For now.*

Morgan put his hands up. "I'm unarmed. No speak Italian."

The man in uniform reached Morgan first. He made no move to restrain him.

The young man stepped up next to him. "Dr. Morgan. I am so glad we found you. Excuse the dramatics. My name is Riki. Riki Vitelli."

Morgan studied the boy. Medium height. Dark hair and well-tanned. Strikingly handsome features. "Vitelli? As in Cardinal Vitelli?"

"He is my grandfather's brother. He asked me to assist you."

"You know he's been shot?" Morgan asked.

"Yes. He will recover. He said you must complete an important mission for the church. My father is a policeman. He will help us."

"Does he speak English?" Morgan asked.

"Not a word," Riki said. "But that is not a problem. I am expertise. I spent a year studying in your country."

"You mean expert?" Morgan said.

Riki waved away the comment. "No matter. I will help you."

"How old are you?" Morgan asked.

"Eighteen. We need to find your two women before the Swiss Guard do." Riki pulled out a tablet and showed Morgan the screen. "They claim you shot Commandanté Berger." He grimaced. "The police revere the Swiss Guard. They will shoot you on sight."

"I didn't shoot anybody."

"I believe you," Riki said. "And, because of the Cardinal, my father believes you. But the other officers will want vendetta."

Morgan's heart pummeled his ribcage. *There's no overturning revenge. How the hell do we ever get out of Rome?* He glanced back at the end of the alley. "My daughter and girlfriend are out there. We were running from the sniper that took out Berger. And now the police. We're screwed, aren't we?"

"Leave your escaping to me," Riki said. "First, we must find your companies, ur, companions."

Morgan eyed the policeman. "You're sure he's on the same page about us?"

Riki smiled and put his arm around his father. "Papa is here to assistant me, to help the Cardinal. And to help you."

"Okay," Morgan said. "Up here."

They strode to the corner where they discovered the side street deserted. Then to the next intersection. Still no sign.

"Which way?" Riki asked.

"We didn't have much time to coordinate," Morgan replied. "The Cardinal is sending us to Patmos. I told them to go to the US Embassy in Greece."

Riki whistled. "Patmos. The place of legendaries. I have always wanted to go."

"First things first," Morgan said. "Find my daughter and girlfriend before the police, the Swiss Guard, or the sniper." The magnitude of their situation hit Morgan square in the gut. "How would they discreetly get to Athens?"

Riki pondered the question. "The train station is being watched. Same for the bus." He snapped his fingers. "I would go to Civitavecchia, find a captain with a yacht that can go to Greece, and also can sneak in and out. There will be many choices. Smuggling is our second biggest industry."

Morgan surprised himself by chuckling. "What's first?"

"Pickpockets."

Before Morgan could react, a curdling scream rose from a distance.

"That's Taylor!" Morgan set off as fast as his dress shoes would carry him. Riki kept up, but the officer fell behind.

As he reached the second intersection, Morgan saw Linda and Taylor a half block to the right, surrounded by four young men covered in tattoos, looking like gangbangers back in Salem. "Hey! Leave them alone!"

The men didn't budge. One of them opened a switchblade.

"Do not challenge them," Riki said. "They will not react well."

Morgan slowed, but continued toward the circle. "Taylor, Linda, you okay?"

"Do we look okay?" Linda said. Her bare feet were scuffed and red.

The youth with the knife stepped forward. "*Smettila di immishiarti.*" He waved the knife around in a circle.

Morgan ignored the fear circulating through his system and moved closer. "I don't want any trouble. Let my daughter and girlfriend go and we'll walk away."

The youth pointed the tip of the blade at Morgan. "*Smettila di impicciarti!*"

"What now?" Morgan asked Riki, keeping his focus on the gang in front of him.

"He wants you to back off."

Morgan took one more step, which caused a chain reaction. The lead banger pushed the knife toward Morgan's face. *So, this is how I end. Not to a demon, but to a punk in Rome.*

Riki stepped even with Morgan, standing tall. "*Alt!*"

The knife's edge nicked Morgan. He felt a sticky ooze leaking.

Riki grasped the boy's arm. His eyes bored into the assailant who withdrew the blade.

"*Alt!*" Riki's father caught up with them and flashed his badge at the scum. In sync, the four boy's eyes widened. Riki let go, and they scampered into the night.

Morgan rushed to Taylor. Her eye mascara was running with tears. "Did they hurt you?"

She wiped her face and stared at Riki. "No."

"You sure?"

"We're fine, Richard," Linda said.

Morgan noticed Linda's abused feet. "Your feet say otherwise. Want your shoes back on?"

Linda winced. "Too swollen."

"We'll get you some tennis shoes in the morning. Are the ones you have a hassle to carry? Should we ditch them?"

She looked at the heels in her hand. "No way. These are like a weeks salary for me. Remember, I'm just a community college teacher now." She wiped his throat with her finger. It came back with a single drop of blood. "Are *you* okay?"

"I'm fine."

Taylor hugged him. "What were you thinking?"

Morgan exhaled. *Yeah. What were you thinking? You're not fucking James Bond, you know.* "Just protecting my girls. It all worked out."

Taylor nodded toward Riki and his father. "Aren't you going to introduce us?"

"This young man is Riki Vitelli. Related to the Cardinal. And that is his father, a member of the Rome police."

"The police?" Linda said. "Is that a good idea?"

Riki stepped forward and kissed Linda's hand. "We are pleased to meet you. I am sorry for the rude reception. Italy is really a very friendly country."

Morgan rolled his eyes toward the stars. *If you ignore the pickpockets. And thugs. And snipers.*

"I'm Linda. Appreciate your help. Is the Cardinal okay?"

"Recovering. I have been assured he will be fine."

Riki released Linda and switched to Taylor. Morgan thought he saw a light go on in both their eyes. Riki took Taylor's hand and kissed it. "And who is this lovely flower?"

Taylor shoved away from Morgan and giggled. "Taylor Morgan. Thanks for rescuing me."

Oh, brother. Like he did anything. But Morgan couldn't help but smile. *Okay, he did something. And, despite everything, Taylor laughed. Maybe she can live her life like a normal teenager after all.*

Riki held on a little longer than necessary, then stepped over to Morgan. Taylor's eyes followed him. "We need to get to Civitavecchia. Then you can skip Athens and go straight to Patmos. I will take you and handle the negotiations."

Before Morgan could decide whether that was a good idea, Taylor stepped in. "Thanks. We accept."

Morgan frowned at her. "Excuse me," he said to Riki.

He pulled Taylor aside. In hushed tones, he said, "What are you doing? We don't know this guy."

"Oh, come on, Dad," Taylor whispered. "He saved our lives." She gazed at Riki.

"I appreciate your input, but let's leave the decisions to me,"

Taylor stepped back, hands on hips. "I'm not a child anymore. I'm turning sixteen. It's time you treated me like an adult."

Morgan stared at her. *Where is this coming from?* He glanced at Riki. *Oh, right.* "I know you're not a child, but you're not an adult either."

She stood up straighter. "I'm not afraid. Of Lilith, or anyone else. It's time I learned to take care of myself."

That's fine. I'm afraid enough for both of us.

Linda stepped between them. "Can I interject something?"

"Sure," Morgan and Taylor said in unison.

"Riki and his father know their way around here. If they were part of Drakul's gang, we'd already be captured. I say we take advantage of their offer."

Morgan looked at Linda. *Et tu, Linda?* He glanced at Riki, who looked like a puppy at the pound. He moved back over to Riki. "Thank you. We'd appreciate your help."

But before they could start their journey, Riki's father spoke again. *"Alt!"*

Instead of a badge, he held a gun, aimed at Morgan's heart.

CHAPTER 11

Morgan stared at the threatening pistol aimed straight at him in the dark alley. He took a step forward, but stopped when he saw the cop's trigger finger tense.

"Papa?" Riki said. "*Che stai facendo?*"

The cop didn't look at his son. "*Il mio responsabilità.*"

Responsabilità. I think I know what that means.

Riki pressed ahead, "*Ma, Cardinale Vitelli chiesto ci aiuto.*"

The cop shook his head.

"What's going on?" Morgan asked Riki, taking a step back to protect Linda and Taylor.

"The precinct chief found out my father left with me while still on duty. He called him to ask why. My father told him everything. They ordered him to turn you over to the Swiss Guard."

"Will he really shoot me?"

"I would not chance it." Riki glanced at Morgan. "Let me talk with him."

Morgan checked the streets in all directions. "Please hurry. We can't afford to be spotted."

Riki nodded and stepped up to his father. They whispered back and forth in brisk Italian accompanied with wild hand gestures. After several arm waves, Riki turned to Morgan. "He feels he has no choice, under the law."

"You said he'd help."

Riki stared at the ground. "I know. He changed his mind."

"The Swiss Guard think I killed their boss," Morgan said. "That's why Cardinal Vitelli sent you. They'll kill me. Please help us."

Riki looked from Morgan to Linda to Taylor. He stopped at Taylor and seemed to find a new level of resolve. He argued with his father, which earned him a harsh slap on the face.

Morgan took Linda and Taylor in his arms and whispered. "Listen. He'll stick with me if you two run. Get to the US Embassy in Athens. Then, to Patmos. You might have to do this without me."

"Dad, no!"

Linda rocked her head. "Richard, there's too much corruption here. You can't trust the Guard, or the police."

"I know. But what choice do we have?"

"I'm not leaving without you," Taylor said.

Linda piled on. "Me, neither. We have to find another way."

The arguing between Riki and his father grew louder. Morgan turned to see Riki, crimson-faced, a stream of blood cascading down his cheek.

Would the old man really shoot us in front of his son?

A siren blasted from a few blocks away. The police officer's radio went off, and voices collided with each other at breakneck speed. As Riki's father answered the call, Morgan decided they had no choice. "Now!"

The three of them broke for the alley twenty feet away. Morgan took up the rear, trying to protect Taylor and Linda. He glanced back. Riki was standing between his father and them, trying to impede the man.

A police car with flashing lights skidded into view. Riki turned to Morgan and yelled. "Piers 4. Tell the captain I sent you."

Morgan took Linda and Taylor by their hands and fled.

* * *

After offering an excessive wad of American dollars to buy a cab ride and the driver's discretion, they arrived at Civitavecchia an hour later. The cabbie dropped them off at Varco Vespucci, the port's main vehicle entrance.

A giant cruise ship loomed on the far side of the harbor. The stench of fish overpowered the smell of the sea, and a stiff Mediterranean breeze chilled Morgan, still wearing his light blazer. A sign for Piers 2 through 13 pointed to the east.

They walked to Pier 4. A luxury yacht at the end of the pier appeared deserted. Raindrops started to fall.

"What now?" Linda asked.

"Find the captain and hope he's willing take us to Athens," Morgan said.

Taylor shivered. "I'm cold, Dad."

Morgan thought back to Taylor's transformation in Salem, and her love of the cold nights. He shimmied also, but for a different reason. "The yacht will have blankets."

"Maybe this wasn't such a good idea," Linda said. "Should we catch a train to Athens?"

"And won't the police come looking for us?" Taylor said. "His father had to hear Riki tell us to come here."

"If the police were coming," Morgan said, "they'd be here already. I don't think Riki's father understood him." He swallowed. "I hope."

A creak on the wood behind them froze Morgan. "Come on." They bolted for the yacht.

Linda looked back toward the noise. "Is that the police?"

"Stay low," Morgan said. "With the rain the visibility's bad. Maybe no one will spot us."

Hunched now, they reached the end of the dock. The swells intensified, along with the rain. The fifty-foot yacht bobbed and weaved.

"What now?" Taylor asked. Her summer dress was soaked, and her shakes had intensified.

A distinctive sound edged toward them. Footsteps. On the old wood. Approaching slowly.

"Richard?" Linda said. Her tone said it all. *The music is about to stop, and we're a chair short.*

Morgan put himself between the women and the advancing steps. "Climb onto the yacht and hide. I'll handle this."

The steps got louder. But the rain created an opaque curtain obscuring Morgan's view.

Whoever this is, he's close. Morgan tensed himself, ready to vault at anyone trying to capture them, or worse.

Two simultaneous screams sucked the air from Morgan's lungs.

On the yacht, a round man smoking a pipe and brandishing a shotgun screamed in Italian at Linda and Taylor, who stood on board.

Ahead, a younger voice called out. "Dr. Morgan?"

Riki!

Riki stepped through the downpour, drenched, but alone. A welt under his eye.

Riki recognized the threat to Taylor and launched himself up the ladder and over the railing onto the yacht, yelling in Italian. He stepped between Taylor and the armed captain.

Morgan followed him, pulling Taylor and Linda into a tight circle. "What's he saying?"

The captain stared at Riki, then recognition set in. He set aside his weapon and hugged the boy.

They spoke in hushed tones. The only words Morgan recognized were *Cardinale Vitelli*. Riki pointed to Morgan, then the women, and finally, to the yacht. The captain nodded enthusiastically.

"It is okay," Riki said, as if all the day's catastrophes were under control. "You just startled him. He lives on the boat, and there are some shady characters on the docks, so he is cautious."

A two-ton bag of sand fell from Morgan's shoulders. "He will help us?"

"He is my friend's uncle. He will help us."

"Won't your father expect this?"

"No," Riki said. "He does not know my friend, or about the boat."

Morgan pointed at Riki's eye. "Your father do that?"

Riki looked ashamed. "I did not give him much choice. He is a good father. And a good policeman."

"But you let us escape," Morgan said, "and wouldn't tell him where we were going."

"Something like that." Riki turned to the captain and spoke in Italian. After a few exchanges, Riki approached Morgan. He spoke so softly Morgan could barely make out the words in the rain. "He will take us all the way to Patmos. You have cash? It is a long, expensive journey."

"I have plenty of American dollars."

"That is fine," Riki said. "I will get supplies for the trip. Then we will leave."

"We?" Morgan said.

Riki pawed at the water rising on the boat. "I go with you." He glanced at Taylor in a way that made Morgan nervous. Taylor returned his smile, and Morgan's apprehension grew larger. "I have not much future here. I'll be safer on the sea."

Damn. He saved our asses. I can't just leave him here, can I? Morgan checked on Taylor. Her eyes were riveted on Riki. Much too riveted. Taylor seemed to sense she was being scrutinized, glanced at Morgan, and blushed through her golden complexion.

Morgan put a hand on Riki's shoulder. "If I allow you to come, you'll follow orders? I can count on you to behave? Be a gentleman?"

Riki rose onto his toes and crossed his heart. "Absolute."

Morgan scratched at a day's beard growth. "I don't suppose your Greek is better than your English?"

"Oh, yes," Riki said, his bravado overflowing onto the wet pavement. "I am an *expert!*" His emphasis on getting the word right came with a puffed-out chest. "I can be a big helper to you."

A flash of lightning struck nearby. The boat shook.

"All right," Morgan said. "Let's get those supplies. Starting with comfortable walking shoes."

"Is it safe?" Linda asked. "I mean, the storm."

"No problem," Riki said, waving his arms. "Our captains are experts at dealing with any problem the Mediterranean might throw at us."

Another expert. That's just great.

CHAPTER 12

Morgan kept watch on the yacht while Riki went for supplies. The rain persisted, but there was no sign of the police or Swiss Guard along the pier. The wind had calmed to a steady flow, and crisp sea air replaced the overpowering stench of dead fish. A tradeoff Morgan could live with.

Riki, clothed in all black, returned with a continental breakfast, jackets and shoes for the women, and a change of clothes for everyone.

The captain, now a spitting image for Popeye the Sailor Man in his shirt and cap, barked orders that only Riki understood. Linda and Taylor came up from belowdeck under thick blankets. Taylor's frown turned to a smile at the sight of Riki.

"Any trouble?" Morgan asked Riki.

"I have to avoid a few search parties," Riki said with clear bravado, "but I am an expert at blending in. No sign of the police?"

"Nope." Morgan crossed his fingers. He passed out the food and joined the others in scarfing it. "We should get out of here before our luck changes."

The captain barked an order to Riki.

"We will be shoved now," Riki said. "First light will be any minute."

"I think you mean shove off," Morgan said.

The rain ceased, and the first of the sun's rays peeked over the horizon, creating a shimmering effect in the clouds.

"Thank you for going out there," Taylor said to Riki. "It must have been dangerous for you."

Riki stood taller. "It was nothing." Meaning, it was something.

Morgan grinned. He wasn't too old to remember when he had a crush at that age. "Okay, Mr. Expert, let's get out of here."

A dog barked in the distance. A deep, angry, bark, like a German Shepard on the trail of someone. Then excited yelling.

"The police!" Riki said, his face no longer filled with puppy love. "Everyone below deck!"

Morgan trailed as the four of them ducked below deck, leaving only the captain at the helm, and in sight from the pier. Morgan huddled with Linda and Taylor up against the hull with Riki trying to squirm into the circle. Taylor made room.

"Stay down," Morgan said. "Hug the walls."

"The dog may have my scent," Riki said. "If so, they will find us." He pulled a Berreta out of his waistband. "Here. Take this with you. It's armed."

Morgan delayed, but stuck it in his own waistband. He considered his options. *Hide? Run? Fight?*

Above, the captain yelled. Morgan signaled for everyone to be quiet as shouting went back and forth.

The dog's growl penetrated the hull.

Shit. The dog has Riki's scent. He considered pulling his pistol. *Too many of them. It'll just get us all killed.*

More growls. Another shout. More insistent. The captain shouting back. Footsteps coming up the stairs onto the yacht which swayed as the weight balance shifted up top. Morgan's equilibrium ditched along with the sea.

Morgan looked at Linda. "Any ideas?" he whispered.

"They know I am here," Riki whispered. "But they do not know you are." He smiled at Taylor. "I will give myself up. Convince them I am alone."

"Once they find you," Morgan said, "they'll search the boat."

Riki broke free. "A slim chance is better than none." He blew Taylor a kiss and started up the stairs. "I am expert at convincing." He disappeared through the opening to the deck.

Rapid orders broke loose above. A body slammed onto the deck. Riki's voice, urgently responding. Water lapping against the hull.

And then, silence. The dog, quiet. The police murmuring to themselves. Riki's voice, louder this time, calling out his father, "Papa!"

His old man's here. Is that good, or bad?

The father's distinguishable voice, harsh, but somehow compassionate, spoke in Italian from the pier. Riki responded, in a tone that begged to be trusted.

He's telling him he came alone. That we're not here. Will his dad buy it?

The captain's voice rumbled.

"The captain claims he's a stowaway," Taylor said. "Says he didn't know he was here. He's giving us cover."

"He wants his payday," Linda said.

More shouts. Footsteps leaving the yacht. Riki's voice trailed off.

"I think it worked," Morgan said. He lay his forehead against Linda's. "That was close."

"What'll happen to Riki?" Taylor asked.

"They don't know he helped us," Morgan said. "His father will probably just ground him."

"You think?"

I have no idea. "I'm sure."

The yacht's engines fired up. Morgan took a chance and peeked out the window. No police. No Riki. "I think they're gone."

"Riki saved us again," Taylor said. "We'd be in jail if it weren't for him."

"He did," Linda said. "Don't worry. He'll be fine."

"He's nothing like the boys back home," Taylor said.

Morgan frowned. "He *is* older than the crowd you hang with."

"Just two years," Taylor said, her voice rising.

The yacht moved forward. Morgan watched the pier fall back until they passed the jetty and were on the Mediterranean. Once at sea, the yacht rocked more, and Morgan felt queasier.

"I think we got away," Linda said.

Morgan shook. *But to what fate? A battle with a demon? With lamias?* He stared at Taylor. *Putting my daughter in harm's way?* "I need to get on deck before I barf."

"Gross, Dad."

"Seasickness is why I went into the Army rather than the Navy."

They walked up the stairs. The clouds were dissipating, and a blue sky greeted them. Their craft approached an anchored midsize cruise ship on their port side.

"You can handle a cruise ship, right?" Linda asked.

"Never been on one," Morgan said. He glanced back at Linda. "You like cruising?"

"I *love* cruising. I'll get you a patch."

Morgan gulped. *A patch? I don't even like baths.*

His attention drifted to Taylor. He tensed. Her eyes had the same blank look they'd had in Salem, before the trip. *When the demon invaded.* "Taylor? You okay?"

She stared at the cruise ship. Drool fell onto her dress.

"Taylor?" Linda said, closing in on her. "What's wrong?"

Taylor didn't respond, but a booming voice came barging from the cruise line's Promenade. A girl about Taylor's age, fully protected by the shade of a canopy, waved to them, her eyes afire.

Morgan's mouth lost all its moisture, and his throat gagged. He tried to warn Taylor to get back below deck, but all that came out was a dry grunt.

"Taaaaylooor!" the girl yelled. "Come to me!"

As much as Morgan had prepared himself for the reality of facing Lilith and more lamias, his body had other ideas. His knees buckled, his chest heaved, and he couldn't breathe.

Taylor took a step forward, toward the railing. Morgan pushed back the crippling anxiety and held her in place. He found a raspy voice. "Taylor, it's Dad. Snap out of it."

But Taylor kept fighting to get overboard.

Linda joined Morgan in holding Taylor.

The girl on the cruise ship opened her mouth, exposing elongated fangs. She cackled like Taylor had when she'd been infected, just weeks earlier.

"A lamia," Linda said, her voice catching. "It's started, hasn't it?"

"Yeah," Morgan said.

"Has there been enough time to turn her?"

"Maybe not. Maybe Lilith is still in that girl. Lingering while the transmutation completes."

The sun cast its deathly glow near the girl, and she retreated deeper into the shadows. They passed the cruise ship, and Taylor fought to board it. They held her tight until she collapsed against him.

They eased Taylor into a deck chair. Morgan checked her vitals. "She's breathing," he rasped, "but it's strained."

From a distance, the girl called out, "We all see you soon"

That same use of incomplete sentences. The lisp. She's turning into a lamia, all right. Perspiration poured from Morgan's brow, stinging his eyes. *She said* all. *How many lamias has Lilith created already?*

He shook his head. *No. It takes time to transform. She's got to be the girl from the Vatican. Lilith is messing with me. Again.*

"Lilith has message for Arrogant Loser," the girl yelled. "This time, you and whore die."

Arrogant Loser. Lilith's name for me.

"Do you think that's the original girl from the Vatican?" Linda asked.

"It has to be."

"If she's already turned enough to show symptoms, she can infect other girls. The plague will spread." Linda wiped the sweat off Morgan's face with her sleeve. "We should turn around. Kill the host. Trap Lilith again."

Morgan looked at Taylor. His stomach erupted. He scrambled to the railing and lost his breakfast. Once he stabilized, he returned to a concerned Linda.

"Something's off," Morgan said. "Why would it risk exposing itself to us? We almost killed it. Wouldn't it lay low and complete its mission?"

"It has a monstrous ego."

Morgan paced. "Fair enough. If we chase Lilith now, we may lose our chance to confront Drakul on Patmos. Vitelli thought that was critical. That killing Lilith was no longer enough." He glared at the cruise ship, now in the distance. "My gut tells me to go to Patmos. Somehow, this Drakul guy is key. Vitelli called him the head of the snake. What if Lilith is just part of his plan?"

"Okay, then." Linda sighed. "I sure hope you know what you're doing."

Me, too.

CHAPTER 13

Patmos, Greece

Under radiant blue skies, light Mediterranean breezes, and a warm midday sun, Morgan stood at the front of the yacht, watching it dock deep within the smuggling alcove of the port of Skala. Linda and Taylor climbed on deck and joined him.

"How you feeling, Dad?"

"Getting by." *Which is code for: as long as I don't eat, my stomach is stable.*

"Look at the island," Taylor said. "Beautiful."

"Did you see the beach?" Linda said. "It's like the South Pacific. Without the humidity."

Morgan scanned the hillside that rose close to one thousand feet. "It's amazing. Look up there." He pointed at a brown castle rising above white buildings at the top of the hill. "That's the monastery. A World Heritage Site."

"And," Taylor said, "below that is the Cave of the Apocalypse, where John received his vision and wrote the Book of Revelation. My teacher says it's considered one of the holiest places on Earth."

And maybe something else. Maybe the home of Cardinal Drakul's group, trying to bring forth the end time. We should start there.

As the captain had assured them, nobody asked for their identification on this section of the port. After getting assurances that the local businesses would not check their passports Morgan led his party onto shore.

"What now?" Linda asked.

"We find a hotel." Morgan turned to Taylor. "I don't suppose your language skills include Greek?"

"Nah. But I heard this place is a big-time pilgrimage and vacation spot. I bet it won't be hard to find people who speak at least a little English." She pointed to a hotel up the beach. "We should stay there. Ocean views." She cocked her head. "If it's not too much."

Morgan admired his daughter. *All this turmoil and stress, and you're cool and composed. And my kind of travel agent.* "Sounds like a plan. Lead the way."

"Look at the water, Richard," Linda said. "It's so clear. I bet the diving is spectacular."

Now you want me to go diving? He thought back to his last encounter with the ocean when he'd failed to save Michelle from drowning. "I'm sure it is. Let's stay focused on the task, okay? Once we get a room, we have work to do."

"Find the Lilith lady," Taylor said. "Or the Dracula priest. Got it."

"It's Cardinal Drakul," Morgan said. "But, yeah."

"Can I have my own room?" Taylor asked.

Morgan put his arm around her as they started toward the hotel. "Not happening. You're not leaving my sight."

"But, Dad."

"No buts. I know you're in a hurry to prove you're a grownup, but safety first." He almost laughed. *Safety first. We're chasing a demon and probably walking into a trap. Yeah, that's safety first.*

She hugged him as they started for the hotel. "Thanks for looking out for us."

"It's what Dads do."

The Skala Hotel came through big time. A third floor room with two single beds and a rollaway. Jaw-dropping ocean view. Furnished balcony. All charged to the untraceable Vatican card. If Morgan didn't know better, he'd have thought he was in paradise.

He knew better.

Taylor stuck her nose up from a hotel directory. "There's a snack bar at the pool. Can we get something to eat?"

"Sounds great." Morgan led the way. "Then, rest. We can start our quest when we're refreshed."

The rectangular pool had a shady awning hanging over bar seats near the shallow end. The three of them found a table with a big ocean view.

"I've never seen the sea change color like that, even on the beaches in South America," Linda said. "Near shore, it matches the brownish gray of the sand, then gradually adds shades of green, until it darkens and adds blue."

"Costa Rica was like that," Morgan said. He shivered.

"Do you think Cardinal Vitelli really knows where Drakul is?" Linda asked.

"He better." Morgan signaled for a waitress. *And what if he doesn't? What do we do then?*

An hour later, after scarfing up many authentic Greek delicacies, Morgan crashed onto the bed closest to the door. Linda lay on the other bed, leaving the rollaway for Taylor.

"Can I sit on the balcony for a little while?" Taylor asked.

Morgan frowned.

Taylor preempted a clear rejection. "Just for a few minutes. You can take turns showering, and the other person can keep an eye out. We're on the third floor. Nobody knows we're here. I'll be fine."

Morgan's stomach cramped. *Nobody knows we're here. Why don't I believe that?* "Just until we turn in."

He set the Beretta on the night stand. But before he could decide who should shower first, he fell asleep.

* * *

He woke up to the sound of the wind rustling trees outside. *Taylor!* He sat up. Taylor was snoozing in a lounge chair on the balcony as the sun set.

"She's okay." Linda had joined him on his bed, a tight, wonderful, fit. She smelled of coconut and orchids from her shower. "I'm watching her. And I made her come in and lock the slider while I showered."

"How long was I out?"

"About an hour."

Morgan turned to her. "You've been awake all this time?"

"Too bright. And I've been thinking about my daughter. She'd be eighteen next week."

Morgan lay back and pulled Linda closer. "I'm sorry. Sometimes I'm so focused on Taylor, I forget about your loss."

She stroked his cheek. "Nothing to be sorry about. We both need to protect her. She's the only daughter we have left."

We? Wow. He hugged her tighter. "Thank you. I don't think I could do this without you."

"And you'll never have to find out."

They lay in silence for several minutes until Morgan whispered. "You know the worst part for me? The eyes. Those dead, black eyes Taylor got when the demon possessed her. The red eyes, when she was a lamia, they were bad. But the black eyes were worse." He shivered. "That must sound crazy."

"No. I understand. For me, the black eyes in my daughter were a reflection of the darkness building in my soul. A darkness that allowed her to be killed by the Costa Ricans dedicated to stopping the plague."

Morgan squeezed her. "I don't know what I'll do if I see those eyes in Taylor again." He didn't want to wake her, but he found himself unable to control the volume of his own voice. His teeth chattered. "I don't think I'd survive another possession."

Linda crawled on top of him and kissed his lips. "We're going to destroy Lilith. Nothing will happen to Taylor. Got it?"

He answered her with a kiss. "Got it. I better shower before you dump me. I've got all kinds of ripe going on here." He slid out from under her. "Taylor. It's time."

He felt relief when she came inside and locked the door.

Along with the grime, the warm shower temporarily washed away some tension. But his mind still churned as he tried to fall asleep that night.

CHAPTER 14

Morgan woke to a scuffling sound from the direction of the balcony.

Taylor!

He grabbed the Beretta and flew out of bed, his vision blurred from the deep sleep, unable to see either Taylor or Linda in the black of night. "Linda, Taylor, wake up!"

Neither answered.

He kicked a nightstand on his way to the balcony. Pain emanating from his big toe raced up his leg. "Shit." He pogoed the rest of the way until he crashed into the closed lanai slider. He peered through the glass. The slightest orange hue peeked over the horizon as the sun prepared to rise, giving Morgan enough light to check the balcony. *Nobody out there.*

A scratching noise shook him like a volcano erupting. He whirled around. "Who's there?"

The room's doorway creaked open. A column of hallway light widened across the three empty beds. *They're not here. Could I have slept through their abduction?*

The door opened further. Linda stepped in, followed by Taylor, carrying a paper sack. Linda held three coffees.

Morgan relaxed enough to breathe again. "Jesus, you two scared the hell out of me."

Linda gave him a puzzled expression. "We picked up breakfast."

"Yeah, Dad. Lighten up. We can take care of ourselves. Look. My first coffee."

Her first coffee. Another red letter day for losing my daughter to adulthood. "I hope you loaded up on cream and sugar."

Taylor glowed. "Nope. Straight up."

"So," Linda said, "what's our first move?"

Morgan stretched. "Start at the caves. Then the Monastery."

"Do we need more guns?" Taylor asked.

Linda handed him a coffee. "They clearly won't hesitate to shoot *us*."

Morgan ran his thumb across his lips. "Right. But we can't just walk into a store and buy a firearm. We entered the country illegally. They must have some kind of checks."

"What, then?" Linda asked.

"I bet they have a cool black market." Taylor bit into a muffin. "I can go find us a source."

Morgan choked up coffee. "How do *you* know about the black market?"

"My computer science class. The teacher had us do lots of cyber security stuff, including accessing the dark web. Don't worry. It was all supervised. He wouldn't let us see anything juicy. But I read a lot about the black market."

Morgan stared at his little girl. *Wow, I really have no clue what goes on in your world, do I?* "You're not going out to find anything."

"I'm not a child, Dad. I can help."

And I'm not ready letting you out of my sight. "It has nothing to do with how old you are." He shrugged. "Well, it has a little to do with that. But we're sticking together. This Drakul is after you. I'd insist even if you were my age." When Taylor protested, he put his hand up. "That's final, Taylor. Don't go wandering off."

"Yes, Dad."

Morgan took Linda's hand. "You ever fire a pistol?"

"Growing up in Peru, we all handled guns. But I've never used one on a person."

"Trust me," Morgan said, "you don't want to start now. Just the one firearm then. But I'm going to get supplies for our mission. Stuff that won't require an ID check."

"Your Army training got us out of Costa Rica alive," Taylor said. "I thought we were goners."

Morgan bit into a scone. *Are we crazy? We don't know anything about our opposition. Do they know we're coming? Are we sitting ducks? Am I walking Taylor into another demon possession?* He tried to shake the thoughts away, but they wouldn't leave. Even more disturbing, Linda and Taylor had fallen into a quiet funk, as if contemplating all the risks.

"It'll be okay," Morgan said. But his voice couldn't mask the truth.

* * *

After Morgan purchased gear at a local hardware store, the three took a cab ride on multicolored cobblestones up to the Cave of the Apocalypse. Dropped off in front of a "RADIO TAXI PATMOS" sign post, they stared at the cave entrance.

All the signage was in Greek, with English translations below. The building itself shined like fresh snow, its white walls smudged with roof residue from a recent rain, a stark contrast to the brown soil surrounding it. A mosaic was set above the entrance, with a portrayal of Saint John the Theologian and his disciple Prochorors, who translated John's vision into Greek.

The structure was carved into the hillside and reminded Morgan of a fortress. He counted four stories, and dozens of windows. "It's huge. I was expecting something more like a cave. Big enough to house Dracul's group."

Taylor turned her back to the entrance. "Look at the view." A cruise ship was docked in the commercial side of the port. "Open ocean as far as the eye can see."

The bell in the tower rang out eight chimes, and the front entrance opened. A short man in a beige uniform and oversized straw hat appeared. He waved them over with a smile.

Morgan moved toward the entrance. An uneasiness ripped through his gut. *We're being watched.* He checked the windows above, looking for evidence his instincts were right.

At the second-floor window above him a shadow flashed across the glass. Morgan reached for his Beretta, poised to defend Taylor and Linda.

An old woman appeared in the window frame. Morgan's finger tensed on the trigger. She lifted a large cloth and shook it. Dust floated down and sprinkled Morgan's face.

He kept the pistol in his waistband and wiped the debris from his hair. *Get a grip.*

"You okay, Dad?"

"All good. Let's go inside." He smiled at her. "Before the cleaning crew launches another assault."

Taylor giggled and Linda laughed. The docent took their money, handed Linda a brochure, and pointed inside.

"Excuse me," Morgan said. "Is there any Catholic clergy inside?"

The docent squinted. His features turned stiff. His face turned scarlet.

He knows something.

After a long pause, the docent put his hands up. He recited a litany of indecipherable words.

Maybe he doesn't understand. Odd for someone greeting people. Their eyes locked. *What's your story, old man? You look scared.*

The docent lowered his eyes and pointed inside. Morgan peered into the shadows, found no one, and led Taylor and Linda across the threshold into the darkness.

Ground-up gravel scraped under his shoes. The air turned stale and smelled of mold. A single wall torch provided scant light.

"Everyone okay?" Morgan asked as he pressed ahead, the hair on the nape of his neck at attention.

"It's creepy," Linda said, a hitch in her voice.

"I think it's cool," Taylor replied.

They arrived in the cave, a room deep in the recesses of the hillside. Chairs, half filled with nuns, were set up arm-to-arm behind two rows of benches, to allow for viewing of the sacramental display. Gray boulders made up the roof, lit by spotlights. There were lit candles throughout. The air, cool and reverent, seemed thick as glue. The hum of prayers bounced off the walls.

"Just think." Taylor's soft voice echoed through the chamber. "This is where John had his vision of Christ returning." She ran her shoe along an indentation in the smooth stone floor. "See this? They claim this is where John lay his head as he received the vision. Like a stone pillow."

"The end time," Linda said. "It's like you can feel the holiness within the air."

"It *is* magnificent." A calm passed over Morgan, and his eyes drooped as if ready to sleep. He shook himself. "As for the end time, I'd prefer that come on God's terms, not some whack job's."

He ducked to get under the boulder to get a closer look. A glass case. Paintings and etchings portraying the key figures of the early church. A tapestry in Greek. Towering candelabras of gold and silver. "Either of you see any clues that Drakul's using this as a base? I don't."

"Nothing unexpected," Linda said.

"Ditto," Taylor said. "We should totally check out the rest of the building."

Morgan led them back into the main building where they meandered through hallways and up and down stairs. At every turn, Morgan's spine shivered. Eventually, they stepped outside through a side door. "I can't shake the feeling we're being watched."

"Something feels off," Linda said. She scanned their surroundings. "It's kind of creepy."

Taylor skipped past them. "You two are such drama queens. Let's find someone who works here and knows English."

Morgan checked out the brown castle looming up the hill, nestled above white buildings. "Maybe we'll find more answers at the monastery."

An elderly man holding a newspaper approached them from the direction of the road. Morgan tensed as he approached in his white long sleeve shirt and proper gray slacks. The gent tipped his Panama hat as he reached them. He spoke in a British accent. "Good day."

"You speak English?" Morgan asked, noting the man's features didn't match an Englishman. *Looks more middle European.*

The man stopped to give him a once-over. "I speak the *Queen's* English."

"Do you work here?" Linda asked.

"Visiting the monastery." He looked out over the panoramic view. "I stop here on my way up the bugger of a hill to have my morning biscuit."

Morgan glanced at the newspaper. A cruise ship loomed above the fold, with the caption CRUISE SHIP NIGHTMARE.

Morgan's knees weakened, and he braced his hands on his thighs. "Excuse me. Have you read the paper? I can't help but notice the headline and photo." He thought back to the cruise ship they'd passed leaving Italy. "I think I saw this ship in port a few days ago."

The Brit grunted. "Shocking, really. A cruise ship under attack like that."

"What kind of attack?" Morgan asked.

"Well, the story goes that girls are being cut around the neck. They made an emergency stop in Monaco. Authorities are searching for clues as to the villain, but nothing yet."

"Is the ship under quarantine?" Morgan asked. *Maybe the plague is contained.*

"Quite so. Nobody off until they get to the bottom of it." The Englishman nodded to them. "Good day, folks. I'm off for that climb. Perhaps we will meet again." He scuttled away.

"Odd fellow," Linda said.

"He seemed nice enough," Morgan replied.

"Are the attacks that Lilith lady?" Taylor asked.

Morgan looked at Linda for answers on how best to respond, then at Taylor. "Yeah."

"Should we go back?" Linda asked. "While the plague is still contained?"

Morgan held his head. *Vitelli sent us after Drakul for a reason. He must be here.* "I think we need to find Drakul. Somehow, in ways we don't understand, stopping Lilith isn't enough."

"You are right, Dr. Morgan."

Morgan spun around to find himself face to face with Romanoff, who stuck a pistol in his temple.

CHAPTER 15

Morgan recognized Romanoff despite half his face being hidden under a floppy canvas hat. "Romanoff. You son-of-a-bitch."

The cold steel of Romanoff's pistol dug into Morgan's temple. "Not fan, eh?" Romanoff pocketed Morgan's firearm and motioned for Linda and Taylor to walk toward the road. "Car is waiting."

"We're not going anywhere with you," Morgan said.

"Big talk for a man with gun to his head." Romanoff laughed. "You go, or I kill you and your girlfriend right here. We have no use for you." He eyed Taylor. "Your daughter, on other hand, we have big plans for."

Something snapped inside Morgan. He disregarded every ounce of self-preservation he owned, channeled his army training, and spun around, catching Romanoff by surprise. He wrestled Romanoff back toward the building, pointing the pistol toward the sky. The crack of Romanoff's head slamming against the stone sounded like a gunshot, and Romanoff released the weapon.

Morgan pinned the unarmed assailant against the stucco with his forearm. Romanoff's eyes bulged as his source of oxygen disappeared. "Where's Drakul?"

Romanoff glanced toward the monastery before he passed out. Morgan gave him one last shove of anger and let Romanoff crumple to the ground. Only then did he recognize the cramping pain in his legs. *You're not in the same shape you used to be. Better be careful, or you'll end up blowing the whole bad-ass deal you've got working here.*

"Geez, Dad, you're always so calm at home. First in Costa Rica, now here. Where is all this Jason Bourne stuff coming from? You're like a Jedi or something."

Morgan turned to Linda and Taylor. *We all know what happened to the Jedi Knights and their moral high ground.* "Just paternal instinct, backed by some useful training." *I wish I was Jason Bourne right now. Or Rambo.* "You both okay?"

Linda looked like she was in shock. "I don't know. I thought I was up for this fight, but everywhere we turn it gets more dangerous."

Morgan pulled her into an embrace. The cramping in his leg muscles ramped up a notch. "I know. It'll get better. I promise." *Well now you just sound like a dope. Or a con man.*

Linda wiped a tear away. "You won't hurt anyone if you don't have to, right? You're still bound by the Hippocratic oath."

"I know. Romanoff will be fine." *Not that he deserves to be fine.*

While they hugged, Taylor picked up Romanoff's pistol.

Morgan froze. "Here, sweetie. Point the firearm away and hand it to me."

Taylor stared at Romanoff. "He worked at the Vatican. How can he be so evil?"

Morgan didn't have a good answer for her question. But he could see her hatred and stepped in between them. *Last thing we need is for Taylor to shoot this guy.*

Linda's voice shook. "What should we do with him?"

Morgan had no good answer for that, either.

"He'll keep coming after me, won't he?" Taylor said. "He and Lilith and the Dracula guy."

Morgan reached for the pistol. Taylor gradually released it into his hand and he activated the safety. He took his own firearm from Romanoff's limp body and tucked Romanoff's pistol into his belt.

Tears formed in Taylor's eyes. "I miss Mom. Life was simpler then."

Morgan choked back his own bile. *Oh, Jesus, was it ever.* "I know." He glanced at Linda, who nodded her okay to him. "I miss her too. I'd give anything to have that day to do over."

Taylor lay her head on Morgan's chest. "I'm sorry about what I said in Costa Rica. I know you tried to save her."

Morgan's muscles clenched. "Oh, sweetie, that means more than you can imagine."

"Suppose I owe Azra an apology, too."

Morgan's calf tensed, and he tried to rub the cramp away. "You don't owe her anything. Not because she didn't do her best to save your mother. She did. But, she's not part of our life now." *And she tried her best to impede saving you.*

Linda came up and wiped the tears from Taylor's face. "We can't do anything about your Mom, and I know it sucks, but we won't quit until your life is yours to live again."

Taylor moved into Linda's arms. "I'm glad you're here. You make us happy."

Morgan blinked away his own tears. "On to the monastery. That's where we'll find Drakul."

"He obviously knows we're here," Linda said. "He'll be expecting us."

"Romanoff said there's a car," Morgan said. "We incapacitate the driver, lock him and Romanoff inside, bind and gag them, then take the car."

"What if the driver's armed?" Linda asked.

"Don't worry," Morgan said. "If he poses a threat, I'll take him out."

Taylor's eyes grew wide.

Linda fidgeted. "Take him out?"

"I'll try not to hurt him. Promise." After a moment of silence, Morgan took Romanoff by the belt and dragged his listless body. "Stay behind me."

A black Mercedes S-series purred around the corner, only ten feet away. The driver stood in a dark suit to the side, staring away from Morgan toward the sea.

Morgan handed Romanoff off to Linda and rushed the car. Before the driver turned, Morgan had the advantage. "Don't move." He stuck his pistol into the man's back. Morgan found the henchman's firearm and pocketed it. "If you cooperate, I'll leave you unharmed. If you don't, well, you get the idea. Where's Drakul?"

"I tell you nothing."

"Good, you speak English." Morgan found a small knife in his gear and jabbed him in the arm. The man screamed. "How many men does Drakul have?"

The driver refused to answer. Morgan shoved the knife in deeper, and the man succumbed. "There are a dozen members on the island."

Counting Romanoff, that means ten left. "Members of what?"

"The order of Patmos."

"Are the Monastery monks in on it?"

The driver's face cringed with pain. "The monks think we're on a research pilgrimage from the Vatican. They leave us alone. Jesus, I can't believe you stabbed me."

"Do they leave the monastery unlocked?"

"No. We knock, and they let us in."

"How many are armed?"

"Everyone, except the Cardinal."

"Where exactly will I find Drakul?"

The driver hesitated, and Morgan reminded him of the cost of not cooperating with another jab. The man screamed again, then coughed up spit. "In the back, beyond the monk's cells. The conference room and the library. Closed to the public. Drakul will be there."

"Good man." Morgan pulled out the duct tape. "Are all you guys with the Catholic Church?"

"We report to Cardinal Drakul."

"You know what he's up to?"

The driver glanced at Taylor and narrowed his eyes. "God's work."

"God's work, my ass. You guys are in cahoots with a demon, for Christ's sake. Attacking my little girl. I should kill you right here." He made a poor-man's tourniquet. Morgan put his hand on the man's chest. "You're lucky *I'm* a believer."

Morgan forced him into the trunk. Linda came up and tied his hands and feet, then gagged him. Next, they repeated the procedure with the unconscious Romanoff.

Morgan took the wheel, with Linda riding shotgun and Taylor in the back. "Ready?"

They nodded.

The car climbed the steep hill where the road dead-ended at a deserted parking lot next to a closed gift shop. Stairs led to the monastery.

The monastery must be closed to tourists today. That's good. Then the bad news struck him. *Shit. There's someone in a priest's robe at the top of the stairs.*

The priest called out, "You killed Morgan and his girlfriend? Saved us from lugging them upstairs?" The accent sounded Eastern European.

Morgan didn't flinch. *Can he see me through the smoked glass from that distance?* He tightened his grip on his pistol.

The priest's expression altered to one of recognition and panic. He pulled out his own pistol and aimed it at Morgan.

CHAPTER 16

Morgan felt a violent chill. *I don't want to shoot a priest.* But the priest didn't fire. Instead, he retreated into the monastery.

"Why didn't he shoot?" Linda asked.

Morgan's leg cramped tighter. "He has orders to deliver Taylor alive to Drakul. Can't risk hitting her."

"But now they know we're here," Linda said. "We'll have an army on us in no time."

"The driver said they keep the door locked." Morgan raced out of the car. "Maybe I can catch him before he warns anyone."

He ran up the stairs. The priest was rapping on a monumental door with his back to Morgan.

There's still time. Morgan raised his weapon. "Stop! I *will* shoot."

The priest hesitated, then spun around with his own pistol raised.

Morgan didn't match his delay. He shot the priest in the lower leg, giving him a flesh wound. The priest crumpled to the ground, screaming as he fell. His pistol fell impotently next to him.

Morgan rushed him and secured the stray pistol. "Cooperate and I'll let you live."

"But *you* will die," the priest cackled. "No one can stop the revelation."

Linda and Taylor reached the top of the steps. They looked like seasick ghosts. "What happened?" they said in unison.

"Just winged him. He'll recover."

"What do we do with him?" Linda said.

Morgan inspected the monastery. The wind, stronger at the top of the hill, blew leaves past him. Fifty-foot-high walls and a reinforced door made it clear there would be no insurgencies. Above the main entrance was a small opening.

"What's that?" Taylor asked. "For spying?"

"For defense," Morgan said. "They could pour burning oil on anyone trying to break in."

"Oh, yeah," Taylor said. "I remember learning that."

"I'm digging the whole history lesson, but a monk might show up any second," Linda said.

The priest violated Morgan's instructions and yelled for help. Morgan kicked him in the teeth, knocking chipped, white fragments across the ground. "Bad listener." He drove the man's pistol into his scalp, knocking the priest out cold. "Help me tie him up. By the time someone finds him, we'll have Drakul." *I hope.*

Linda and Taylor helped Morgan get the priest tied up out of sight. Morgan secured all three firearms, and then returned to the front door. Linda and Taylor followed.

Morgan tried the door and found it locked as expected. "Drakul and his men should be in the back. Probably didn't hear any of the screams or gunshots." He knocked.

"One problem," Taylor said. "We don't fit the profile of being from the Vatican. Two women? And look how we're dressed."

"Leave that to me," Morgan said.

The door creaked open inch by inch. Morgan couldn't stand the suspense and peeked around.

A monk in a brown robe and sash pulled the door ajar. Small of stature, he grunted as he pulled.

"Greetings," Morgan said. "English?"

"Yes," the monk said. "I only one. Why I answer door."

"We're just in from the Vatican." *Damn, I could use a cross right about now. At least Taylor has hers.* "Linguistic specialists for Cardinal Drakul's research team. He and his Vatican priests have scrolls for us to translate. May we come in?"

The monk studied them. For too long. Morgan began to perspire. *Come on. I don't really want to push a monk around.*

The monk opened the door further, allowing them passage. Without an utterance, he motioned for them to enter.

The main courtyard had a pebble and stone floor, with a covered holy water well in the center. Centuries of construction and reinforcement resulted in floors at different levels, depending on which direction Morgan looked. The hum of Byzantine hymns rose from the main chapel.

"Which way?" Morgan asked.

The monk strained to close the door. He nodded toward the chapel of The Virgin Mary. "Library beyond chapel, past refectory. I take you."

"No need." Morgan perused the area, then moved forward. "Stay close." Taylor followed, with Linda bringing up the rear.

They passed the chapel and walked along the dim hallway. On their right, light passed into the hallway from an adjacent open doorway. Morgan slowed. He pulled out his own firearm. Linda took another pistol from his waist.

"You sure?" he asked.

Linda nodded. "We may need it." Her voice trembled.

Morgan took a deep breath and stepped into the gap, his firearm poised.

A dozen monks sat around two marble tables, eating. Priceless artwork adorned the walls. The monks paid him no mind.

They eased farther along. No matter how softly he tried to walk, each step echoed in the hallway, and he paused before taking another one. *They'll hear us coming. Not good.*

Ahead, a large wooden door loomed, this one closed. Morgan listened.

Shuffling sounds. *Someone's definitely in there.* He reached for the brass handle.

But the door opened from the inside, and Morgan found himself face to face with the British gentleman from the cave. The gent saw the weapon and shivered. "You again. What on earth are you doing waving that around?"

Morgan lowered his pistol. "What are you doing here?"

"Why, I told you I'm visiting."

The chap was alone. Bookcases lined the walls. Manuscripts covered a half dozen tall tables, surrounded by high wooden chairs.

"This room is off limits to visitors," Morgan said.

Linda and Taylor edged in. Linda still had her firearm.

"Ah," the gent said, "your ladies are with you. Smashing. Care to come in?"

Morgan didn't budge, weighed by confusion and suspicion. "You didn't explain how you're allowed in here." He raised the pistol slightly.

The gent put his hands on his hips. "Now, see here. I've done nothing but be kind with you. I must insist you put that loathsome thing away."

Morgan stared into his calm, blue eyes. *There's something off about you, old man.* "You work for Drakul?"

"Who?"

"Have you seen any Catholic priests around?" Linda asked. "A cardinal, perhaps?"

The man rubbed his chin. "Well, the place has forty monks in residence. But actual priests, I don't think so."

Morgan locked onto the man's eyes. "We know they're here. They have access to this library. You sure you haven't seen them?"

"I'm certain. But I only have access to the library. No further."

Morgan considered that. *It's possible. There must be hundreds of rooms back there.* He relaxed his grip. "Can you point us toward the conference room?"

"Oh, that won't be necessary."

The cold steel of a firearm lodged itself yet again into the back of Morgan's head. Linda and Taylor squealed as two Vatican priests nabbed them.

Cardinal Drakul stepped from the shadows. His eyes were exactly like his photo. Dark and menacing.

"You see," the gent said, "there's no future for you in there." He grinned devilishly at Taylor. "But, you, my dear, you have quite the future in store."

Cardinal Drakul bowed toward Taylor. "Allow me to introduce myself. Cardinal Drakul, Head of the Order of Patmos." He raised up straight to look her directly in the eyes. "But you can call me Savior."

Morgan half-turned and saw who had the pistol on him. *Romanoff! How did you escape?*

"We have been watching you all along," Drakul said. "My man Romanoff is very upset about the way you treated him. When we woke him in the trunk he was quite motivated to come deal with you personally."

Prepared to die trying to save Taylor, Morgan tensed to strike. A blow to his head caught him by surprise. He fell to his knees, and the room faded to black.

CHAPTER 17

Taylor stared at Drakul. *You don't look so tough. I'll kick your ass.*

She scanned the room. Drakul was vulnerable to a rush, and the Vatican priest holding her used a light grip. Almost respectful. Like she was not to be harmed.

She broke free and rushed Drakul. "You sick bastard." She lunged at him with outstretched hands. "Leave my Dad alone!"

The Brit seized her hair. Then two strong hands tied her wrists behind her. They weren't gentle about it, and her eyes watered at the pain.

She checked on her dad. Still out cold. His hands were tied, like Linda's. "What is it with you, anyway? How do you even know us?"

Drakul studied her. "He hasn't told you." He rubbed his hands together. "How delicious."

Taylor stared at Linda. "What's he talking about?"

"Don't listen to him. He's a deranged, evil man."

Drakul howled with laughter. "Evil? I will bring about the ultimate salvation." He waved to his surroundings. "And I owe my inspiration all to this place. Studying here and in the cave, I found the answer. And then you brought me the demon, the jackal we need." He winked at Taylor. "And *you* will be the most important piece."

Taylor gulped. *This guy's lost it.* She thought back to something her father had repeated many times. *Only a fool isn't afraid of a crazy man.*

Drakul motioned to his henchmen. "Take the good doctor and his girlfriend. Dispose of their bodies where they'll never be found." He beamed at Taylor. "I have a story to share with our girl."

"No!" Taylor screamed. But Morgan and Linda were hauled away, and Taylor was alone with Drakul. She tried to wrestle out of the binds but only scraped her wrists on the rope.

These nut jobs are serious. They mean to kill my Dad. I have to save him.

"I'm not afraid of you," she spit out.

"Congratulations. Now, sit over there, and I'll tell you why you are the chosen one."

"The chosen one?"

"Oh, yes. You, of all the women on earth, will deliver salvation to the human race. You should feel honored."

"Whatever it is you want, I won't cooperate."

Drakul smiled. "Fortunately, your cooperation is unnecessary."

Taylor's face drained. *What's he talking about?* "Just try to come after me. I'll make you wish you hadn't. And my Dad, he'll kill you."

"Oh, dear, I won't do anything to you. But Lilith? That's something entirely different."

CHAPTER 18

Morgan woke to a pounding head and blurred vision in a dark, square room with walls of gray brick. The sink and toilet next to him smelled of excrement and lye soap. A thin layer of slime on the floor reeked of mold. His initial attempt to raise his head resulted in sharp pain. *Ugh, that's probably a concussion. Take it slow.*

He tested his ankles and wrists and found them bound. He squinted at a shape near a dim light.

Linda crouched there, bound by rough twine and gagged with a dirty rag. A floor lamp shone next to her. Her wide eyes warned him of imminent danger.

A crack on Morgan's head dropped him back to the floor.

"You think you tough guy?"

Romanoff. Hippocratic oath or not, I should have killed you.

"I will show how impotent you are," Romanoff continued. "I torture your girlfriend. Then kill her. You watch. Then, favorite part. Torture you, kill you in front of daughter."

"You're not man enough to do any of that."

Linda's face turned red as Romanoff approached her, a knife in his hand.

"You better deal with me first," Morgan said. "Oh, wait. I almost forgot. You're a spineless coward."

Romanoff ignored him and took Linda's hair in his fist, the knife poised. "Your mind games will not work on me."

Morgan needed a different distraction. He squirmed to one elbow. "Answer me one thing."

Romanoff put the knife against Linda's scalp. "Pay attention. You don not want to miss this."

"What is Drakul going to do with Taylor? If you want to torture me, nothing can hurt me more than knowing her fate in the cardinal's talons."

Romanoff considered this, then eased the pressure on Linda's head. "You are right. That will be much worse for you." He released Linda and stepped halfway to Morgan. "I will tell you about all of it. And how *you* made it possible."

Morgan swallowed. *Keep buying time. There has to be a way out of this.* "Tell me about the Order of Patmos."

Romanoff's chest puffed out. "We are selected few within Catholic Church. Not part of Pontiff's Catholics. True believers. Not politicians, like Pontiff."

He wants to tell me. Take him right where he wants to go. "You must be special to be one of the selected few."

"Not me." Romanoff teared up. "Drakul leads. Will save us all."

"I want to believe you, but I'm struggling with one thing. You're aligning with a demon. You'll infect girls and turn them into lamias. How can that be God's plan?"

"You not seeing big picture." Romanoff took a step closer.

One more step, and I can reach him.

"You know where we are, right?" Romanoff asked.

"Yeah. The place where John received the Revelation. So?"

"The Order of Patmos created by true believers to make prophecy of revelation come true. Cardinal Drakul will bring Antichrist. Which is first step in Christ's return to earth. Our ultimate salvation."

Morgan pretended to be sore and shifted closer to Romanoff.

"The Antichrist's a bad guy, right? A thousand years of misery and war. Stuff like that?"

"Necessary step. Now, here is best part. You in prophecy we found in caves."

Morgan glanced at Linda. She looked as puzzled as he felt. "What are you talking about?"

Romanoff inched even closer. "My people discovered clues for executing prophesy in cave. Then we found out about you and Taylor from Cardinal Vitelli. And Lilith. Easy to put all together."

"Put what together? Releasing a plague on girls? How does that do anything good?"

"Not a question of *good*. Question of what *has to be*. What is *preordained*. We are making end time happen."

Morgan judged the gap between them at five feet. *If I can get on my feet, I can knock him over. Maybe he'll hit his head.* "What does conspiring with Lilith have to do with the Antichrist."

Romanoff shook his head. "What is first step in birthing Antichrist?"

Morgan flashed back to the cemetery scene in *The Omen*. The jackal in the grave. *The Antichrist's mother.* "You're looking for a jackal?"

"Do not be stupid. The jackal in prophecy isn't *literal*."

"I'm still not following."

Romanoff looked pleased with himself. "That is the discovery, the link, we made in cave. The jackal is actually a demon! To birth the Antichrist we need a demon."

Morgan's mind whirled. *Where's he going with this?* "Lilith?"

"There you go. You catching up now."

"But that makes no sense. Lilith can't give birth."

Romanoff laughed. "And that is where your daughter comes in."

Dizziness rushed Morgan. He lurched toward Romanoff but fell flat on his face. His nose split open and spewed blood. "You touch Taylor, I'll kill you."

"No need for anyone to touch her."

Morgan lost focus as tears flooded his eyes from the damage to his nose. "How can you be this stupid? A demon isn't a prop. It's *evil*. And *dangerous*."

Romanoff paused as if to savor the moment. "We far from stupid. We only ones with answer. This demon has powers beyond turning people into vampires. While possessing a girl of childbearing age, it can also impregnate the host."

Morgan wondered if he'd heard correctly. He fought nausea. "What century are you living in? That's biologically impossible." Each word drove a spike into his head from his nasal passages.

Romanoff laughed. "So was Virgin Mother. Taylor will be second to give a virgin birth. The Antichrist."

The crazy bastard believes it! Morgan involuntarily choked on his own blood. *Lilith can't do that.* Then, a dark thought floored him. *I didn't think Lilith could turn her, either. I was wrong. What if I'm wrong again?* Somewhere deep inside, where he didn't want to admit even existed, he suddenly believed the hideous idea Romanoff proposed. "No. You can't."

"Oh, we can. Lilith busy turning girls, waiting for Drakul to bring Taylor. So we have multiple approaches. Demon moving from city to city on a cruise ship, with offspring spreading plague globally. And, at same time, we have Taylor birthing the Antichrist. By time Antichrist is old enough to lead, world will be in chaos, almost destroyed." He cackled like the demon he coveted. "By then, people will welcome the Antichrist."

Morgan's world faded to black.

CHAPTER 19

Morgan woke in a bloody mess. His face stuck to the floor when he tried to move. "Linda?"

No answer.

He coughed, then spit up blood. He pulled his face from the floor and rolled onto his back. The pain in his nose reverberated throughout his entire body. He tested his hands and feet. Still bound. "Linda! Where are you?"

He scanned the rest of the room. No Romanoff, either. *Why would they leave me alone?* He forced his upper body up to a sitting position. *Romanoff claimed he planned to torture her in front of me.* He spit out more blood. *Did he change his mind?*

The door squealed open and Romanoff stepped in, a sinister grin on his face. A sick feeling lodged in Morgan's stomach.

Romanoff lit up. "Good. You awake. Afraid you'd miss out on watching Linda die."

"Where is she?" Morgan asked. "And where's Taylor?"

"Don't worry. Your girlfriend is down hall. Taylor is with Drakul. Off to meet Lilith."

"Look, you can do whatever you want to me. Just don't hurt *them*."

Romanoff stepped further into the room. "You got me fired." He pulled out his knife. "I will make you watch while I kill your friend."

Morgan's stomach cramped and bile rushed up his esophagus. He decided on a plan of action. He swallowed blood until the churning reached a crescendo and he vomited his stomach's contents on Romanoff's shoes.

"Look what you did." Romanoff put his knife in its sheath and took a step back. "Jesus, that reeks." He glared at Morgan. "I will be back, and we will get started."

A shadow showed itself beyond Romanoff. It grew larger as Romanoff slowly backpedaled.

Please be a monk. Call for help.

Romanoff took a final step into the hallway, and the shadow lunged. Romanoff toppled over.

Riki Vitelli stepped into the room, holding a bloodied rock.

"Riki! Thank God. Careful, he's got a knife."

Riki took the knife and kicked Romanoff in the gut. "He is out."

"How'd you find us?"

Riki untied Morgan. "I knew you came to Patmos. The cave and monastery were the obvious choices." His smile faded. "Where is Taylor?" He blushed. "And Linda?"

"Linda should be down the hallway." Morgan shook his hands to get the circulation flowing. "Drakul has Taylor. They're gone."

Riki's face darkened. "Do we know where?"

Morgan bent his legs at the knees and stretched. "My guess, the cruise ship Lilith attacked. Docked in Monaco."

"Can you walk?"

"Yeah."

"Then no time to waste. Come. We find Linda." He stared at Morgan. "Your nose is sideways. Let me fix."

"That's okay."

Before Morgan could stop him, Riki reached out and tweaked Morgan's nose. Pain radiated through his face, then subsided.

Riki nodded his approval. "Better."

Morgan gingerly touched it, and found it mostly straight. "Let me guess. You're an expert at fixing broken noses."

Riki waved him on. "Save Linda. Then Taylor."

"Hang on." Morgan moved over Romanoff and slapped him.

Romanoff groaned, then opened his eyes.

"Where's Drakul taken Taylor?" Morgan asked, while Riki kept the knife at Romanoff's neck. "You have five seconds."

"I never tell you."

"Four."

Romanoff glanced at Riki. "A million dollars to kill Dr. Morgan. Plus, a seat at table when we unleash Antichrist."

"Three."

Romanoff grinned at Morgan. "We both know you won't have the boy kill me."

"Two."

Romanoff defiantly glared at Morgan.

"One."

The time expired, and Romanoff laughed.

Morgan pushed the knife away. "You're right, I won't ask him to do it." He took Romanoff's head in his hands and twisted with a rush of adrenalin, snapping Romanoff's vertebrae. "There. Now you're really fired." He released the head, and it slammed against the floor.

Morgan wiped his forehead and checked on Riki, whose skin sparkled in sweat. "Sorry you had to see that."

"He would have killed you. He took Taylor."

"Yeah. There may be more of them. And they're armed. You up for this?"

Riki flashed the knife. "Don't worry."

"I know. You're an expert. But I hope we don't have to put that to the test. It's no fun." *And we* are *bringing a knife to a gunfight.*

They eased down the hall, passing open doors and empty chambers until only one cloud door remained. A light glimmered through a crack underneath. Morgan brushed against the door, listening, careful to keep his feet from casting a shadow under the door.

Something inside moved. A shuffling sound. Morgan took the knob in his hand. He turned it slightly, but it announced his presence with a rusty squeak.

"Romanoff?" came a hushed British whisper from inside.

Morgan lowered his voice and did his best Russian accent. "Yeah. Open."

Footsteps approached the door, and Morgan tensed. He nodded to Riki. "I'll rush him." *And if he's not alone?* Morgan shook that thought away.

The doorknob rotated. The instant the door moved, Morgan shoved it with his shoulder and stumbled in.

The Brit, holding an automatic weapon, fell back. Morgan lost his balance and crashed to the floor. *Oh, shit.* He expected bullets to rip into him at any moment.

Instead, a swoosh flew by him, and a gargling sound came from the Brit. A knife stuck out of his throat, and his eyes glazed over. The man fell to the floor as Riki retrieved his knife.

Riki stepped in and helped Morgan to his feet. "Look." He pointed to a table where Linda lay, strapped and gagged, her eyes closed. Morgan rushed to her and undid the gag. "Linda. Talk to me." He checked for a pulse. "She's alive."

He patted her face, and she responded with a faint smile. "I knew you'd come. Taylor?"

Morgan released the straps holding her. She appeared unharmed. "Drakul has her." He stepped back so she could see Riki. "Look who I found."

She forced a wider smile. "Riki! How'd you find us?"

Morgan helped her sit up. "He's an expert, remember?" He gave Riki a nod. Riki put his hand up for a high five. Morgan rolled his eyes and gave him one.

"Romanoff?" Linda asked.

"Dead." He shrugged. "And, yes, I killed him. He refused to give up Taylor's location. I think the rest of the cult went with Drakul."

"He left you no choice, right?" she said.

No choice? Kind of. "I did what I had to do."

Linda stared at him for a moment, then blew out a breath. "Where to then? You must have a plan."

"The cruise ship," Morgan said. "It's time we face the demon. And free Taylor once and for all." He turned to Riki. "You have a phone?"

"I brought a burner." Riki pulled an old-fashioned flip phone from his shirt pocket. "Thought you'd want to be off the grid."

"Good thinking." Morgan took it and dialed Garcia. "I should check in with Javi. He deserves to know."

The phone rang twice before Garcia answered. "Hello?"

"Javi!"

"Pennywise! Where are you, man?"

"Patmos. On our way to Monte Carlo. Listen, Taylor's been kidnapped."

"What? By who?"

"A rogue group calling themselves the Order of Patmos. A Cardinal Drakul has her. He's taking her to Lilith. He says Lilith can impregnate her after it takes possession. He's trying to bring about the Antichrist."

After several seconds of silence, Garcia whispered. "Antichrist? A Cardinal? I don't understand. Listen, Smokey and I are in Rome, looking for you."

"What?"

"We're here, man. Is Linda with you?"

Morgan's heart picked up the pace. "She's okay." He winked at her. "Meet us in Monaco. I'll call when we arrive."

Morgan verified he still had the Vatican credit card. "Let's go. The ferry to Athens, then a train to Monaco."

CHAPTER 20

Taylor woke from a drugged sleep in a pitch-black space. The last thing she remembered was fighting with Drakul at Patmos. But she sensed she was far away from there now.

Far away from Dad. She steeled herself and sat up.

The room came into focus. A bed. A dresser. And a crib.

A crib? Who's that for?

She swung her legs over the side of the bed. Her bare feet scraped against the pebble and stone floor. Definitely not the Ritz.

She found a lamp on the nightstand and pulled the chain.

As light flooded the room, a nursery with black walls and furniture appeared. *Who paints a nursery black?*

The door opened, startling her. Drakul, wearing a black robe that got lost in the background, carried in a tray of food and dirty water in a plastic glass. "Ah, you're awake. Excellent."

"Where am I?"

Drakul set the tray in front of her. His eyes reflected the black bedding. Taylor shivered. *I've seen black eyes like that before.* But she couldn't recall where.

"You're in your new home. Eat. You'll need your strength."

Taylor shoved the tray away. "I'm not hungry. And this isn't my home."

"Don't be obstinate. You need nourishment. The drugs will dehydrate you." He pushed the tray back toward her. "Drink. It won't help you to suffer."

"Where's my Dad?"

Drakul didn't answer. Instead, he sat across from her in a chair. "I will do what your father never did. Tell you the truth."

"My father never lies."

"Did he tell you who Lilith is?"

Taylor shifted uncomfortably. "Some kind of bad lady who infected me and my friends."

Drakul grinned, showing yellow, pointy teeth, which made Taylor cringe. "Lilith isn't a bad *lady*. She's a demon, straight from Satan's lair. Been around for thousands of years. She possessed you and turned you into your own special kind of monster, and *you* infected your friends."

Taylor peered into his eyes, looking for any sign of deceit. She found only blackness. "That's crazy. You want me to believe I was possessed? Like in a horror movie?" She remembered watching The Exorcist with her father and not being able to sleep afterward. He'd sat with her all night.

"It's true. And, deep inside, you know it."

Taylor sank into the bed. The clanging of "Tubular Bells," a memory she couldn't quite place, ran through her head. "Monster? What's that mean?"

"It turned you into a lamia."

Taylor's stomach roiled. "What's that?"

"It's a special vampire. One that feasts on girls and turns them into more lamias. One possession can end up infecting thousands, millions of girls. And, without women, there are no children. The human race dies off." His eyes danced at the thought.

Taylor took a drink from the plastic glass before she even realized. "You're lying. There's no such thing as vampires."

"A commonly held belief."

Taylor felt lightheaded. "You put something in this?"

Drakul took the glass from her. "Rest. You have a special guest on the way."

"Dad?" she stammered.

"No, dear. Your father is dead." He let that sink in. "I'm your father, now."

Taylor gasped, then slumped onto the bed. The tainted water did its job. She fell asleep and entered a realm of horrifying nightmares.

CHAPTER 21

Salem, Oregon

Dr. Azra Khan paced circles around her sterile confines at the Salem Medical Examiner's Office. She stared at the metal slabs in the autopsy room through her office window, trays that had been full of live, infected girls just weeks before. Nigel Rathbone, her mentor from the CDC, and the one who'd approved her quarantine request, was waiting for her in the conference room, along with an FBI agent. This was her big moment, and she wasn't about to let her ex-fiancee ruin it unless he admitted his mistake and begged her to reestablish their relationship.

Richard, why won't you take my calls? I didn't want it to come to this.

She dialed Morgan one last time. Again, no answer. No connection to voice mail. Nothing.

She pocketed the phone in her white medical coat and narrowed her eyes. *You'll be sorry you treated me like this. It was bad enough you abandoned me for that deranged bitch who put all these crazy ideas about demons, exorcisms, and vampires into your head. But to cut off all contact? Disrespect me like this? Disrespect our medical training? You'll pay for that.*

She picked up two file folders, ones she'd spent days carefully crafting, making sure they could honestly withstand the most stringent scrutiny. Azra's mentor and a fortyish African-American man in sunglasses, both in dark suits, sat impatiently. She slapped the folders onto the metal table. "Results of the contagion diagnosis here in Salem."

Rathbone, spoke first. "Dr. Khan. Nice to see you again. This is Special Agent Collins." After handshakes, he continued. "Give me the highlights."

Azra settled into a chair opposite them. "We found a previously unknown virus in the bloodstreams of the victims. We treated each victim with a different antiviral. Before we could establish an effective countermeasure, the virus ran its course and the girls all recovered on their own."

"You're certain it's an unknown virus?" Rathbone said.

"Nothing like I've ever seen. Of course, the CDC database is far more extensive. You have everything you need to do your own check."

"If it went away that quickly, why are we here?" the FBI agent asked. He was a good foot taller than Azra. His red tie screamed "I'm in charge here."

Rathbone opened the file and perused it. "We always flag new diseases from remote locations. Many of the world's most dangerous contagions originate from places like the jungles of Costa Rica."

"Okay," the FBI agent said, "that explains why you're here. Why call the FBI?"

Azra narrowed her eyes. "As we tracked the virus, we noticed it mutating just before it vanished."

"Mutating how?" Rathbone asked.

Azra thought back to the freaky quarantine. "It was dividing and spreading quickly. The girls were getting worse, showing frightening symptoms, like patient zero."

"What kind of symptoms?" the FBI agent asked.

"Pain in their mouths. Unusual growth in some teeth. Eye and skin color changes. Variations in their normal speech patterns. Hostility."

"That was all in your preliminary report," Rathbone said. "But you didn't mention anything about a mutation."

"We didn't recognize it right away. As the symptoms retreated, and the girls recovered, we assumed the changes were part of that healing. Only after we analyzed the data did we realize it mutated."

Rathbone frowned. "You have the tissue samples that show this?"

"Of course."

The FBI agent rifled through the pages. "I still don't understand why you insisted I come to this meeting. Seems like a job for the CDC."

Azra addressed the agent. "Because patient zero, Taylor Morgan, and her father, Dr. Richard Morgan, broke out of our quarantine and fled to Europe."

"Is she a risk to others?" the FBI agent asked Rathbone.

Rathbone rubbed his chin. "Based on this new mutation revelation, it's possible."

Azra leaned in. "It pains me to say this, but Dr. Morgan fully understood the stakes, and the risk." She paused for effect. "He took her on purpose."

"Why?" the FBI agent asked.

"He fought us at every turn when we were trying to contain the virus. I think he's got some unknown agenda." She drifted in further. "It's as if he wants the virus to spread, and he knew he had to get out of our jurisdiction to make that happen."

The FBI agent exchanged glances with Rathbone. "That's a serious accusation."

"I know," Azra said. "Richard and I go way back, and he's not the same guy I used to know and respect. He's mentally unstable."

"Do you know where they are?" Rathbone asked.

"You've seen the news in Monaco? The symptoms match. What better way to move it around Europe than on cruise lines that hit a new port every day?"

The FBI agent stared at the file. "Okay. I'll call Interpol and have them alert law enforcement."

"And I'll contact the World Health Organization," Rathbone said. "Give them the background about this pathogen. I know they're all over that cruise ship." He paused. "But, if it mutates, it might not be as easily defeated as the victims here in Salem. It could create a dangerous epidemic."

"I'm certain they caught it from Taylor Morgan," Azra said. "I need not to tell you how dangerous Dr. Morgan and Taylor are if allowed to roam the planet."

The FBI agent nodded. "Don't worry, Dr. Khan. In a few hours the entire world will be looking for them. There's nowhere they can hide."

Azra smiled.

CHAPTER 22

Monte Carlo, Monaco

Morgan, Linda, and Riki de-boarded the train after a half day's travel from Patmos, feeling exposed without their weapons. Linda tried to pull the wrinkles out of her sweat-stained blouse. Morgan settled for hand-combing his now oily hair.

The train station floors looked clean enough to eat on, and the walls reflected their shadows in the fluorescent lighting.

Darkness had fallen, and crystal stars lit up the sky. The cruise ship rested in the harbor. "There it is."

"What's the plan?" Linda asked.

Morgan squinted at the security staff surrounding the ship. "Find out if Taylor's on there. And if Lilith's *still* on there. Save Taylor. Kill Lilith."

"How are we going to get aboard?" Linda asked. "It's still under quarantine."

"I don't know. But if they got Taylor on, there must be a way."

"They'll have a list of anyone who boards," Riki said. "Right?"

Morgan agreed. "Should. Let me try Javi." He gave up after a dozen rings. "Not answering. Let's catch a cab."

Morgan started to hail someone when something familiar caught his eye. He shifted his attention to a wall in the station. His picture stared back at him from a flyer. *Wanted for questioning. Contact the authorities. Do not approach.* "That's not good."

Linda came up. "The Swiss Guard must have put them on to you." She pulled him away from the streetlight and into the shadows. "You need to lie low."

"I need to find Taylor."

Riki cleared his throat. "They're looking for Taylor, too." A second flyer on a connected wall displayed her picture, with the same caption. "Why would the Swiss Guard want her? They know she didn't shoot my great uncle."

"But they don't know what happened with Berger," Morgan said.

"Then why nothing about me?" Linda asked.

"Good question," Morgan said.

Riki peered around the corner. "No police. But this is bad. Interpol. The Swiss Guard. The Order of Patmos assassin who took out Berger. All looking for us."

Morgan noticed the use of the word *us*. *I like this guy more all the time.* He closed his eyes. "Maybe I should turn myself in. Not to the Swiss Guard, but to the Monaco police."

"What?" Linda said. "Why would you do that?"

"They may be our best chance at saving Taylor." Morgan opened his eyes and rubbed them. "Based on the flyers, they're already looking for her. Maybe we can help them find her. Before Drakul gets her to Lilith."

Linda's face washed out. Morgan could almost read her mind. *They may already have Taylor on that ship, and she may already be possessed.* He shivered.

"And if they lock you up for murder?" Riki asked.

Anxiety crashed onto Morgan. "You're right. Our only option is to find out if Taylor's on that ship."

"But how?" Linda asked.

A gruff voice spoke from behind. "I have an idea, Doc."

Morgan spun and came face-to-face with Lieutenant Smokey and Garcia. Smokey had his trademark unlit Cuban Montecristo. Garcia was casually dressed, with his white collar.

"Javi!" Morgan rushed to embrace him. "Boy, am I glad you found us." He blushed at ignoring Smokey. "You too, detective. Guys, this is Riki Vitelli. He's Cardinal Vitelli's great nephew, or something like that. And an expert at many useful things."

Riki beamed as he shook hands. "A friend of Dr. Morgan is a friend of mine."

"Likewise," Smokey said.

"We've been so worried," Garcia said. "I talked to Cardinal Vitelli at the Vatican, and Smokey spoke with the European authorities. The police say you tried to murder a Cardinal, then killed the head of the Swiss Guard? And now, you're intentionally trying to spread Taylor's virus across Europe?"

Morgan swallowed. "Taylor's virus? How would they get that idea?"

Garcia looked down. "Azra convinced the CDC and the FBI you're dangerous. They contacted the WHO and Interpol." His eyes rose to meet Morgan's. "She's pretty pissed."

Morgan took a moment to digest that. "There's nothing I can do about her right now. Smokey, you said you have an idea?"

"The Padre and I did reconnaissance at the cruise ship. Between my badge and his collar, we got a hint of what's going on."

"Tell me," Morgan said.

"First," Smokey said, "as a professional courtesy they let me see the log of everyone going in or out. No girls have gone on board since they contained the plague."

Morgan's face warmed. "So no Taylor." He turned to Linda. "Could we have beaten Drakul here?"

"If he has to move slowly to keep Taylor concealed, maybe."

"They've got fifteen girls showing symptoms," Smokey continued. "Isolated in the showroom. Doctors and nurses from the WHO are trying to treat them. The rest of the passengers and crew have been taken off the ship, so the ship's a ghost town. Security is high, of course."

"So," Morgan said, "if we can find Lilith's host, we can kill Lilith before she gets to Taylor."

Garcia swallowed. "If Lilith is still there. She may have fled."

"She's there," Morgan said, his voice hiding his own doubts. "It takes more time to turn the original host." *I hope.*

"What are we going to do about the girls?" Linda asked. "None of the WHO medicine is going to do any good. They don't understand what they're treating. Do we have to destroy the girls?"

Morgan felt dizzy. "One step at a time. We have to get on that ship and make an assessment."

"The cruise line hired private security to control access to the ship," Smokey said. "The local cops are watching the dock, but they won't go on the ship unless asked. They also have three patrol boats in the bay."

"So we have to sneak past the cops and talk our way onto the ship," Morgan said. *Which will take a miracle.*

Smokey grunted. "We might have a solution to that. They allow the parents of the infected girls to board and talk with the doctors. They just can't go inside the quarantine area."

"And that helps us how?" Morgan asked.

Garcia handed Morgan a badge. "I got this from a girl's father. It might get you past the police on the dock and the security guards at the ship."

Morgan looked at it and saw a mild resemblance between the fuzzy picture ID and himself. "How'd you get this?"

Garcia pawed at the ground. "I kind of stole it. I was consoling a dad, and the opportunity just presented itself."

Morgan laughed. "*Kind of stole it?* Javi, what have I done to you?"

"Let's not mention it ever again, okay? But you have to hurry, man. The dad will figure out he doesn't have the badge the next time he goes to visit, and he'll report it."

Linda squeezed his hand. "What if their security force has *your* picture? The cops do. Can't someone else do this?"

"No." Morgan looked at the badge. "It's my job. Let's go. I'll have a better chance of passing for this guy at night."

Linda let out a loud breath. "What if you do find Lilith?"

Morgan's stomach growled. "I've been thinking. That poor girl is turning, and infecting others, but if the transmutation isn't done, Lilith is still in the host girl. We can exorcise her again."

Garcia gulped. He wiped excretion from his forehead. "I don't know, man. Will it be susceptible to the same routine? And, don't forget, we don't have the shaman."

"He *was* critical," Linda agreed. "What about the silver to contain Lilith?"

Riki could stand no more. He stepped in front of Morgan. "Exorcism? Nobody said anything about an exorcism."

Morgan set his hands on Riki's shoulders. "You're right. We haven't told you everything. Lilith is a demon. It possessed Taylor recently. Now, it wants her again. To possess her, and worse."

Riki narrowed his eyes. "A demon?"

Morgan swallowed. "Lilith turns girls into vampires. That's what's happened on this ship. That's why we're here. To put an end to this human and spiritual carnage." He smiled at Riki. "You've done more than we could ever have asked. It's time for you to head back to Rome."

Riki stared at Morgan for a full minute while the rest of the crew watched in silence. "A demon? I must admit I'm not an expert at exorcisms."

"There are no experts, kid," Garcia said.

Riki rubbed his chin. "It would be interesting. Something to tell the Cardinal. And it will impress my friends."

Garcia moaned and grasped Riki by the shirt collar. He shook him. "It's not something to brag about. A battle with the devil is the worst experience a human being can go through." He gave one last shove before releasing him. "Understand?"

Riki wiped the smile off his face. "I'm sorry." He turned to Morgan. "Why didn't you tell me?"

"I considered confiding in you on the way here, but I worried I'd be robbing you of whatever semblance of adolescence you have remaining. The topic sucks the life out of you. That's why I never told everything to Taylor."

Linda cleared her throat. "Clock's ticking, guys. And we need that silver container."

"I know where there is a silver box," Riki said. He pointed to the hill above the harbor. "I need an hour."

"You sure?" Morgan asked.

"Positive. I can get it for you."

"That's good. But maybe we won't have to do an exorcism." Morgan put a finger to his lips. "I wonder what happens to Lilith if her host dies while she's still in there."

"You want to kill the girl it's possessing?" Garcia asked.

Morgan looked at his long-time friend. "No. But what if I can get it to possess me, and I jump overboard? Will I kill it if I drown while it's inside me? Avoid the need for an exorcism?"

"Richard!" Linda exclaimed. "You can't be serious."

I am serious. If it'll work, I'd be willing. But, could I actually commit suicide when I'm not sure? So many things could go wrong. It could escape while I'm plunging to my death. I just don't know. Morgan choked back more bile. "If it saves Taylor, I'm absolutely serious."

Riki came up to him. "I should let it possess me. She will need her father to get through this."

Morgan smiled at Riki. "I appreciate the gesture, but I can't let you do that. Besides, I have a history with it. We whipped it in Costa Rica. I'm sure it remembers. How about you settle for getting us that silver box?"

Riki nodded. Morgan could see the satisfaction in Riki's eyes. *Yeah, this guy's a keeper.*

"I'll go with him," Garcia said. "But, Pennywise, Lilith only attacks girls. What makes you think it'll go into you?"

Morgan shrugged. "It went into the bat at the exorcism. It was in a bat when it infected Taylor in Costa Rica. Why not an adult? I'm pretty sure it's pissed enough to want me."

"Then, after we get the silver box, I have to come with you," Garcia said. "You can tell security you brought the family priest. They won't deny me access."

"We should all go," Linda said. "Once Drakul and his henchmen show up, we'll need all hands on deck."

They stared at each other. Smokey broke the tension. "Come on, Doc. Let's go kill the bitch."

CHAPTER 23

Garcia and Riki stood in front of Saint Nicholas Cathedral in Monaco-Ville under faint moonlight. The Romanesque Revival architecture reminded him of many churches across Europe.

"You sure you can do this?" Garcia asked.

"I'm Italian. Pockets. Locks. All the same."

"But aren't there alarms? Video surveillance?"

"We are in the Bermuda Triangle of surveillance in Monaco. The Prince's Guards have responsibility for security near Grimaldi Palace, which is close by. But the Cathedral is not their primary concern, so their patrols are intermittent. Because of the proximity to the palace the police force also doesn't patrol here often. And we have another big advantage."

"What's that?"

"I run very fast."

Garcia stared at Riki. "That's your plan? Outrun armed guards?"

"Well, yes." He puffed out his chest. "I was a track star in school."

"What about me? I'm a short, paunchy Mexican-American. I don't run so fast."

Riki frowned. "Then I will go in alone. You put on your priest collar and walk back now. Priests are commonplace here. They will chase me, not you."

Garcia put a hand to his head. "This is crazy."

"You have a better idea?"

"No."

"Then it is settled. If you are stopped, hope it is by the police. The Prince's Guards are a military unit."

"That's comforting."

Riki nodded toward the church. "Have you seen the graves of Princess Grace and Prince Rainier?"

"First time in Monaco."

"Too bad you can't come in. They are majestic. I've seen all of Grace Kelly's pictures. You?"

"We didn't have many Grace Kelly nights in the barrio."

"But she's an American princess, right?"

Garcia regarded Riki with a mix of amazement and confusion. "I'm a Catholic Priest. We're not allowed princesses. Even ones that *are* Catholic."

"Too bad. She was very pretty."

Garcia couldn't help but laugh. He put on his collar. "Look, I appreciate the whole nostalgia deal, but we need to steal that box. Our friends are counting on us."

Riki saluted. "Yes, sir. You go. I suggest you stroll by Jacques Cousteau's Oceanography Museum. You can tell your friends."

"I'm not planning to tell *anybody* about tonight. Ever. Hurry. It'll be daylight soon."

Riki picked the lock on the Cathedral entrance.

"Two thefts in one day. And a break-in." Garcia crossed himself. "I'm forging quite the legacy."

"Go," Riki said. "I've almost got it."

The priest retraced his steps toward the cruise ship. *On the road to Hell. Or a third exorcism.*

Then the alarm sounded.

CHAPTER 24

Against the backdrop of the spotlit white cruise ship a hundred yards away, which showed a layer of grime from a week of stagnation, Morgan heard the alarm go off atop the hill above the harbor. *Javi! Riki!* "Damn. Now what?"

"Don't panic," Smokey said. "It might be something else."

"It doesn't sound like something else," Linda said. "Sounds like our guys got caught."

"Setting off an alarm and getting pinched are two different things. Give the Padre a chance."

Morgan fidgeted. "I should go up there."

"And do what?" Smokey said. "The police are looking for you. We need to focus on getting aboard that ship whether or not we have a silver box. The guy in charge is a cruise line executive. No security chops. You can see in the security guard's eyes they want to get paid and not catch whatever's on that ship. And, the executive's *wearing a cross.*"

"You think Javi can persuade him to let us all on?" Morgan asked. "What if they've seen my mug shot?"

"Cops don't like to share with private security," Smokey said. "We show up with a priest, a US lawman, and you as the grieving father, who brought his family to say one last goodbye, I like our chances."

The alarm shut off. Linda pointed to the road descending from the hilltop. "I see Garcia." She turned to Morgan. "I think he's okay."

The priest was almost to the bottom of the hill.

"But where's Riki?" Morgan asked.

"There," Smokey said.

Sure enough, Riki raced down the hill. He blew by Garcia, who broke into a jog for the last fifty yards.

"Get ready," Morgan said. "This looks bad."

Riki arrived first. "I got it." He displayed a silver box large enough to hold a large rat.

Garcia chugged in a moment later, wheezing. "Remind me to never go on another crime spree. Bad for my physical *and* spiritual health."

"I probably don't want to know where you found that," Morgan said.

"Oh, man, definitely not," Garcia said.

"It was in Saint Nicholas Cathedral," Riki blurted out. "My first church heist."

Garcia winced toward Morgan. "And there it is." He glanced toward the heavens. "My finest spiritual moment."

Linda hugged the priest. "It's okay, Father. God understands."

"Thank you. Someday, Saint Peter will decide if you are correct."

Smokey twirled his cigar. "You better give me the box. Just in case God *is* pissed and strikes you both."

Everyone laughed, though Morgan sensed underlying apprehension. "Thanks, Javi. I know that wasn't something you had on your bucket list."

Smokey took the box and put his pistol inside it. "My Salem badge will get this through security."

Morgan pulled a baseball cap he'd picked up in Athens over his eyes. "Let's go."

They reached the police checkpoint first. Two white vans with police markings blocked the entrance to the path leading to the cruise ship. Four policemen stood guard.

Smokey approached first and flashed his badge. "Detective Smokey from Salem, Oregon. I'm here with a local contingent supporting my friend, whose daughter is inside."

Morgan clipped his access badge to his jacket. "My daughter is in critical condition. I brought my family priest to give a blessing while I confer with the doctors. I know it's early, but my friends have a flight out of Nice later this morning."

A police officer checked Smokey's badge, Garcia's collar, and Morgan's clip-on. "Look at me," he said to Morgan.

Morgan fought for control, and his body shook. *Stay calm. The light's poor. You can do this.* He lifted his head and stared into the officer's eyes.

The officer glanced at Morgan's face, then at the access badge. "I am sorry about your daughter." He bent closer. "Is it as bad as they say?"

"It's bad. I'd stay off that ship if you can."

"I plan to. None of us wants anything to do with it." The guard nodded to the other officers to let them pass. "You're a good father."

"It's what we do, right?" Morgan said, and all four officers nodded. "God bless you all." *And God, thank you for granting my prayer. One miracle down. One to go.*

He corrected himself. *At least one to go.*

Garcia took the lead, and they marched in single file to the ship's security checkpoint. After several minutes of pleading and looking grief-stricken, they were each handed a badge that allowed access to the WHO coordination center in the main dining room.

Morgan led them up the gangway where their badges were scanned by more temporary guards. Once cleared, they found themselves in the main lobby. The overhead lights were off, and the ship struck Morgan as haunting. A guard pointed along a roped passageway toward the main dining room in the aft of the ship.

They moved until they were out of the guard's line of sight, settling next to a photo gallery. Pictures of elated vacationers still hung on the display.

"Now what?" Linda asked.

Morgan pointed at Smokey and Riki. "They verified Drakul didn't bring Taylor on, but we need to know the second they arrive. Can you two keep watch while Linda, Javi, and I sneak back to the showroom to check out the infected girls?"

"Are we looking for patient zero?" Garcia asked.

"Any evidence of Lilith's current location," Morgan said. "I'm afraid our arrival might get a reaction."

Garcia gulped. I need a glass of water. I'll bless it, and we'll have holy water. If God's still listening to me."

Garcia ran off and Linda gripped Morgan's arm. "You feel the vibe in here? Reminds me of the Bribri Village in Costa Rica during the exorcism." She tensed against him. "And the silence on this huge ship. It gives me the creeps."

Me, too. But best if I don't admit that. "Don't let it get in your head. It's just a ship." *Right. And Dracula's castle was just a lodge.*

Smokey retrieved the silver box and handed it to Morgan. "The gun's inside."

Morgan took the silver container and its content. "Call out if you see Drakul or Taylor. Do whatever you have to to free Taylor."

"Got it, Doc." Smokey turned to Riki. "Ready?"

Riki nodded, and they went back toward the entrance.

Morgan tapped the box. "The box won't do us any good without a bat. I have no idea how to locate one of those. And that's assuming Lilith's really here."

"What we need is an axe." When Morgan gave Linda a puzzled expression, she continued. "What if we have to destroy the infected girls?"

The horrifying truth felt like a spike driven through Morgan's head. "Jesus, Linda."

"I don't know what we'll find in there, but if any of them are too far gone, it's the only humane solution." She blushed. "You know it's true."

I was prepared to do it to Taylor. Seems like a million years ago. "Killing those girls is signing our own death warrant. I'd be abandoning Taylor."

"There's only two ways to save those girls." Linda teared up. "Exorcize the demon out of the host, like we did with Taylor in Costa Rica, or destroy them, like they did to my daughter in Peru."

Morgan held her while she cried. "Sorry you have to relive that."

"Not your fault."

Garcia returned carrying a drinking glass full of water. "Okay. I'm locked and loaded." He recognized Linda's tears. "What's wrong?"

Linda wiped them away. "Nothing. Let's get on with this."

Morgan, Linda, and Garcia crossed under a rope and stepped to the other side of the ship. A stairwell led them up a floor. They moved solemnly aft toward the showroom.

A twitchy guard in a rent-a-cop uniform stood nervously at the starboard showroom door. A plastic sheet with a slice to allow access covered the entrance.

When the guard saw them approaching, he stood up straighter and fear etched his brow.

He thinks I'm checking up on him. Why else would I be here? Use that. "Anything to report?"

The guard rattled his head. "Nothing, sir."

"Who's in charge?"

"The World Health doctor is in there with a bunch of nurses. They're in white smocks and masks. The doctor's the tall woman with red hair."

"Thanks. Stay alert."

"I will. There's weird shit going on."

You have no idea. Morgan walked past him, through the slit in the plastic barrier, and into the showroom.

Then froze. Linda and Garcia bumped into him, and he took one hesitant step to allow them in.

Morgan counted fifteen girls lying in rows of beds filling the stage. They all looked the same. Matted hair. Skin pale and inhumanly putrid. Red eyes staring at the ceiling. *Jesus. A fucking nest of lamias.*

Six nurses lingered around the beds, their backs to the exits. Their postures screamed 'I want out of here.' The doctor sat facing the stage in the first row, writing at a table. A loud air recycler purred by the patients.

Morgan eased toward the stage, followed by Linda and Garcia. *Good. They didn't hear us.*

"It's worse than I imagined," Linda whispered. "Smells like death."

Morgan studied each girl. "Taylor's not here. And no black eyes, so no sign of Lilith."

"She might be in one," Linda said. "She can stay hidden if she wants to."

"Right," Morgan said. "Check everyone. See if we can get Lilith to show herself. Remember, Lilith speaks articulately. The lamias can barely structure a sentence."

"We still don't have a way to exorcise her," Linda reminded him.

"I know. But we need to identify the host girl before we can do anything useful."

Garcia ambled ahead of them, spilling holy water in a shaking hand. "We're not prepared. We should leave." He turned to Morgan, his face mortified. "Pennywise, we shouldn't be here."

Morgan reached out to steady him. "This is where the fight is. There's nowhere else to be."

"You don't understand," Garcia said. His teeth chattered. "Once we came in here, I heard Lilith's thoughts. I think she's connected to us after the exorcism. She's been waiting for us. And the message is clear. Lilith intends to kill us all."

CHAPTER 25

Then demon Lilith stirred within its young girl host. *Within the hour, the transmutation will be complete. This host will be a lamia, and I can move on to the bitch,* my *Taylor.*

Something familiar tugged. Lilith sharpened its focus on the surrounding area.

The Arrogant Loser is here! And Father Chancho.

Lilith rose to the surface of its host.

I've been expecting you.

CHAPTER 26

The showroom lights flickered, then dimmed. The nurses backed away from their patients, exchanging glances and checking the exits under the emergency lights.

A deep voice bellowed from the stage. "Arrogant loser!"

Morgan's legs cramped. *Lilith!*

The nearest patient rose to a sitting position and hissed. Her eyes shifted from red to black, and her complexion burned in the subtle light.

"Chancho!" the infected girl yelled, pointing toward Garcia. "This time, without your Awà, you will die."

Garcia dropped the glass. It shattered and water splashed against their shins. Morgan caught the priest just before he passed out.

"Javi, hang on," he said, then looked at Linda, who was mesmerized by the scene before her. "Linda, we have to get Javi out of here."

The nurses screamed, then ran for the opposite exit.

The doctor, a woman of tall stature, stood. "Get back here!" But they were having none of it. She reached for a loaded syringe.

Morgan lifted Garcia into his arms and carried him through the protective barrier, followed by Linda. The guard was gone. Morgan set Garcia's unconscious body on the floor. "Can you stay with him?"

"Where are you going?"

Morgan took a deep breath. "Back in there."

"To do what?"

He didn't answer. Because he had no answer. He stepped back inside the breeding ground and gasped.

The girl, standing now, had the doctor by the neck, holding her high in the air. The doctor's face turned purple, but she managed to plunge her syringe into the girl.

The effect was immediate. The girl's eyes flickered. She loosened her grip, and the doctor extricated herself. The girl growled at the doctor, then fell to the floor.

Tranquilizers! Of course. They worked on Taylor. For a while. Morgan found his legs and ran to the doctor. "You okay?"

The doctor struggled to breathe. "I guess. Help me get her back onto the bed." Once they had the girl situated, the doctor paid Morgan more attention. "I appreciate the help, but you're not supposed to be in here. WHO personnel only."

"You looked like you could use some help," Morgan said. "Sorry if I broke containment protocols."

The doctor frowned. "Well, thank you. We've seen no sign of the infection spreading, so we were going to remove the plastic, anyway." She looked past him toward the exit. "I can't believe my nurses left."

"I think the circumstances would scare anyone." *Especially if you understood what you're dealing with.*

"I'm Dr. Hollister. Word Health Organization. Who are you?"

"I have some experience with what you're dealing with. I'm here to help."

Hollister hesitated. "Funny, I don't recall seeing you before." Hollister stared at his badge, then at him. "I need to make a call. Excuse me for one second."

Something tells me your call isn't about the patients. "Sure."

Hollister walked backstage, turned her back on him, and put the phone to her ear.

Linda joined Morgan at the base of the stage. "We found the host," Morgan whispered. "We need to take her."

"Where?"

Morgan eyed Hollister. "If we can get her into a stateroom while the sedative is working we can regroup and make a plan."

"Are you thinking an exorcism? Because our priest is passed out in the hall. And how do you plan to get access to a stateroom?"

"I'll blow the lock off."

Morgan glanced at Hollister, who was waving her free arm as she talked. He was about to pick the girl up when he caught movement a few feet away in one of the girls.

One infected girl rose, then another, until all fourteen were sitting up. Their stringy hair reeked like garbage. All at once they turned to Morgan, their eyes a fiery red, and grinned, each with protruding fangs and wretched breaths.

CHAPTER 27

The overhead lights in the showroom dimmed further. Morgan could think of no logical explanation, which left only the supernatural. He heaved the sedated girl over his shoulder and backed away from the stage, keeping his eyes on the fourteen lamias. "Linda, get ready to run!"

"What about the doctor?"

Doctor Hollister still had her back to the lamias, talking on the phone. *Shit. She's trapped back there.*

The fourteen girls slid off their beds. The scene was entirely different than when Taylor and her friends had been in the throes of the plague. Taylor had looked menacing, but these girls were well beyond anything he'd seen before. *They're rotting.*

"Hollister!" Morgan hollered as he backed away. "Get out of there!"

Hollister glanced over her shoulder at the commotion and froze.

The she did so the back row of lamias split off from the front row and turned toward her. The front row shuffled toward Morgan, their arms now outstretched. Long fingernails protruded from their hands as they glided off the stage zombie-like.

Instead of running, Hollister stayed in place, her face a contorted mask of terror.

The lamias picked up their pace. Their shuffling noise was the only reason Morgan knew their feet were touching the ground. The closer they got, the stronger their stench. *Remember Taylor's speed and strength? We'll never outrun them.*

"Linda, take the girl! Get yourself to safety."

Linda lifted the girl and trudged toward the exit, moaning under Patient Zero's heft. Morgan retrieved his pistol. The lamias hissed. Their claws reached for him.

He broke away from Linda. "I'll keep them occupied." A shriek from Hollister nearly floored him. "Hollister! Hang on! I'm coming."

Morgan jumped back onto the stage and ran between the two packs. "Hey! Over here!"

But the lamias from the front row marched toward Linda and the girl who had created them. The back row of lamias swarmed Hollister and slashed her face. The lamias slurped Hollister's blood and a joyous hum emanated from them.

Morgan fired his weapon over the heads of the lamias attacking Holiister. "Get away from her!"

The lamias attacking Hollister turned methodically. Their burning eyes bore into Morgan. His soul felt the heat. "Hollister? You okay?"

The lamias took a synchronized step toward him.

Lilith is directing them, like a conductor. All expendable. A mental spike drove into his head. *It can always make more.*

"Hollister?"

"I'm here." Her voice trailed off, weak and frightened. "What's happened to them?"

"No time. Get out."

The lamias picked up the pace until just ten feet separated him from the hive. He remembered Taylor's offspring had been slow and deliberate in their movement, unlike Taylor, who was blazingly quick. *Maybe I can hold them off.*

Morgan backpedaled faster. Each step the lamias took toward him created a larger escape route for Hollister. "Go for the open exit. Get help in the lobby."

He glanced over his shoulder. Linda had reached the exit. Four lamias pursued her like monsters in a B-horror flick. *Four?* He checked the open exit. The other three had moved there, blocking Hollister's path. His heart, already in overdrive, amped up the pressure.

He stopped and closed his eyes. *Think. How do I disable them without killing the girls?*

His pause cost him. A knife-like fingernail tore into Morgan's cheek. He gasped and stumbled backward, collapsing to the stage. His firearm fell to the floor. Seven lamias surrounded him, hissing with excitement.

CHAPTER 28

The demon Lilith commanded its host, the girl over Linda's shoulder, to awaken and attack Linda. But the girl stayed unconscious.

Lilith screamed to the bowels of Hell.

The demon turned its attention to the fourteen lamias, each of whom was following her orders. Seven had Morgan pinned. *Make the Arrogant Loser bleed. But don't kill him. Save that juicy moment for me.*

The priority for the others was to free the girl with Linda, Lilith's host. *The transmutation is minutes from completing. Then my host will be immortal. She and her offspring will infect millions.*

And I can go to my *Taylor.*

Lilith sent a message to the lamias pursuing Linda. *Save your parent, within whom I live. Kill the human.*

CHAPTER 29

Garcia stirred into consciousness, his mind muddled. *Did I really pass out? Just when Pennywise needed me most? And did I dream that gunshot?*

He opened his eyes. The spotlight in the beige ceiling blasted heaven's accusing glow at him. He rolled onto his side as Linda appeared in the plastic sheathing. "Linda? What's happening?"

Linda was carrying a thin teenager. Garcia jumped to his feet and helped her rush the body across the threshold. "One of the infected girls?"

"Patient Zero." Linda's words stumbled over each other. "Sedated, for now. Richard thinks Lilith's still in her."

Garcia's chest tightened as he took the girl. Her breath reeked of spoiled meat and dead carcasses. "Where's Pennywise?"

"In trouble. Take the girl to Smokey." Linda pointed to the plastic. "I have to go back."

"No. It's time I stepped up."

Their debate ended as the plastic sheet shredded open, and four lamias lurched through. Their eyes cast an orange hue in the hallway and their talons wiggled menacingly.

Garcia thought he'd seen enough horror for one lifetime in Costa Rica, but he was wrong. His head spun and his knees buckled.

Linda's scream jolted the priest back to reality. Two lamias flailed at Linda's face. Her attempts to cover up failed, and blood splattered her outfit.

The other two came at Garcia, hissing the lyrics of Satan's Greatest Hits. Holding Patient Zero over his shoulder, he blocked one attack with his free arm, which received a painful cut. He kicked at the other lamia, landing a solid blow. The lamia fell back into the two attacking Linda, and that set off a chain reaction. The two lamias turned on the offending beast, attacking viciously. Even the fourth broke away from Garcia and piled on.

"Take the girl," Garcia said. "I've got Pennywise." He dashed through the plastic before Linda could protest.

The scene on the stage forced him to one knee. Morgan was buried beneath a pile of lamias, thrashing to protect himself, a pool of blood expanding under them. *Jesus. They're killing him.*

A lady in a doctor's coat watched, seemingly unable to move on the other side of the stage. Three lamias were steadily advancing on her. *She's in shock. Doesn't even see the approaching threat.* "Doctor! Snap out of it!"

Nothing.

"Pennywise!"

No answer. Just the sound of slashing and grunting.

Garcia stood and pulled out his cross. He held it firmly in front of him, but his hand and voice wavered. "By the power of Christ, I compel you to stop!"

The attack paused and all seven of the beasts stared at him. One stood and cocked its head. "Father Chancho! Glad you join us. But have to wait turn."

Christ. The lamia voice again. Irritating. He stared at the talons spiking from the hands on the lamias.

The plastic flap shredded open. He turned to see four lamias, slashed and oozing blood, stagger toward him.

CHAPTER 30

Morgan took advantage of the pause and wiped the blood from his eyes to clear his vision. Pain surged throughout every cell in his body. *Find the pistol! No mercy! They're no longer little girls.*

He scrambled for the weapon on the floor amidst the lamias.

They hissed and sliced into his non-shooting arm, forcing him into a crouch. He dropped onto his back and he planted a bullet into the shoulder of the nearest lamia. The beast crashed backward and lay motionless.

The rest of the nest went batshit crazy, as if all communication with their coordinator had been severed, and they didn't know what to do. They bumped into each other, hissing and slashing at fellow lamias.

The ones surrounding Garcia and Hollister did the same. Hollister took the opportunity to run.

Garcia reached Morgan. "Christ, Pennywise, you need a doctor."

Morgan got to his feet. A chunk of his left arm hung from the elbow, exposing muscle and bone. *Too much blood. I'm going to pass out.*

The lamias suddenly stopped and stood up straight. They turned to Morgan and Garcia.

Morgan and Garcia watched in horror as the lamia's gunshot wound closed, leaving a mere smudge.

Jesus. Shooting them doesn't even slow them. "Their wounds heal." Morgan raised the pistol. "I have to go with head shots."

"They're little girls who can be saved."

"It's them or else, pal."

"*Please*, Pennywise."

"I'll try one more time. Maybe taking out a kneecap will cripple them. Maybe their bones don't heal as fast as flesh wounds."

This time, the attack was swifter. All fourteen lamias descended on Morgan in a rush that caught him by surprise. They reached him before he could get a shot off. They forced his weapon from his hand. *No!*

He covered his eyes, but the rest of his body was a moveable feast. *So this is how I end.*

A shot came. He felt nothing.

The hissing turned to screams, and the slashing stopped. Morgan peeked over his arm. Another lamia was down with an arm puncture, and the others were whirling around it.

"Let's go!" Garcia yelled, holding the smoking pistol.

With Garcia's help, Morgan dragged himself off the stage, and limped up the aisle toward the exit. "Thanks, Javi. I can't believe they moved that fast. Must be a sign they're getting stronger as they mature."

"Don't thank me yet."

They reached the plastic just as the screaming stopped. Morgan glanced back. *The lamias are back on Lilith's frequency.* "Better give me the pistol."

Garcia handed it over, and Morgan aimed for their knees. He fired twice into the throng of charging lamias. Two collapsed, their hit legs exploding in steam and blood. Then the chaos started all over again. The shrieking grew louder, and a burning stench rose from the wounds.

"I sure hope those girls survive," Garcia said, crossing himself. "They can still be saved."

"Worry about us. If they get any faster, or stronger, we're toast." Morgan bent over in debilitating pain. "If they can heal from that, I'll have no choice but try head shots."

They crossed into the hallway and saw Smokey and Riki racing toward them, followed by two cruise line security guards. Smokey and Riki reached Morgan and Garcia. The guards ran into the showroom.

Smokey surveyed Morgan. "Jesus, Doc."

"Linda?"

Riki put Morgan's arm over his shoulder, holding him up. "They have a training kitchen for the passengers as part of their culinary cruise package. Found it unlocked. She and Patient Zero are in there."

Morgan winced. "By herself?"

"We heard the gunshots," Smokey said. "Linda made us come after you."

"The sedative could run out any minute," Morgan said, his voice barely a whisper. "Linda can't be alone with it."

Before they could move, screams emanated from beyond the plastic. Adult screams.

"Give me the gun, Doc." Morgan handed it to Smokey, who checked the ammo. "Only four rounds left. Riki, take them to the kitchen."

"What about the guards?" Garcia protested.

Gunshots rang out within the showroom. Followed by screams that were cut off by gurgling.

Jesus. It sounds like they're slitting the throats of the guards. And, adapting to losing members of their clan. Shooting one might no longer distract them.

"Hurry!" Smokey yelled.

"We're trying not to kill the girls," Garcia said.

"Padre, that time has come and gone. Riki, get them to Linda!"

Riki shoved Garcia toward the lobby and clutched Morgan by the arm. "You heard him. Let's go!"

Morgan stood his ground. "Detective, you can't stop all of them. We all need to retreat."

"If I don't slow them down, you'll never make it." Smokey took a deep breath that struck Morgan as accepting his fate. "You know I'm right."

The plastic exploded in front of Smokey. A blur of lamias stepped through. Meat hung from their talons.

They assailed Smokey. He fired off four rounds, dropping four with head shots, before the rest engulfed him.

No! Save him! Morgan tried to get to Smokey, but Riki and Garcia pulled him away.

Smokey vanished in a cloud of lamias. Blood splattered the ceiling.

CHAPTER 31

By then, early morning sunshine splashed thorough the ship's windows. But Morgan saw only darkness. He lost his balance and fell into Riki.

Riki and Garcia dragged Morgan toward the kitchen..

"The kitchen's on the other side of the stairwell," Riki said. "Stay with me."

"They killed Smokey," Morgan said. "I can't leave a soldier behind."

"There's nothing we can do for Smokey now," Garcia said. "We have to get to Linda and Patient Zero in that kitchen."

And then what? We have no way to defend ourselves.

The feasting stopped, replaced by footsteps.

"We have to kill Patient Zero." Garcia's voice shook. "Then they'll all stop. Won't they?"

"Don't know," Morgan said. "We only know exorcising Lilith frees them."

The approaching scuffling ramped up. Morgan glanced back. *Jesus. They look so hungry.*

"There!" Riki said. They reached the demo kitchen. Floor to ceiling glass walls made viewing easy.

Jesus, they can break through that glass.

Linda swung open the glass door, and they stumbled inside. She slammed the door shut and latched the deadbolt. Morgan reached for her cut face.

"I'm fine," she said.

Right. And I'm Van Helsing.

Seconds later, a throng of eight lamias smacked into the glass, which surprisingly held.

Morgan recognized the sound. *It's plexiglass. That'll hold a little longer.*

The lamias scratched at the window, leaving long marks stained in blood.

Smokey's blood. What have I done?

"Where's the girl?" Morgan asked, his tone like the rough steel of a knife sharpener.

"Over here." Linda led them to the girl, still passed out on a polished chrome cooking counter. "She hasn't budged."

The scratching on the window switched to pounding. Sixteen red eyes flared at them. Their incisors had grown.

"What now?" Garcia asked. "Kill her?"

"Can you exorcise Lilith?" Morgan asked.

Riki moaned. "Your detective friend has the silver box. Don't we need that?"

Garcia hovered over the girl. "I don't have my Rite of Exorcism with me." A crack appeared in the plexiglass. "An exorcism takes time. Time we don't have."

"If we kill the host while Lilith's still in there, we might kill Lilith too, right?" Linda said.

Morgan examined Patient Zero. *A random victim. None of this is her fault.* He shook his head. "Either way, she'll wake up soon, and we have no tranquilizers. If those lamias are this strong, imagine what *she* can do to us."

"How would we do it?" Riki asked.

"It's a kitchen. Find the knives."

More pounding came from the windows on the promenade where two lamias had taken a position to box them in.

"Lilith! I know you're in there." Morgan gripped Patient Zero by the throat with one hand and gave an adrenaline-infused squeeze. "It's over. I'll crush this girl's windpipe, and you and your lamias will perish with her."

Patient Zero's eyes popped open, revealing a red glow unlike anything Morgan had ever seen. He felt a burning in his hand, and he released her.

Then, her eyes shifted to black.

Morgan stopped breathing. *That's Lilith in there! Kill her! Now!*

"Too late," the girl growled.

Morgan wrapped both hands around her neck, ignoring the pain of the heat surging from her body. "You leave my little girl alone!"

The window to the interior hallway shattered. Followed by the window to the promenade. Morgan prepared for the onslaught of vampiric attacks, but none came. Instead, the ten lamias surrounded him and gazed at the girl hosting Lilith. They stood in reverence.

"You see," Lilith said via the girl, "it is done. This one has completed her transmutation. She is immortal now. She no longer needs my protection. She will protect her children, and they will spread her greatness worldwide."

"We'll see about that." Morgan gave up trying to save the girl and squeezed with enough force to crush anyone's windpipe.

But not hers.

She grinned at Morgan, mocking his effort. Then she slapped him with the back of her hand, launching him across the floor.

A sea gull landed on the cracked window leading to the promenade and squawked. It struck Morgan, bizarrely, as an interested spectator.

Lilith continued lecturing. "I'd wanted to play with you, make you watch while *my Taylor* changes the world, but now you bore me." The girl nodded to the lamias. "Feast on the others after I leave. The Arrogant Loser is *mine.*"

Morgan, smothered with blood where he'd skid, got up on one knee, then both, and finally to his feet. "You forgot the first rule of combat."

The girl's eyes dimmed slightly.

"When you need to kill someone, don't talk about it," Morgan said. "Just do it."

Linda had sneaked up on Lilith's host. She shoved a carving knife into Patient Zero's back.

The ten lamias freaked. Shrieks shook the walls. Pots hanging from hooks in the ceiling crashed to the floor.

But Patient Zero didn't scream. Instead, she grasped the knife blade sticking through her chest and pulled it forward, as if enjoying the experience. The handle caught in her back, but she pulled the knife blade harder, and the handle squeezed through her body.

Morgan wobbled. *How can that be?* He thought back to vampire lore he'd read as a child. *That should have pierced the heart.*

The wound healed instantly. "I told you," Lilith said via Patient Zero. "She's immortal." She smiled fiendishly at Morgan. "Now, where were we?"

"Going to Hell," Garcia yelled as he swung a meat cleaver at the girl's neck.

The girl's eyes switched back to red, just as the cleaver sliced through her. Patient Zero's head flopped onto the floor, setting off a chain reaction with the lamias, who fell themselves. The eyes of the decapitated girl reverted to blue, and those of the ten lamias returned to human colors.

Garcia dropped the cleaver. He looked to Morgan with watering eyes. "I killed an innocent child. God help me."

"You saved us," Morgan said.

"There's no sign of The Savior in my sin." He knelt over the decapitated body, his knees surrounded in blood.

"I guess the legends are true," Riki said. "That's how you kill a vampire."

Morgan clutched a counter to hold himself up. "We need to check all of them. Check for a pulse. Look for any sign of Lilith's black eyes."

Morgan staggered to the first girl. Out cold, but breathing normally. Her skin returning to a human hue rather than the chalky green as a lamia. And, neither red nor black eyes. The next girl checked out as well. He and Linda checked them all, and found no immediate health risk, and no signs of possession or lamia traits.

Linda raised her eyebrows at Morgan. "We did it."

Garcia pulled out his cross. "Silence, please. Patient Zero deserves last rites. Then I'll go find Detective Smokey and the four girls he killed." He whispered last ministrations and prayers.

Squawk!

Morgan glared at the bird still on the cracked window ledge. *Shut up!*

The gull flapped its wings, brandishing dead black eyes Morgan knew all too well.

Morgan fell to his knees. *No! It can't be.*

The gull squawked shrilly and flew off.

Garcia finished his rite and joined Linda at the window. "I killed this girl for nothing?" He broke out in sobs. "Smokey died for nothing?"

"No," Morgan said, barely hanging on. "We stopped a plague. You did what you had to do."

Garcia plopped onto the floor. "There'll just be another Patient Zero. And another. We can't win."

Morgan slid over and joined his friend. "Lilith's after Taylor now. We bought the world a little time. After this, people will believe. We can warn them. We can beat this." He swallowed. "We have to." *For Taylor's sake. For everyone's sake.*

Linda stood next to them, staring out at the sea. "What about the girls? They'll wake up soon."

"We must contact their parents," Garcia said. "Get doctors in here to treat them."

Morgan nodded. "And arrange for Smokey's body to make it home. Then we find Taylor."

"You need a hospital," Linda said. "And the police and WHO needs the evidence."

Garcia looked at the girls. "Their teeth are already changing back. They'll be no evidence to see. Just a dead detective, and five dead girls. A decapitation by an axe with my fingerprints on it, and four fatal head shots with Smokey's gun. And, Pennywise, you're already on their watch list. We're screwed."

Morgan swallowed, then sank against the wall. *And we have no idea where Taylor is.*

CHAPTER 32

Morgan gagged as he gathered Smokey's mutilated body with blankets from housekeeping. The physical damage went beyond anything Morgan had seen in either medical school or the army. *They didn't just want him dead. They wanted to punish him. Because he helped me.* He wiped away tears. *Fucking demon.*

Linda emerged from the showroom. "I wrapped the four dead girls in sheets. I guess their recuperative powers end when they die. They still show the elongated incisors, fingernails, and that ghoulish skin tone."

"I guess that's good. Gives our story some credibility."

"Not so good for their parents, though."

If the authorities even allow them to see their bodies. They won't be eager for this story to get out. Imagine the panic. "And the guards?"

"I didn't touch what's left of them. I'll go back to the kitchen and help Garcia watch the girls, in case they wake up."

"Where are the cops? Riki went to get help ten minutes ago. Why haven't they stormed the place?"

Just then loud footsteps announced the security force Riki had summoned. Ten police officers, equally split between men and women, ran in dressed in blue slacks with a vertical red stripe along the side, white shirts, and blue caps with horizontal red strips above the bill. Each with drawn pistols. "Do not move!"

Morgan and Linda raised their hands, which were swiftly handcuffed.

"We're not armed," Morgan said. "We've saved ten of the infected girls. They're in the demo kitchen."

"Silence!"

Morgan persisted. "You need to get medical personnel in here right away."

The lead officer smacked Morgan. "First, a break-in at the Monastery. Now this shit storm. You know Monaco has the largest police presence in the world? Today is a disaster! I'm in no mood."

Morgan's vision blurred. "Hey. Take it easy. I'm trying to help."

The officer cupped Morgan's jaw and forced his head up. "Typical American obstinance. I neither need nor want your help."

One officer approached from the rear, holding a flyer. "Captain, this came in from the Criminal Identity Department. He's the man Interpol flagged. Wanted for murder and biological warfare."

The officer released Morgan and stepped back. "Biological warfare? We need the Specialized Intervention Unit in here. Make the call."

Morgan sagged. *No! This can't happen. I'll rot in jail. Taylor will be doomed. The world will be screwed.*

A familiar woman's voice commanded, "Leave him alone!"

Morgan peeled away the cobwebs clouding his brain. *Hollister! You came back.*

Doctor Hollister, still in her white smock, white surgical mask, and medical gloves, parsed her way through the police and reached Morgan and Linda. She was every bit as tall as Morgan, and her pale skin advertised too much time indoors. Even after all the bloodshed and running, she smelled like a cluster of orchids. *How does she do that?* Morgan noticed lighter brown streaks in her hair.

She pulled out her World Health Organization ID. "Stand down. This is a medical quarantine emergency, and I'm in charge here."

The officer glared at Hollister. "You are a guest of the Principality. You have no authority here. This man is the subject of an Interpol manhunt. Not to mention the crimes committed here."

Morgan made eye contact with Hollister, leading her attention to Smokey's body. She understood and exposed the detective's chewed up face. "Here's my authorization."

The guards stumbled backwards.

"Your government is cooperating fully with the WHO to stop an international pandemic. And, trust me, you and your men want no part of what's on this ship. Unless you want to end up like this."

Her declaration brought mumbles and more retreating amongst the troops. Followed by the faint smell of urine.

"Now take those handcuffs off," Hollister continued. "These two aren't the enemy. They're risking their lives to help me contain this."

The officer uncuffed Morgan and Linda. "But we have bodies. Fatal gunshots. Maulings. A decapitation, for Christ's sake. Interpol claims he's spreading a disease."

"That's old information," Hollister said. "You and your men need to get off this ship while we decontaminate everything."

"A disease doesn't put a bullet in someone's brain, or chop little girl's heads," the officer countered.

"No," Hollister said, "but the bacteria eats you alive and alters your behavior. You've seen what it can make people do. I have a decontamination unit on the dock. You and your men need to go there now."

The cop blanched, and his men stepped farther back. "Are we in danger? Were we exposed?"

"You need to hurry," Hollister said. "The longer you're in here, the higher the risk."

But the lead officer didn't budge.

"Boss," another policeman said, "we gotta go. I have a wife. Kids."

"Hang on," the officer in charge said. "These are criminals in Monaco's jurisdiction. I won't let them get away with what they've done."

"They're not going anywhere," Hollister said. "You're welcome to wait for them on the dock. When I'm done with them, you can have them."

The lead officer frowned, then signaled for his team to leave. All but he rushed away. "Okay. But I will expect them outside." He gave a stern nod, as if to say "I'm still in charge, and this is my idea." Then he ran for it.

Morgan rubbed his wrists. "You okay?" he asked Linda.

"Just another day at the office."

Morgan wanted to laugh at her sarcasm, but couldn't find it in him. He turned to Hollister. "I'm surprised you came back."

"I'm surprised I came back, too. But you saved me in there, and you seem to understand what afflicted those girls. I need to know what you know. I was getting nowhere."

"You could have found that out without sending the cops away," Morgan said. "And making up that whole flesh-eating bacteria thing."

"I'll call the police back if I think you're guilty of something. But my gut tells me you're one of the good guys, trying to stop whatever this is, not spread it like they claim. Where are the patients?"

"Ten survived," Morgan said. "Father Garcia is watching them in the demo kitchen. Our fourth, Riki Vitelli, went looking for help." He lowered his voice. "Detective Smokey killed four of them to allow us to escape. And before you condemn him, Smokey's a good man, better than me. He risked his life, for me, for you, and for the world."

"Your Riki is with my team, ashore awaiting instructions." Hollister pulled the blanket off Smokey's face and cringed. "This your detective Smokey?"

Morgan choked up. "Yeah."

"The patients did this to him?"

"Yeah."

Hollister covered the body again. "What kind of disease would cause the girls to behave like that? I saw unexplainable physical changes."

"Are you a religious person?" Linda asked her.

"Not particularly. Why?"

"Because," Morgan said, "the root cause of this is a demon. It possessed the first girl we called Patient Zero, who then bit the other girls and turned them into a kind of vampire. A lamia."

Hollister stared at them both. "I risked my reputation sending those policemen away, and this is the bullshit you repay me with? Vampires? Demons?"

When neither Morgan nor Linda replied, Hollister paled. "You're serious."

"I'm afraid so," Morgan said. "A fringe cult that infiltrated the Vatican has my daughter, and this demon is after her. That's why we're here."

"So my patients are vampires?" Hollister said.

"Not anymore," Linda said. "When we killed Patient Zero, their transmutation was reversed. They should recover fully."

Hollister ran her tongue around her lips. "You know how this sounds, right? Do you have any evidence? I can't send in a report that claims we have vampires among us without ironclad proof." She paused. "Hell, I might not send it in even *with* proof."

"The girls Smokey shot still have elongated incisors and fingernails," Morgan said. "An autopsy might give you what you need."

"Might?" Hollister said. "That's not good enough."

"It's all we've got," Morgan said. "But you have to convince people this threat is real. The demon escaped, and it will strike again. More girls will be turned. The world needs to be ready."

Hollister folded her arms. "And what am I supposed to do with you?"

"We have to find my daughter before the demon gets to her. She's its next target." Morgan cocked his head. "Will you help?"

Hollister thought for a full minute. She pulled out a walkie talkie. "This is Hollister. Bring the team on board. Ten survivors, seven dead. And send the boy up. Check." She clicked the mic off. "My team will process the scene. The ten girls will be checked out thoroughly and eventually reunited with their families. Riki will join us momentarily." Hollister rushed past them toward the lobby. "Get your priest and come with me."

"Where are we going?" Morgan asked.

"I have an emergency vessel on the opposite side of the ship, in case we had to evacuate patients without exposing the people at the checkpoint."

"You're letting us go?" Linda asked.

"Not exactly. If there's a world-wide health risk, and you're the only ones I can count on to help stop it, I'm going with you."

CHAPTER 33

The gull glided through wispy clouds over the Mediterranean, its course to Taylor charted by Lilith. Lilith used the time to reminisce about times long past.

Mesopotamia. My origin and my home. How I long to return one day. With the Antichrist. There we shall rule. And God, who banished me, who castrated my demon husband, Samael, who couldn't protect his beloved Adam, and then Eve, from my temptations. He will rue the day I destroy His kingdom and all these pathetic humans he holds so dear.

The gull squawked.

What shall I call myself when that time comes? Lilith, the name Satan chose for me? Bé, the one the Costa Ricans used? Or a new one? It must be an appellation for the ages. For songs and paintings will capture my beauty, like Rossetti's sonnet and his masterpiece, Lady Lilith. Or van Haarlem's The Fall of Man. Goethe's Faust: The First Part of the Tragedy, *where I am described as The Pretty Witch.*

Yes, The Pretty Witch captures my beauty. Much more accurate than others used in the Bible and other religious blasphemy. Lamia. Lilith the Sinful. Screech Owl. Night monster. Night creature. And, the worst of all, Night Hag. Hag? Are you fucking kidding me?

Yes, they feared me then. They will come to fear me again.

The gull sped up.

But my favorite passage is from The Seductress. *"Her gates are gates of death, and from the entrance of the house She sets out toward Sheol. None of those who enter there will ever return, And all who possess her will descend to the Pit." Yes. That describes me perfectly.*

The gull defecated. It turned its head as it passed Italy and approached Greece. The light blue sea contrasted with the off-white structures and brown cliffs.

Ah, Greece. Some of my best work. Hundreds possessed. And, with every possession, I learned everything the host knew. Language. History. Culture.

Millions turned. I redefined Greco-Roman mythology. The origin of the lamia. All me. They called me child killer. A cannibalistic appetite for children, they said.

Well, partly right. While I can possess anyone, or any animal, I prefer girls. They allow me to spread my seed by turning them into lamias. Humans thought me to be the lamia, but they failed to realize I was their superior, creating them. My offspring did the dirty work while I watched and laughed.

The gull spread its wings.

Italy. That's a mixed bag. Many successes. But also, the Vatican and their fucking priests, capturing me in the fifteenth century. Trapped in a silver box. Eternal damnation. And then, the miracle. Being shipped to Costa Rica to get me off their continent.

But Costa Rica was actually serendipitous. Rather than confined within the vaults of the Vatican, I was released into a rich environment. So many bats and wild animals to call on. And the indigenous Bribri tribe with its legend of demons. I became the demon they already revered and feared. But the Awás were a dangerous enemy. First, I relocated to the island off Nosara. From there, I possessed my *Taylor, and went with her to America, and a whole new world opened up for me.*

And then the failure in Costa Rica, where the Arrogant Loser and Father Chancho exorcised me from my *Taylor, and repeated my humiliation of capture.*

But you can't keep a good woman down. More serendipity as the delusional Drakul and his merry band of morons let me go. They think they are using me. Did their biblical scholarship teach them nothing about demons? Do they not realize demons were the first to recognize who Jesus was? Only demons understood the order He brought to the realm of chaos we worked for. Only demons saw the threat.

And now, the ultimate victory. Just hours away from my *Taylor, and a new beginning. This time, I will remain in her, and be beautiful again. For eternity. And with her, my revenge for God's arrogance.*

My ascension to run the kingdom.

And the end of God's vile humans.

CHAPTER 34

Nice, France

Dry leaves scratched across the cement walkway at the pier in Nice. Morgan shuddered, then glanced at his arm, treated and bandaged by Dr. Hollister. *Sounds like lamia nails.*

Tourists ambled along the boardwalks in front of multicolored buildings housing restaurants, apartments, and businesses. The aroma, a mix of salt air and French Riviera delicacies, wafted over them in a soothing breeze.

While Hollister passed Riki the aft ties, Morgan examined her flawless skin and pink hue from the boat trip. After she'd changed, her short white smock gave him a view of shapely legs.

He realized he was staring at her, and looked away, blushing. His eye caught Linda's. She glared back at him with an expression of stone. *She's blushing too. Probably not for the same reason.*

Morgan waved to Linda. Her eyes narrowed in Hollister's direction. *Definitely not for the same reason.*

He hurried to Linda and put his arm around her. "Come on, cutie. Let's find some shade."

She grunted, but let Morgan lead her under a canvas overhang shading a restaurant patio. Garcia and Hollister joined them while

Riki finished securing the boat to the dock.

"What now?" Linda asked.

"Finding Taylor is our only priority," Morgan said.

Linda stepped back. "It can't be the *only* priority. We have a plague to contain."

"After we find Taylor."

"Look, I want to find her too. But we have other responsibilities." Morgan's face burned.

Garcia stepped in. "Hey! Both are important, man. Keep it together."

Yeah. Keep it together. She caught me checking out Dr. Hollister, and she's pissed. Don't turn it into a thing. I need a cool head to find Taylor. "Sorry, Linda. I'm just amped up."

Linda glared at him. "You sure that's all you are?"

Morgan pulled her closer and kissed her. She let him. "Of course. Let's get back to work."

Hollister gave them both a puzzled expression. "Now that we're all friends again, I better call in. The WHO is certainly freaking out about our disappearance."

"What will you tell them?" Morgan asked.

Hollister flinched. "Good question. That I'm hunting for the source of the pathogen, I suppose. And I need your help to find it."

A silence descended on them. Morgan finally broke it. "We all know that's not going to fly. Your only option is to tell them we kidnapped you, and you got away. You don't know where we are, or where we're headed."

"I can't walk away," Hollister said. "Not after what I've seen. I know what the stakes are, and you're my best chance to find the source and stop it."

"They'll argue you can do that better with them," Morgan said. "They'll insist you turn us in. They think we slaughtered those girls and guards. And they've been told I'm trying to spread the disease. Not to mention killing the Commandant of the Swiss Guard and trying to kill Cardinal Vitelli."

Riki joined them. "My uncle has already told them you didn't do it. The Swiss Guard should also be after Cardinal Drakul by now."

"Finding Cardinal Drakul is the key," Garcia said. "He's got Taylor. Lilith is on its way to them. Can the WHO help us find him?"

Morgan examined Javi's eyes and saw what his own mind was telling him. *We don't have much time. Once Lilith gets to her, it could be too late to stop this madness.* "Can they?" he asked Hollister.

"Maybe if there's been something reported related to your daughter. Like an Amber alert, or a medical emergency that the WHO flagged. But it's a long shot."

"Make the call," Morgan urged. *Maybe we'll get lucky. Lord knows we can use some.* "I won't blame you for saying we kidnapped you. I'm sure the entire world is after us by now."

Hollister walked a few feet away and dialed. "Director-General, it's Dr. Hollister. Yes, I'm okay. I know what the nurses must have told you. We have a serious health risk out here. I'm searching for the source."

Hollister turned away and lowered her voice, but not so much that Morgan couldn't hear her. "Yes, I bugged out from the ship with Dr. Morgan. The police aren't my concern. This pandemic is."

Morgan heard yelling from the other end of the line. Once her boss calmed, Hollister listened while looking at Morgan. "Can she help? All right. Listen, I've got to go. I'll call you when I know more." She hung up as the voice on the other end complained.

She grinned at Morgan. "You were right. He's not happy."

"I gathered that."

"Say, you know a Doctor Khan?"

Morgan almost sagged to the ground. "Azra Khan? Yeah. Why?"

"They called her in to help the WHO. She's the one who claims you were trying to spread this disease?"

Linda moved in and took Morgan by the arm. "Oh, Richard, she won't stop until you're punished."

"For what?" Hollister asked.

"We were engaged," Morgan said. "It ended badly."

"You think?" Linda said.

Hollister shrugged. "Well, it really changes nothing for us. We have to find your daughter."

"I have an idea about that," Garcia said. "I've been thinking about Drakul's plan, birthing the Antichrist. The Book of Revelation isn't specific about where that occurs, but he won't pick a random place. He'll want somewhere that makes historical sense to him."

"And?" Morgan asked.

Garcia ran his foot along the ground before sharing his idea. "I think Taylor's in Nazareth. It's where the angel Gabriel told Mary she'd bear a child. And it's where Jesus studied as a boy. Cardinal Drakul will like the parallels."

"You sure?" Morgan asked.

"Hell, no. But it's my educated guess."

Morgan pulled out the Vatican black card. "Money's no problem. But getting into Israel isn't like hopping Euro countries. We'll need to show our passports, which means they can track us."

"Not exactly," Hollister said. "My WHO credentials will get us through customs without being logged."

Morgan studied Garcia and Riki. *I've got nothing better to suggest.* He took a deep breath. "Okay then. On to the Nice airport, and the next flight to Israel."

CHAPTER 35

Taylor woke from a nightmare, her body drenched in perspiration in an oversized black tee-shirt she didn't recall putting on. Someone had removed her shoes and socks. In the dream she'd been under attack by gargoyles with oversized wings and claws. She'd been brutally cut and beaten. She awoke just before her inevitable death.

Drakul sat next to her on the bed. "Good. You are awake."

Taylor preferred the nightmare. "What do you want?" A clarity of thought and senses pulled at her. The sedatives had mostly worn off, and she could see clearly for the first time.

Drakul placed a black gown between them. "Put this on. Lilith will be here soon. You should look your best for her."

"Her?"

"Yes. Lilith is female. You couldn't tell when she possessed you?"

Taylor gagged. *That's never happening again, you sick old man.*

Drakul stood, but when he stayed in the room, she glared at him. "Are you going to stand there and watch, you perv?"

Drakul slapped her, hard. "I am a Cardinal in the Catholic Church. You will show me some respect."

Pain radiated from Taylor's jaw. She rubbed where he'd struck her. "My Dad taught me to show respect when people earn it. Is hitting girls the new standard for behavior at the Vatican?"

Drakul's face turned crimson. "How dare you?"

"Go screw yourself. And take your stupid dress with you. I'm not wearing it."

"You will wear it, even if I have to dress you myself."

"You'd like that, wouldn't you?" Taylor threw the dress on the floor. "Try it, and we'll see how tough you really are when you're without your supply of tranquilizers."

A priest in a black robe with a white collar entered. "Pardon, Excellency. There's been a development."

Drakul frowned at the interruption. "What is it?"

The priest's face matched his collar. "Romanoff is dead. Morgan and the woman escaped."

Drakul's eyes narrowed. "That is unfortunate. I should have finished Morgan myself." He scratched his ear. "His only move is to go to the cruise ship."

Steam formed on the priest's face. "Morgan and his cohorts killed Lilith's host, and the batch of lamias."

Taylor sat up straighter. *Dad! You're okay!*

Drakul absorbed the news. "And Lilith?"

"Unclear."

Drakul hissed an expletive. "With the host gone, Lilith will delay no longer. She will come here. For Taylor."

Taylor cringed.

"But how, Excellency?"

"Don't worry about that. She'll find a way. What about Morgan? Is he under arrest?"

"Missing."

"Missing?" Drakul paced. "Missing? How is that possible? Every cop in the world is looking for him. He should have been trapped on that ship. If not by the police, then by our team."

"I do not know how he escaped."

"He's coming to save me," Taylor said. "And kick your ass."

Drakul considered her. "My dear, he has no idea where we are. Lilith, on the other hand, knows exactly where we are. The next visitor will not be your father, but a demon capable of giving you a child. A child to end our suffering."

"You're insane."

Drakul dismissed her with a shrug. He turned to the priest. "Tell the guards to stay alert, just in case Dr. Morgan discovered our location."

"But how could he?" the priest said.

"Does it matter? Maybe Lilith divulged it, just to raise the stakes of the game in her desire to torture Morgan. Nothing would surprise me. See to it."

"Yes, Excellency." The priest bowed and left.

Drakul's attention returned to Taylor. "Kick my ass? You are such a child. I am leaving to see about dinner. When I return, you better be wearing that dress." He surged to the door. "Don't confuse my being a Cardinal with an unwillingness to harm you. I make my own rules unbidden by the church and have no tolerance for disobedience. I can, and will, hurt you if you don't behave."

He slammed the door on his way out. The deadbolt clicked into place.

Taylor kicked the dress across the floor and tested the door. *Bolted. But he didn't drug me this time. I can think. Fight.* She scanned the room. No window. Only the one door. *Come on. There must be a way out of here.*

Then, a shiny object caught her attention. She approached it cautiously as if a sudden movement might scare it away.

A ring in the floor board! If that's a handle, there must be a door!

She grabbed the ring and pulled. Dust and dirt flew throughout the room. A wooden-slatted door creaked open.

Yes!

No. Hard-packed, moist dirt filled the opening. She pawed at it, but the soil didn't give. *Damn it.* Taylor clutched her stomach, which lurched. She thought about her yellow lab back in Salem. *Where's Bear when I need him?*

She slid the door back, and the base snapped off amongst rotted wood. A sharp screw stuck out from the back end of the base.

She moved to the wall opposite the door. The wood was moist to the touch. *I wonder.* She poked the screw into the wall, and a small chunk of wood chiseled out. A few more pokes made a divot. *This wood is damaged. Maybe I can dig through it.*

She checked the door. *Need to hurry, girlfriend. He'll be back any sec.*

She put all her might into scraping wood away. Chunks fell off, and she pushed even harder, adrenaline now coursing through her veins.

One mighty lunge poked through the wall completely. She withdrew the screw and peeked in.

Darkness. Nothing visible. *Shoot. Just another room in the house.* But she smelled something awful. *What is that? Poop?*

The wall came apart faster now that she had an opening to leverage. She chipped away until she could fit her head through.

The smell knocked her back. *What the hell is that?* She held her breath and tried again.

Her eyes stung and watered, but this time they acclimated to the darkness. Through her misty vision, she realized the shadows were bodies.

Dead bodies. Dozens stacked in piles.

Taylor dropped to her knees. The stench assaulted her. She pulled back into the room, but it did no good. She vomited.

I have no way to seal that. Dracula will smell it and know what I did. She stared at the hole in the wall. *I have to go through.*

To where? It's a black pit with a bunch of rotting corpses. What makes you think you can get out of there?

Yet it was the only way out of the prison disguised as a macabre nursery. She returned to the wall and hacked at the decaying wood.

The Night Hag

Within minutes she formed a passageway large enough for her slender frame to fit through. She took an extended breath, choked back the bile it caused, and plunged into the darkness.

CHAPTER 36

Taylor squished as she landed in the pit. She found herself in an enclosed room with no obvious doors or windows. No light streaming in. No other way out.

Bugs scurried along the floor. An insect flew into her mouth and she spit it out. Spiderwebs stuck to her face.

Ignore the smell. Ignore the bodies. Ignore the bugs. Ignore whatever it is you're standing in. Find a way out!

Hold on. These bodies got in here somehow. That's the way out. What would Dad do?

Her head tilted back. *The ceiling. It has a dark gap in it. A chute for dropping the carcasses in.* She stood and raised her arms toward black space, but couldn't reach it. *Need something to stand on.*

Taylor considered her options. *Go back, knock down the wall, and bring furniture through. No. Not enough time, and the Dracula guy will hear me.*

She focused on the dead bodies. Several were piled up under the shaft. *If I pile up a few more, that might work. But, so gross!*

Taylor set her revulsion aside and reached for a corpse. She imagined it coming to life when she touched it, like some sort of zombie. But she grasped ahold anyway and pulled.

Jesus, that's heavy. I guess that's why they call it dead weight. I'll never be able to move and lift enough of these.

You can't stop! Dad is alive! He's looking for you! This is your only shot!

Taylor gritted her teeth and renewed her effort. With a strength she didn't know she had, she dragged a decaying body on top of the others in her target area. She now had a pile two feet high. *One more should do it.*

She corralled another body, but the decomposed arm cracked off the torso. Taylor lost her balance and fell backwards into the muck. *No, no, no! Not cool.*

She dry-heaved into the shifting floor. Then slimed her way to her feet and fought off the urge to wipe her face with her disgusting hands. Instead, she seized another body, which thankfully held, and stacked it on top of the others.

Taylor carefully placed a knee on the pile, which didn't fall apart. She then pushed off with her right leg and had her right foot on a chest cavity. The rib cage crackled under her weight, and she almost lost her balance, but her hand caught the edge of the overhead chute, and she held on. Pain immediately ran along her arm, and she felt blood where her hand had grasped the sharp metal. But she dared not let go for fear of having to start over.

Taylor pulled herself up with one arm to get her second hand inside the chute. She felt the metal slicing into her palm, but refused to stop. The escape route had a narrow rim around the edges, and she shifted her hands so her arms were facing forward. From there, she executed a pull-up until her head entered.

The stench magnified within the narrow confine, and she gagged, spilling bile over her shirt. Part of her wanted to let go, go back to the nursery, and get washed up. *Don't stop, girl! You can do this!*

The deadbolt jiggled in the nursery. *Dracula's coming. Hurry!*

Keeping her head in the chute, she lifted her legs up and through her arms like she'd practiced a hundred times in high school gym. *Thank God for Miss Germain. I'm sorry for all the trouble I caused you.* Pinning her legs against the sides, she arched her back and reached up until she found the chute's entry point.

The door to the nursery screeched open. Followed by a muffled roar. Scrambling feet. A flashlight into the pit below.

Taylor pulled herself up and out before the beam followed her up the chute. The light afforded her a look at her surroundings. She recognized the room immediately. *The loft of a barn.*

Bundles of hay lined the walls. A ladder led into darkness below. Two open windows.

They'll come up the ladder. Use the windows.

She bolted for the nearest one and climbed onto the structure's roof. Stars like back home blanketed the sky, and she paused to gaze. *Boy, I sure miss home.* But there was no sign of light. Just a tree-filled forest up a hill.

Panicked yells, followed by footsteps, rose from the stairs. She shook herself and looked over the edge. Guards patrolled the building's entrance. *No! God, please give me a way out of here.*

She ran along the edge of the roof until she found what she was looking for. A stack of hay twenty feet below, with no guards present. She jumped.

As she fell she imagined a pitchfork within the bale. She landed and her mind played tricks on her. *I've been impaled!*

But the imagined pain vanished. She rolled off the stack and ran for the cover of the trees.

From the barn, Drakul's unmistakable voice screamed. "Taylor! You can't escape. Lilith is a part of you. She will always know where you are."

Even as she ran, Taylor felt a chill up her spine. *Need to find Dad.*

CHAPTER 37

Nazareth, Israel

Cardinal Drakul screamed hellishly at his crew of armed priests. "Find her! We can't let her reach the community at the end of that forest."

The priests raced into the woods.

Cardinal Drakul snagged one priest before he got out of arm's reach. "Father Hampton. Stay with me."

Father Hampton bowed. "As you wish, Excellency. But don't we need every resource looking for Taylor?"

"I need you here."

Father Hampton shifted uncomfortably. "Are you displeased? Did I not do well picking this place? A former Mossad safe house, recently abandoned. Isolated. Hills to the north. Vacant land followed by more hills to the south, toward the city. No lights in sight. Rumors of horrors executed here mean the locals don't dare come near us. And, of course, near the hallowed ground of Joseph and Mary's home."

"I expect Lilith will arrive soon. I'll need you to help me."

Father Hampton shivered. "Help you, how?"

"Our plan must change." Cardinal Drakul put his hand on the priest's shoulder. "We assumed Taylor would be here when Lilith arrived. With Taylor gone I need a temporary host."

The priest pulled away. "You intend to use *me*?"

"I need to communicate with Lilith. Don't worry. Once we find Taylor she will leave you and take possession of her. You will suffer no damage."

"But, Excellency, she's a demon. Maybe the most vile and evil one our world has ever known. I can't."

Cardinal Drakul's face flushed. "You can, and you will."

A squawk interrupted them. A gull swooped in and landed at Cardinal Drakul's feet. He pointed at Father Hampton. "Your temporary home."

Father Hampton turned to run, but froze after two steps. He turned back to Cardinal Drakul. His eyes were black and his voice deep. "Where is *my* Taylor?"

"She is nearby. We are searching for her."

"You allowed her to escape?"

Cardinal Drakul heard the threat in Lilith's voice. "She can't have gone far, and there's no one to help her. With your past connection to her, you can find her, right?"

"I can signal those I possess, or turn. I can control them. I can sense others I recognize when close. But I can't locate them if too far away."

"Then I suggest you cripple Taylor so she can't run. My men will find her."

CHAPTER 38

Taylor stumbled over a tree root and fell to her knees, cutting them on sharp nettles, but the pine forest and its glorious smell invigorated her. Her feet were raw from her escape, and her cut hands throbbed, yet she had to go on.

Have to find Dad.

She scanned the area. *Nothing but trees. I wonder how deep this forest goes.* Voices rose from the direction of the barn. *Get up, girl. You've got to keep moving.*

Her next step brought a shooting pain up her right leg. *Dang. Something's seriously wrong in there.*

But she didn't stop. she moved away from the barn, toward an expanse of open, flat land. *At least I'm wearing black. Maybe I can get to safety before they see me.*

I have to!

She amped up the pace, ignoring the crippling assault from her nerves. Looking ahead, she focused on the path, knowing another fall could doom her.

Then, a new sensation. A recognizable voice. This one in her mind. *My Taylor! I am here for you.*

She froze in terror. *No! Get out of my head!*

She clutched the crucifix. "I am a child of God. You have no power over me."

Lilith's voice responded in her head. *Shall we test your faith against mine? Come back and see how your God protects you.*

"Leave me alone, you sick bastard," Taylor screamed. She plopped onto the ground and recited, "God save me, God save me," trying to tune Lilith out.

CHAPTER 39

Morgan pulled his rental SUV into Nazareth at midnight. The Basilica of the Annunciation towered over the city, providing more light than the street lamps. Dozens of people milled around. "Javi, where to?"

Garcia, in the back between Riki and Hollister, pointed to the right. "There are several places of biblical relevance. The Basilica on your right. St. Joseph's Church, built on the site of Joseph's carpentry shop, Mary's Well, and the Synagogue Church, where Jesus studied."

Linda squirmed in the front seat. "I think we're going about this all wrong."

"What do you mean?" Morgan asked.

Linda half turned to face Garcia. "Don't get me wrong, Father. Drakul *would* come here. But he can't afford to be in any of these public places. He'll be where Taylor's screams can't be heard."

Morgan pulled up next to the Basilica. "I think Linda's right. They'll want a place to keep Taylor for the duration of her pregnancy. Too complicated in a populated area. Who's got the map?"

"I have it," Hollister said. "We're in the center of Nazareth. But the city limits extend into some remote spots. Especially to the northwest." The map crinkled in her hands. "Also, there's this

Nazareth Village to the west. Looks like an open-air museum that reconstructs life in Jesus' time. I'm wondering if they might have underground tunnels and rooms throughout the town."

"The church has sponsored many digs around here," Garcia said. "There are many passages."

"I'm confused," Riki said. "Look at the people. They're all wearing traditional Arab gear."

"Seventy percent of Nazareth's population is Muslim," Garcia said. "The rest are mostly Christian, and most tourists are Christian. If you're wondering where the Jews went, they built their own version of Nazareth just north of here."

"But Drakul won't care about any of that," Morgan said. "He just needs a quiet, isolated spot."

"Agreed," Garcia said. "He may even plan to take Taylor to Bethlehem for the birth."

Morgan moaned. "Javi. Let's not go there, okay?"

"Sorry, man."

A van passed them and Hollister gasped. "Jesus Christ, they found me."

"What?" Morgan asked. He checked out the white van Hollister was staring at. The light blue insignia of the WHO were magnetically stuck on the side. "How'd they get here?"

"Don't know," Hollister said.

Linda tried to make herself smaller in the front seat. "You think they tracked us?" She turned on Hollister. "Or did you tell them where we're going?"

"I didn't tell them anything. And I resent your implication."

Morgan put his hand up, calling for silence. "They didn't stop. I don't think they're following us."

"Maybe," Garcia said, "they have another lead. Maybe somehow the symptoms have been spotted, and they'll lead us to Taylor."

Morgan gunned the SUV. "It can't hurt to follow them."

CHAPTER 40

The wind whistled through the trees surrounding Taylor. Reclining against a pine, she kept her eyes closed, in case Lilith could find her using her own vision against her. Lilith's constant chirping gave her a headache, and the voices of those searching for her were getting closer.

Her right calf muscle cramped, and she dropped to a sitting position. She gripped her toes and pulled back, fighting the cramp. *C'mon God, not fair.* The pain eased, but she realized she was likely severely dehydrated, and subject to further muscle spasms.

A branch broke nearby, and she held her breath. The tension became too much for her and she opened her eyes.

A priest in a black robe was ten feet away. He moved cautiously ahead, but hadn't seen her yet.

Don't move. He's almost past me.

Lilith's voice barged into her head. *Not so fast, my Taylor. Thank you for showing me your surroundings. It's all I need.*

She fell to her knees, quivering. The ground shook. Leaves swirled, like she was the eye of a hurricane.

The priest turned and smiled at her. "There you are, my dear. It's time to take your medicine."

CHAPTER 41

Morgan followed the WHO van onto a dirt road beyond the residential limits of the city, staying fifty yards behind. "Where the hell are they going? There's nothing out here."

"Just the way Cardinal Drakul will want it," Garcia said.

"How come you always seem so steady?" Hollister asked Morgan.

"Professional training, I guess."

"But your daughter is missing. You watched a friend die. It's not normal."

"Suppose we leave the shrink analysis to me. Focus on the job." He brushed away a vision of Smokey and his mutilated body. "That's what gets me through this." *At least that's my story, and I'm sticking to it.*

"Look," Linda said. "At the base of that hill. Is that a building?"

Morgan squinted. "It is. The WHO van is headed straight for it."

"They know something," Hollister said.

"I think you should cut the lights," Riki offered.

Morgan shut off the headlights. "Does the WHO have any authority out here?"

"Not really," Hollister said. "They do fact finding and then try to influence decisions made by the local authorities or international bodies. They can't arrest or detain anyone. They won't be armed."

"So," Morgan said, "they're walking into a mess they're not prepared for. We know Drakul and his followers *are* armed, and not afraid to use lethal force."

Hollister leaned into the gap between the front seats. "Those are my allies up there. We need to warn them."

"Hold on," Linda said. "We expose ourselves now, who's to say they won't stop us from finding Taylor?"

Morgan rubbed his eyes. *Lilith's had enough time to get here. I can't jeopardize finding Taylor.*

"Flash your high beams at the van," Hollister said. "I can convince them to help."

"You don't know that," Linda said. "I say we go in alone." Linda squeezed Morgan's leg. "Right, honey?"

Morgan thought back to the beach in Costa Rica where his ex-wife and then-girlfriend Azra had bickered. *How do I get myself in between two women all the time?* "All I care about is Taylor. Javi, what do you think?"

Linda removed her hand from Morgan's knee.

Garcia pondered for a moment. "We follow the WHO van. For all we know, they're meeting their own people."

"I agree." Morgan looked at Linda, hoping for a smile, but she was unimpressed that he'd taken her side only after Garcia proposed it. He glanced in the rearview mirror. "Sorry, Doctor. We'll reassess when we get to that structure."

"Promise me," Hollister said, "we won't let my friends get hurt. At the first sign of trouble, we go help them."

Morgan rolled his tongue around the inside of his mouth. "I promise." *But, do I? If it's Taylor or them?*

Lights at the structure snapped on, revealing a two-story red barn. The WHO van sped up.

"So much for the element of surprise." Morgan punched the gas. The SUV spun its wheels before lurching forward. Each divot in the road created a violent bounce, and Morgan and his passengers put their hands on the ceiling to protect their heads.

Two robed figures came out of the barn and pointed at the advancing WHO van.

Morgan's hands tensed on the wheel. "That's Drakul!" He jammed his foot all the way down on the accelerator. "I'm coming for you, you son-of-a-bitch!"

Drakul and the priest brandished automatic weapons.

"My people don't understand the risk," Hollister yelled. "We need to get in there."

After stopping ten yards short of the building, the WHO van's driver and passenger doors opened. A man climbed out on the driver's side, a woman on the other. The back double door opened, and four more emerged.

Something familiar caught Morgan's eye. He focused on one passenger who'd exited from the back. Even with only the moonlight, he recognized the size, the shape, the gait.

Holy shit. That's Azra.

CHAPTER 42

Taylor jumped to her feet and faced off against the priest. "Take my medicine, my ass." She snapped off a sharp, heavy branch and pointed it at her assailant. "Come and get me, if you've got the balls for it."

The priest hesitated.

He's afraid. What did Dad always say when we trained? Most battles are won between the ears. Use his fear.

She reached him in three long strides. She jammed the branch into his chest, and he screamed in pain. Another strong jab and the man tripped and fell, landing on his back.

"Please. Don't hurt me."

Taylor swung the business end of the branch into the side of the priest's head, knocking him out.

Automatic gunfire from the direction of the barn caused her to the drop the branch and hold her stomach.

Lilith spoke to her. *Your father is here. Listen to the welcoming party!*

CHAPTER 43

Automatic gunfire pierced the night.

Morgan slammed on the brakes. The SUV skid to a stop behind the WHO van, raising a storm of dust that clouded his view of the shooters. *And their view of us.* "Everybody down!"

Hollister screamed, "No! We have to save the doctors." She opened her door.

But Garcia held her in place. "You can't go out there. Close the door and stay low."

Hollister grunted, but complied. "They're my comrades."

The gunfire stopped. Morgan looked over the hood and singled pout Azra standing between the two vehicles, hunched over. He kicked his door open and ran around the SUV. He grabbed Azra, whose eyes bulged at the sight of him, and retraced his steps, shoving her into the SUV driver's seat.

"Richard?" Azra said. "Where did you come from?"

"Long story." Morgan glanced at Linda, who was glaring at Azra. "You remember Linda, right?"

Azra returned Linda's glare. "How could I forget? She poisoned you with her demon nonsense. You two are wanted big time by the FBI, Interpol, and the World Health Organization."

"Thanks to you," Morgan said. "This lady in the back is Dr. Hollister of the WHO. And she's on board with the demon reality. And the young fella is Riki Vitelli."

Riki pretended to tip a cap. "Any friend of Dr. Morgan is a friend of mine." His eyes showed no fear. Azra's showed anger.

Only the circumstances kept Morgan from laughing out loud. "You all sit tight. We came in without lights, and we're shielded by the WHO van. I don't think they know we're here. But if I'm wrong, get the hell out."

"Where do you think you're going?" Garcia said.

"To get my daughter."

"Pennywise, we have no weapons."

Morgan scanned the area. "Maybe I can catch them unaware."

Riki opened his door. "I am coming with you. I am expertise in sneaking up on people."

"No," Morgan said. "I won't be responsible for you walking into battle unarmed."

Riki smiled. He pulled a pistol from his jacket pocket.

"Where'd you get that?" Garcia asked.

"I picked it up while you all were getting gas. Italy isn't the only country with the black market. It's loaded."

"They gave it to you?" Morgan asked.

"No. I traded an antique Christian relic for it." His face clenched. "One Cardinal Vitelli gave me as a boy. It has always been my good luck charm." He wiped away a tear. "I know it is a sin to sell it."

"Oh, Riki, you didn't have to do that," Morgan said.

"I did. For Taylor."

Garcia hugged Riki, "You're a good man, Riki Vitelli. God understands."

Morgan signaled for Riki to hand the weapon over. "Yes, once again you're a lifesaver. I'll take it from here."

"Who are those people?" Azra interrupted.

"Rogue priests following a deranged Cardinal," Morgan said. "They've got Taylor."

"What? Why?"

Morgan took the pistol. "An even longer story. One you won't believe, so I won't waste time explaining. How'd you find this place, anyway?"

"The WHO called me in, and we went to find you at the cruise ship. You were missing, but we met four priests who were also searching for you. We convinced the local police to pick them up. One of them gave up Drakul's location." She wiped a tear away. "And now this WHO team is all dead. Because I told them you were dangerous." She looked up at Morgan. "I shouldn't have done that."

"No kidding. Look, once I leave, switch seats with Linda. She'll know what to do." Morgan winked at Linda, which seemed to soothe her some. "If I don't make it, it's up to you. Don't let that demon get my daughter."

Azra narrowed her eyes. "What is it with you and this demon foolishness?"

Morgan slapped her. "You get in the way again, and I'll feed you to those killers myself. Understand? They have Taylor and have horrifying plans for her. That's all I care about."

Garcia shook Azra's shoulder. "He's telling the truth, Azra. Don't fight us on this."

Riki exited the vehicle and joined Morgan. "I go with you. For Taylor."

Can I let you do that? Our pistol won't be a match for their weapons. He scratched at the bristles on his chin. *But I can use the help.*

Riki began walking. "It is decided. I go."

Morgan jogged after him. They dropped into a gully that passed by the barn to the north. "This way."

The gully gave them cover, and they moved swiftly to the barn. The loudest bunch of crickets Morgan had ever heard masked their footsteps in the rocky dirt.

The Night Hag

They crept to the far side of the barn. There was no sign of Drakul or the priest. Morgan motioned to advance up the northern edge of the barn. Once there, he intended to pivot around the corner and catch the priests unaware. *And then what? Tell them to drop their weapons? If they turn and fire on us, we're both toast.*

Then I'll just have to shoot them without warning.

Morgan shivered at the thought, but so far nothing he'd tried had worked. *Smokey's dead, because of me. Those WHO doctors are dead because of me. I've tried doing this the right way. Time for a new plan.*

CHAPTER 44

Lilith observed the carnage before her through the priest's dull, black eyes. It pleased her. But, how had they been discovered? That was another matter entirely. "You allowed them to find us."

Drakul continued to scan the horizon. "I don't see anyone else. I've handled it."

"But still an incompetent display. And losing Taylor? Perhaps I made a mistake aligning with you."

"No mistake. We'll have Taylor here shortly."

Lilith reached out to Taylor again. *I have slaughtered your rescue party. Come back, before you force me to kill more.*

But, in reaching out for Taylor, Lilith sensed another familiar presence. *The Arrogant Loser! He is here!*

The priest turned around, pointing his automatic weapon at the edge of the barn where Lilith sensed Morgan.

CHAPTER 45

Morgan tensed as he prepared to launch himself around the barn.

Riki stopped him. "Let me go first. I will provide a distraction."

Before Morgan could stop him, Riki bolted around the corner. Morgan scrambled after him.

Morgan found Drakul with his back to them under the barn's spotlight. But the other priest was tracking Riki. *No!*

As if on cue the priest switched his focus to Morgan.

His eyes! Lilith's in him! That means it's not in Taylor yet! Morgan fired at the priest's chest, drilling him near the heart.

Drakul spun at the noise and caught the priest before he collapsed. But now his automatic was out of commission. Morgan shot Drakul in the shoulder to wound but no kill, knowing he might hold the key to finding Taylor. Both Drakul and the priest fell to the ground.

"Get their weapons," Morgan said to Riki. He went straight to Drakul. "Where's Taylor?"

Blood spread around Drakul's shoulder. When he refused to talk, Morgan dug the toe of his shoe into the wound. "Is she inside?"

"She escaped," Drakul rasped. "Tricky one, that girl. But she can't hide from Lilith. Our work will go on." He looked toward the forest. "My men will find her, then return to kill you."

Morgan pointed the pistol at the cardinal's forehead. "I should end you right now."

Garcia, Linda, Hollister, and Azra ran up to him.

"Pennywise, stop! He's defenseless."

"He deserves to die."

"The Vatican will see he threatens no one again," Linda said. "His reign of terror is over."

Morgan frowned, then kicked Drakul in the side. "Don't move." He switched to the priest. *Barely breathing. And the eyes are still black. Maybe I can end Lilith right now.* "Lilith's in him," Morgan said. "This may be our best chance to kill her."

"Killing the host won't destroy Lilith," Linda said.

Garcia hooked his arm. "All it'll do is make you a killer."

Morgan shrugged Garcia off. *Anything to save Taylor.* He stared into the priest's eyes.

The black vanished.

"No!" Morgan screamed. "It might have gone to Taylor!"

Azra growled. "Not yet."

Azra's pitch-black eyes bored into Morgan's soul.

CHAPTER 46

Morgan revulsed, the stench from Azra's breath choking him. He raised his pistol at Azra's face. He wanted to squeeze the trigger, but his finger froze as he recalled Linda's words. *Killing the host won't destroy Lilith.* "Why Azra?"

Azra grinned and spoke in the demon's voice. "Because she didn't believe."

Hollister pounced, driving a syringe into Azra.

She spun on Hollister and tried to claw at her eyes, but the sedative worked quickly. Before she could do any damage, Azra collapsed. Garcia and Riki helped Azra to the ground.

Morgan willed himself to move. He stood over Azra, like Ali over Liston. Her lifeless black eyes remained open. "Lilith's still in there."

"The sedative must affect the demon, too," Hollister said.

"But for how long?" Morgan aimed the weapon at Azra's forehead. "I can't get the thought to kill Lilith out of my head. What if this is our only chance to destroy her?"

Linda stepped in front of Morgan. "Remember all the evidence I got from the Vatican archives. The word of the *Awá*, Valverde. It can't be killed. Only captured."

"Maybe," Morgan said. "But they never killed a host while sedated like this. It might keep Lilith from fleeing."

Linda nodded. "You're right. We can't be certain. But Valverde killed many lamias sedated with his drugs, and Lilith always escaped. We have to assume killing Azra will only result in her death. Lilith will survive and move to another host."

Garcia put his hand on Morgan's shoulder. "Azra's still in there. You'd be murdering your friend, your ex-fiancee. A person. You'd be destroying your own soul."

Morgan lowered the pistol.

"We'll find a way," Garcia said. "We beat it before, we'll beat it again. We still have the silver box from Monaco. We can trap it like we did in Costa Rica."

Morgan put the weapon away. "Okay, we'll do it your way. Dr. Hollister, you have any more of that sedative?"

"That's it until I can fill a prescription."

"What about the van?" Morgan asked.

"Not a medical unit," Hollister replied. "They don't stock most vans with medical supplies. It makes them a target for local criminals."

"Gotcha." Morgan wiped the perspiration, and sting, out of his eyes. *I hope Javi and Linda are right. This could be our only chance.*

"What now?" Riki asked.

Morgan looked to the forest. "We find Taylor. Riki and I will go after her. Javi, you and Dr. Hollister stay here." He swallowed. "If Azra comes out of it, and you feel threatened, kill her before Lilith can hurt you."

"You know I can't do that," Garcia said.

"Jesus, Javi, it's a demon."

"It's Azra. As much as we might dislike her for what she's done, she's still a human being."

Morgan threw his hands up. "We're just going to let Lilith hang around until it can possess Taylor again?"

"Of course not," Garcia said. "Go find Taylor. Once we have Taylor, we can protect her."

Can we?

CHAPTER 47

Taylor emerged from the north end of the forest and spotted homes in the distance. The wind raced by, bringing with it the sound of crickets and the smell of livestock. *Yes! They'll have phone service. I can reach Dad.*

A car's headlights appeared. *Even better, if the driver has a cell phone.*

If I can trust the driver.

She debated her, then rushed to the street and flagged it down. The car which screeched to a halt.

A figure got out, masked by the headlights. "Can I help you, miss?" Taylor heard the local accent and exhaled.

"Do you have a phone? I need to call my Dad."

"I can help. Come closer."

She rushed toward the car, and the figure came into focus. A priest, with an assault rifle.

Taylor stopped, her knees buckled, and she collapsed.

CHAPTER 48

Morgan and Riki cautiously started for the forest under a partial moon when a gunshot from the woods pierced the night. A bullet spit into Riki, who dropped face-first.

Chaos surrounded Morgan. Screams. More pistol gunshots whizzing by. He fell over Riki. "Everybody down!" He checked Riki's pulse. Still breathing. "Come on, Riki, stay with us, buddy."

Linda screamed. Morgan turned to see Drakul being led away by a priest toward a car that had pulled in. The spotlights on the barn gave him a clear view of the passenger inside.

"Dad! Help!"

"Taylor! No!" Morgan stood up, but a round of gunshots whizzed by and forced him back to his knees.

They loaded Drakul into the back seat of the car and sped off. The gunfire from the woods stopped.

Amazed he hadn't been hit, Morgan checked Riki for a pulse, and found a faint one. *Why did Drakul's men stop shooting? We're sitting ducks here.* "Riki's been shot. Anyone else?"

"We're okay," Linda called back. "But Taylor's in that car with Drakul."

Hollister arrived at Morgan's side within seconds. "Let me see." She checked Riki's vitals and the wound. "He's in bad shape. We need to take him to the ER. Help me get him to the van. Now."

Morgan helped her move Riki to the SUV. Garcia and Linda loaded the black-eyed Azra inside, Morgan took the wheel, and they sped toward downtown Nazareth.

"I don't get it," Morgan said. "They could have killed all of us once they had Drakul."

"Maybe," Linda said, "they didn't know which of us Lilith chose as a host."

Morgan dodged a hole in the dirt road as they approached paved civilization. "I still think we should kill Azra right now."

"Pennywise, you know that won't do any good. Even if it would, it's not who we are."

"He's right, Richard," Linda said. "We have to stay true to our moral compasses."

"Our moral compasses?" Morgan spit out. "Just where has that gotten us? Smokey's dead. Others slaughtered. Taylor's captured again. Lilith is alive and ready to possess her. And you two keep insisting we follow a moral code. Well, I'm done with that."

"Pennywise, I know you're upset."

"No, Javi, you don't know shit. I wanted to kill Drakul, and I let you talk me out of it. Now look where we are. We're screwed. Your faith and Linda's desire to save the world isn't doing me any good. It's time I took matters into my own hands."

"It's not just my faith," Garcia said. "It's yours, too."

"Not anymore. Save Taylor. That's the only religion I know."

CHAPTER 49

Morgan raced toward the emergency entrance of the Edinburgh Medical Missionary Society Nazareth Hospital. "I need sedatives to keep Azra and Lilith under. Doctor, can you get me those?"

Hollister held an unconscious Riki in her lap. "I can. But I won't if you plan to use it to kill someone. Riki's hanging on by a string. Isn't that enough damage for one day?"

Morgan winced. *Riki. If he dies, it's on me.* "Please do everything you can to save him."

Morgan slammed on the brakes in front of the entrance, catapulting his passengers forward. Hollister pulled on the rear door handle and kicked it open. "Nobody's dying today." Linda got out with her and they carried Riki to the automated entry, then vanished.

"Pennywise, I can do another exorcism. We can trap Lilith again when it's forced out of Azra."

A glance in the rearview mirror told Morgan all he needed to know. *Javi's scared shitless.* "I can't ask you to do that. You've already performed two. You might not survive a third."

"I can do it. We'll take Azra to the Basilica. I'll perform the Rite of Exorcism there. Remember when Linda said we'd need the local religious leader in Costa Rica? Well, we'll ask the local priest to help."

"Come on, Javi. You know that's not practical."

"Why not?"

Morgan stared at him via the mirror. "Because it will kick your ass."

"Thanks for the vote of confidence," Garcia said. "Even if you're right, that's better than murdering Azra. Let me try."

It won't work. Morgan held his head in his hands. His stomach cramped. *Maybe nothing will work. I brought Taylor here, and she's going to die. Because of me.*

"Pennywise?"

"Yeah."

"Let me try. Please. My faith is stronger than when we confronted the demon in Costa Rica. You know that's true."

"I do. But maybe faith isn't enough."

"Faith *is* the only tool. Give me a shot. What do we have to lose?"

Just your life. Another one on me. Morgan looked back at him in the mirror. "You sure?"

"Hell, no. But we must put our fate in God's hands."

Morgan half-turned to face him. "Okay. Let's do it." And then, a familiar realization hit him. *If Javi exercises the demon, we still need to trap Lilith. A bat, like Costa Rica, or something else that fits in the silver box. Otherwise, it'll just escape again, and be off to find Taylor.*

"What are you thinking?" Garcia asked him.

"Nothing."

The emergency room door sprang open and Linda rushed out. She climbed in the front seat. "Riki's going into surgery. Dr. Hollister will stay with him." She pulled out two loaded syringes. "She got me sedatives. Said to give them to you as long as they aren't used to cause harm."

Morgan smiled. "Buckle up. We're going to an exorcism at the Basilica."

CHAPTER 50

Garcia paused at the Upper Church's gilt and sandstone interleaved-brick facade of the Basilica of the Annunciation. A cupola towered above them, with glass panels and a cross, the beacon for Christian tourists, and also to the few Roman Catholics who braved living in Nazareth. Two armed Palestinian guards paced near the entrance. *That's not good. We'll have to deal with them.*

"This is the parish church entrance," Garcia told Morgan and Linda. Morgan had the unconscious Azra in his arms. "There's a separate door for the grotto downstairs. That's where Mary lived, and where the annunciation took place."

"What's with the guards?" Morgan asked.

"This is a terrorist target," Linda said. "I've read that the local police force is woefully understaffed, and crime is out of control. Most of the Christians and Jews have fled."

"Maybe they'll move on," Morgan said.

Garcia entered first. He hoped his collar would buy him some priestly cooperation before the tourists arrived at ten. Glass triangles in the Basilica's dome provided sparse morning light. Colorful mosaics of the Virgin Mary adorned the walls. Statues of Biblical figures were set in each corner.

Reminds me of the church in Monaco. Breathtaking. No time for admiration, though.

A priest in a black cassock stood near the altar.

How am I going to explain this to him? Garcia wondered. *And where's a private spot we can stage the exorcism?*

Morgan interrupted Garcia's thought. "How do we know the priests aren't aligned with Drakul? Maybe *they* provided him the safe house."

"I'd think they'd have all hands on deck with Taylor out at that barn," Linda said.

"Maybe," Morgan said. "But stay alert, just in case."

Like I'm not already on high alert. Garcia approached the priest, his shoes squeaking on the freshly polished floor as he passed the two dozen rows of pews in the wide aisle in the middle of the church.

The priest turned and gave the four of them a querying stare. "Can I help you, Father? If you're here for the tour, it starts at ten."

I wish. "I'm Father Javier Garcia. I'm here on official Vatican business." *Well, that's not exactly true. But I'm guessing God will let that one slide.* "Is there somewhere private we can talk?"

"Father Sebastian, Franciscan." He waved at the empty church. "I'm the only one here. How can I help a fellow priest?"

Garcia felt the blood drain from his cheeks. "I need to speak with your exorcist."

The priest blanched. "Excuse me? My hearing isn't what it used to be. My exorcist?"

Garcia reached the priest, leaving Morgan, Azra, and Linda to sit in a pew. "I'm afraid you heard right. I have a possessed woman over there. I'll need another exorcist's help."

"I'm afraid I'm it in these parts." The priest traced a finger around his lips, then peered at Morgan and the unconscious Azra. "I have some informal training, but I've never actually done one. Her?" He gestured toward Azra.

"Yes," Garcia said. "Possessed by a demon that claims to be Lilith."

Sebastian steadied himself against a pew. "Lilith is here?" He sat, his face a white sheet, and scratched at a mark shaped like an opened-winged bat under his right ear. "You're sure?"

Hmm. Pretty dramatic reaction. "Are you okay, Father?" Garcia pointed to the scar. "Have you been burned?"

"Birth mark. It's never hurt like this."

Garcia studied him. *You are the one we need. You just don't realize it.* "You mentioned you've been informally trained to do exorcisms. It was by your family, wasn't it?"

Sebastian nodded. "How did you know?"

"The mark under your ear. I was in the Vatican recently. There was a portrait of a priest with the same mark. An exorcist."

"My great-grandfather. One of a long line of descendants who went toe-to-toe with Lilith."

"Yes. And now that demon is here, in your church. That can't be a coincidence. That's why you feel the burning. Don't you see? You are destined to help us. You can do what your ancestors could not. Defeat your family nemesis."

"I don't know," Sebastian said. "Times have changed. I cannot be the renegade my ancestors were. Have you done the investigative requirements to prove this is a possession? Do you have formal approval from the Church?"

No. "Yes. Approved by Cardinal Vitelli at the Vatican. It's imperative we begin right away."

"Are *you* an exorcist?"

No. "Yes. I've exorcised this demon before."

Sebastian turned toward the altar and stared at the floor-to-ceiling painting of Jesus and his disciples. "But this is a holy tourist site. An exorcism can take weeks, or longer. There's nowhere here private enough to do such a thing. There must be somewhere else." The priest turned back, then winced and rubbed the mark under his ear.

"You have the lower church." Garcia pointed to the spiral staircase leading downstairs. "The Grotto, the Cave of the Annunciation. We could do it there. All you have to do is sequester that area. And convince the security guards to leave us alone."

The priest looked astounded. "I can't do either of those things. The guards don't report to me, and this Church is under the joint authority of the Vatican and the Israeli government. I'd need approval from both."

Morgan stepped next to Garcia, having left Azra with Linda on the pew. "Don't you see, Father, it isn't a coincidence we're here. Your family has a long history of battling with this demon. You *must* help us. Hell, you're probably the *key* to defeating the demon."

"I'm sorry. It's not possible. Neither the Church nor the government will ever allow it."

"Then we won't ask for permission," Morgan said. "This woman is possessed by the demon your family has been fighting for centuries. How can you turn your back on them and your chance to vanquish it?"

The priest laughed mockingly. "Save the amateur psychology." He turned on Garcia. "Father, you know they approve exorcisms only after months of psychological analysis. I bet you're not an official exorcist, or have any such approvals."

Garcia blinked away tears. *Are these tears of defeat or relief? Do I really have it in me to do another exorcism?* "You're right. But I've done two exorcisms. Including once with this demon. I beat it once. I can beat it again. With your help."

Sebastian pursed his lips. "Find another location. Rent a hotel room."

"I'll still need you as second chair," Garcia said.

"You can do much better than me. Take the girl back to Rome. There you can have your pick of experienced exorcists."

Garcia rubbed his chin. "I understand you're apprehensive."

"Damn right," Sebastian blurted. "Aren't you?"

"I'm scared out of my mind. But I chose a side. Good or evil. Me, I'm on God's side. He's calling me to do this."

"There's no time to go to Rome," Morgan said. "Look, that thing is trying to kill my daughter. We have to exorcise it now. It's clear you have to be part of this."

"I'm sorry," Sebastian said. "There's nothing I can do."

Garcia took Morgan by the arm. "Come on, Pennywise. We'll find somewhere else. And someone else."

Morgan shrugged him off. "No. We have what we need right here. He's uniquely qualified. We do it now."

"Pennywise, Father Sebastian said no. We can't *make* him."

Morgan stepped back and pulled a pistol from his jacket. "I'm afraid I must insist, Father. No more delays. Take us to the lower church. You *will* help us."

Garcia's knees wobbled. "Richard, what are you doing?"

"Whatever it takes."

Sebastian stepped up to Morgan. "How dare you bring a weapon into a House of God?"

"I'm a desperate man, Father. Don't test me."

"Richard!" Linda yelled. "Stop!"

Morgan stepped to the side where he could see everyone. "Javi, you carry Azra. Father Sebastian, you lead the way. Linda, you can come with us or stay up here. Either way, we will exorcise this demon."

"What about the security force?" Sebastian said. "One of them does rounds every hour. They'll come looking for me if I'm not up here."

"Get rid of them," Morgan said.

"There's no getting *rid* of them," Sebastian said.

Linda stood and glared at Morgan. Her eyes shimmered. "Richard, don't do this. To Father Garcia. To Father Sebastian. To me. To us. Most importantly, to yourself."

"I know exactly what I'm doing. Saving Taylor. Everyone to the lower church. I'll figure out what to do about the guards later."

CHAPTER 51

Morgan forced Father Sebastian, Garcia with Azra in his arms, and a glowering Linda into the lower church. At the bottom of the spiral staircase they reached an open space surrounded by remnants of the previous Byzantine and Crusade churches. In the room's center sat a marble table covered with a white lace cloth, set on a marble platform. A single light bulb provided subdued lighting. To their left was the Cave of the Annunciation.

A chill raced up Morgan's spine, even though the room was stuffy and warm. They stepped up to the grotto. A pillar on the right looked as if it was holding up the cave's natural rock ceiling. Set in the center was a Carrera marble platform and table-top. Inscribed on the face of the platform was "Verbum Caro Hic Factum Est."

"What's that say?" Morgan asked.

"Here the word was made flesh," Linda replied.

Two lit candles provided the grotto's only light, and their flickering gave an uneven and eerie vibe, offsetting a white vase with a flower bouquet. Stairs beyond the altar led up to parts unknown.

"Where do those stairs go?" Morgan asked.

"Mary's Kitchen," Sebastian said. "It's a small cave with an exit to the yard."

"Is there an entrance up there?" Morgan asked.

"It's locked from the inside," Sebastian said.

"What can we do about access from the upper church?" Garcia asked.

"Not much." Sebastian jogged back up the stairs.

"Hey!" Morgan yelled. "Where do you think you're going?"

Sebastian hung a CLOSED sign on a chain at the top of the staircase. "Doing all I can to keep tourists out." He looked longingly at the upper church, then returned to Morgan. "We only have an hour before tourists arrive. The security force may come inside before then." He winced and rubbed his birthmark.

"Then you two better get started," Morgan said.

Garcia groaned. "Come on, Richard, you know that's not enough time."

"Just put Azra on the table," Morgan ordered, his voice echoing through the chamber. He turned to Sebastian and flashed the pistol. "We don't stop until we trap the demon. Got it?"

Sebastian hung his head. "Yes."

"You have something to secure Azra to that slab?"

"I have cords and rope in the maintenance supply room," Sebastian said.

"Get them," Morgan said.

Garcia lay Azra on the marble slab within the grotto. "Man, that's cold. I hope Azra can't feel that."

"She can't feel anything," Morgan said. "Just hope it doesn't wake Lilith up before we're ready."

Linda sat on a step leading to Mary's Kitchen. "I can't even look at you right now. You're not who I thought you were."

Morgan's chest muscles knotted. "I'm sorry you feel that way."

"You're sorry *I feel that way*. How about, you're sorry for treating us this way?"

"You left me no choice."

Linda lowered her eyes. "Oh, you had plenty of choices. You could have chosen not to betray me." She turned her back on him and walked to the far side of the room.

I'm just trying to save Taylor. Why can't you see that?

Sebastian returned with the rope. He and Garcia bound Azra's hands and ankles, then secured her to the tabletop by looping the rope through a passage under the slab. Once done, the candles flickered in a way that made Morgan's skin crawl.

"Pennywise, is that gun necessary?"

"You tell me. Are we all on the same page about the exorcism?"

Each of them nodded. Morgan inhaled, then put the weapon back in his coat pocket. "Don't make me take it out again."

"You're forgetting something," Linda said. "We need a vessel for the demon to enter once it's exorcised. One that fits in the silver box we stole from Monaco."

Garcia pulled the box out and showed it to Sebastian. "We used a bat last time." He scanned the ceiling. "I don't suppose you have any of those?"

"I don't understand," Sebastian said. "You're trying to control where a vanquished demon goes? What makes you think you have any control? Or any way to predict?"

"This demon," Garcia said, "is trying to get to Dr. Morgan's daughter. It possessed her before. We know it can jump to anyone in proximity, but it prefers to possess an animal that can take it away. The vampire bats of Costa Rica were perfect for that purpose."

"We have no bats," Sebastian said.

"How about rats?" Morgan asked.

Sebastian blushed. "I'm embarrassed to say. We can't seem to get rid of them."

"You have traps?" Morgan asked. "Glue traps that don't kill them?"

"Yes, many."

Morgan looked at Linda. "That might be the answer. Can you go with Father Sebastian and see if they've caught any rats that are still alive?"

"I can, but I won't."

"I'll go," Garcia said.

Linda frowned at Morgan. "And leave me here alone with *him?* Forget it. I'll go."

Morgan stared at Sebastian. "And come right back."

Sebastian nodded. "I will. We're here with a demon that has haunted my family for centuries. I don't appreciate your methods, but I'm convinced this is my fight, too."

Morgan searched for signs of betrayal, but found none. "Thank you."

After Linda and Sebastian took the silver box and went searching for a live rat Morgan and Garcia stood over Azra.

"What do you think Azra feels with the demon inside her?" Garcia asked.

Morgan shook his head. "Taylor remembered nothing, so hopefully Azra won't."

"We can only hope."

Azra's eyes suddenly opened wide. Morgan retreated. He gripped a spasm in his chest.

Azra grinned. "You two. How lovely." The demon voice. Eerier with the echo. "Shall we get started?"

Morgan fought to regain his composure. *Don't show fear. It feeds on that.* "With what?"

"Why, the exorcism, of course. That's your plan, right?"

Morgan closed in, deciding to go on the offensive. "We all know Azra's not who you want. It must be frustrating to keep failing to get to Taylor."

Azra's grin widened. "In time. Would you like me to tell you a secret?"

"Pennywise, don't engage. It's a liar. You know this."

Azra's lip turned down. "That's very mean, Father Chancho. But, I'll ignore your rude behavior and tell you, anyway." She strained against the ropes. "An infected girl got off that cruise ship."

"Not possible," Morgan said. "They quarantined everyone."

Azra laughed. "You are such a fool. They didn't identify the problem until after they'd ported in Italy. Her parents thought her sick and took her home. If you don't believe me, check with the cruise line."

Morgan closed his eyes. *Is that possible? Could there be another lamia outbreak?*

"There can, and there is," Azra said. "It's had days to spread in the remote countryside."

"But you didn't possess anyone long enough to turn her," Morgan said. "You're lying."

"Am I?" Azra opened her eyes wider. "Or was I lying when I told you I needed more time in Taylor to complete her transmutation?" She cocked her head. "Or are you just wrong about your assumptions?"

"Pennywise, Taylor infected girls without permanently becoming a lamia."

"Yes!" Azra yelled. "The pig wins a prize. That girl can infect hundreds, and then those will infect thousands, and, well, you do the math. The only ramification of her not being possessed by me long enough to turn into a lamia is she's not immortal."

"I don't believe you," Morgan said. He fumbled for a syringe in his pocket.

"Suit yourself. But after I escape, have your doctor whore check into it. She'll confirm everything."

"She's not *my* anything."

"Fine. She's Father Chancho's whore." Azra giggled.

"Watch your mouth!" Garcia's face burned crimson.

"Oh," Azra said, "did I hurt your feelings? What do you plan to do about it, preacher scum?"

"I will exorcise you from Azra and kill you."

"Good luck with that. Better priests than you have tried. Just ask Father Sebastian."

Morgan's suspicions elevated. "What about Father Sebastian?"

Azra grinned. "Let's just say his family's track record isn't so good."

"I exorcised you once. I can do it again." Garcia pounded his fist on the marble. "And you know it. You fear me more than I fear you."

Azra closed her eyes and appeared to fall asleep.

"Nice job, Javi. I think you worried it."

Linda raced in with a closed silver box, followed by Sebastian. "We trapped a live rat."

Morgan engaged with Sebastian. "You say your family has been trying to destroy this demon for generations. That confuses me. If your father was a priest, how did he have you? Priests can't marry."

Sebastian chuckled. "No, they can't. That's why every generation has four sons. Only one son becomes a priest. That way, the pipeline stays full." He sighed. "Until now. I am the last of the Sebastians."

"Did your family ever have any success with this demon?" Morgan asked.

Sebastian pondered the question. "Like you, we trapped it once and turned it over to the Vatican. But that has never been our goal. Our goal is to destroy it."

"You know how to do that?" Garcia asked.

Sebastian went to a desk. He opened the top drawer and withdrew a pile of papers. "These were given to my ancestors centuries ago by holy men in Israel. Copies of *The Zohar*, part of the Jewish Kabbalah. There are five books in *The Zohar*, but one segment stands out for our purposes. My family has been translating the original Aramaic for centuries."

Garcia stepped over to look. "I know these. Written in Aramaic, first discovered in Spain in the thirteenth century. De Leon claims a rabbi wrote them in the second century."

"Right," Sebastian said. "I have pages on the translation as well."

"How does this help us?" Morgan asked.

Sebastian flipped to the back. "I'm sure you're aware that there are references to Lilith throughout ancient Jewish texts. *The Bible*.

Dead Sea Scrolls. Various Kabbalistic sources. But see here. This translation is from *The Zohar*. It matches the Book of Revelation and other Biblical passages about demons."

Morgan joined them. "What's it say? Can we use it to save Taylor?"

"It says," Sebastian said, "that demons can be removed to the Abyss. That they will be thrown, along with Satan, into the lake of fire. In the last days."

"I don't see how that helps," Morgan said.

"What if we can recreate those conditions?" Sebastian said.

Garcia scratched his forehead. "Recreate the end time? How?'

"I don't know," Sebastian said. "We have been studying this for centuries. But the answer eludes us." He handed the text to Garcia. "Take it. Maybe you will have more luck."

Garcia reluctantly accepted the papers. "You sure? This is your family's journey."

"Our legacy is to destroy Lilith. Or, as we in my family call her, The Night Hag. But we have hit an impasse. Perhaps the task requires a fresh perspective."

Garcia pocketed the document. "I'll get this back to you."

Sebastian shook his head. "This is the end of the line for me and my family. It's your fight, now."

"It's *our* fight," Garcia said.

"There's something," Sebastian said, "my family has learned in the centuries we've been trying to kill Lilith. She has an enormous ego, even for a demon. There's one moniker in the texts that drives her insane with rage."

"What is it?" Morgan asked.

"Night Hag."

At the mention of the name, Azra's body flinched. She screamed, "I am Lilith. Show some fucking *respect*. After all, it is I who will kill all of you."

"I think you touched a nerve, Father," Morgan said. "Thanks. We can use that."

"Come, Father" Garcia said. "Let's prepare for the exorcism."

Morgan turned to Garcia. "You ready?"

"Is anyone ever ready for an exorcism?"

CHAPTER 52

Garcia accepted Father Sebastian's *Rite of Exorcism*. His heart raced like it had in Costa Rica, and at his first exorcism a decade earlier. He tried to steady his breathing, to no avail. *Come on, I've got this. God is my armor.*

Sebastian placed a miniature statue of the Crucified Christ on the marble slab. Azra lay silently. Morgan and Linda stood back, keeping an unfriendly distance from each other.

"We're ready," Garcia said, though his stomach said otherwise. *Keep it together, man. Taylor's counting on you.* He kissed the cross hanging on his chest. "Be strong and have faith. Just like in Costa Rica, your participation and conviction matter."

"Won't the tourists hear us?" Linda asked.

"The acoustics are working in our favor," Sebastian said. "Our voices get trapped within the cave. They'd have to come down to hear us."

"Enough talk," Morgan said. "Let's go."

Garcia traced the sign of the cross over Azra, himself, Sebastian, Morgan and Linda. He then took out a vial of holy water and splashed it on each of them.

"We begin with the Litany of the Saints," he said, nodding toward his responders. "Lord, have mercy."

Morgan, Linda, and Sebastian responded, "Lord, have mercy."

"Christ, have mercy."

"Christ, have mercy."

Azra's eyes popped open. "Christ is dead, and I shall have no mercy for you."

Garcia ignored the intrusion. He recited all sixty entries. After each name, the responders replied, "Pray for us." Azra mocked each saint with a tale of their hypocrisy.

After reciting the Lord's Prayer and Psalm 53, Garcia prayed. "God, whose nature is ever merciful and forgiving, accept our prayer that this servant of Yours, bound by the fetters of sin, may be pardoned by Your loving kindness."

Azra spit in his face.

He wiped himself and turned to Sebastian, who read, "Holy Lord, Almighty Father, everlasting God and Father of our Lord Jesus Christ, hasten to our call for help and snatch from ruination and from the clutches of the devil this human being made in Your image and likeness."

Azra's face turned pink. She spoke in a new voice. "Why did you leave me?"

Patti, my first exorcism. It used that against me in Costa Rica. "Shut up, demon! That didn't work before, and it won't work now."

Azra narrowed her eyes. "So much blood on your hands. Patti. Now Azra. Then Taylor. All dead, because you weren't strong enough."

I am strong enough. Garcia bore down. "Strike terror, Lord, into the beast now laying waste Your vineyard. Fill Your servants with courage to fight against this dragon. Let Your mighty hand cast him out of Your servant."

Morgan, Linda, and Sebastian chorused, "Amen."

Garcia took a deep breath as Azra's face turned blood red. *This is hurting it. Keep pressing.* "I command you, unclean spirit, whoever you are, along with all your minions now attacking this servant of

God, that you tell me by some sign your name, and the day and hour of your departure. I command you to obey me to the letter, I who am a minister of God despite my unworthiness."

Azra growled. "Stop asking me to identify myself. I told you my name is Lilith. I demand you call me by my name! God will remember me. I'm His worst nightmare. And, soon, I shall be yours."

Garcia laid a hand on her forehead. *Man, her skin is on fire.* "They shall lay their hands upon the sick and all will be well with them. May Jesus, Son of Mary, Lord and Savior of the world, through the merits and intercession of His holy apostles Peter and Paul and all His saints, show you favor and mercy."

The other three replied, "Amen."

Azra thrust herself against the ropes. "Do you know what your friend thinks of you? The Arrogant Loser thinks you can't do this. He thinks you're *weak*."

"The Lord be with you," Garcia said.

"And with your spirit," came the response.

Garcia opened his book. "A lesson from the holy Gospel according to Saint John. John One, verses one through fourteen."

Garcia signed himself with unsteady hands. Half-expecting her to free herself and take his hand off with one chomp of demonic teeth, he continued over Azra on the brow, lips, and heart.

She hissed. "You're right to worry. I can break these ropes and take your hand off whenever I want. Or I could slice your throat open. Maybe I'll crush your windpipe. I'll give you one last chance to stop."

A wave of doubt rushed over Garcia. *I bet it can.* He blinked repeatedly as if that would keep Lilith from intruding on his thoughts.

He returned to his reading from the Book of John. Once completed, Garcia nodded to Morgan, Linda, and Sebastian, who replied, "Thanks be to God."

Garcia took a deep breath and put a shaking hand over Azra.

"May the blessing of the Almighty God, Father, Son, and Holy Spirit, come upon you and remain with you forever." He sprinkled Azra with holy water, which sizzled on contact.

She shrieked, and the room shook. Bits of rock and dust fell on Garcia. Blisters popped up on Azra's skin.

Garcia crossed himself and Azra again, then put his right hand over her head. Even from a distance he could feel the heat. "See the cross of the Lord! Begone, hostile powers! Let us pray. God and Father of our Lord Jesus Christ, I appeal to Your holy name, humbly begging Your kindness, that You graciously grant me help against this and every unclean spirit now tormenting this creature of Yours. Through Christ our Lord."

The floor rumbled in a wave, like an earthquake rolling through. Cracks appeared in the ceiling. If his responders answered, he didn't hear it over the roar.

"In the name of our Lord Jesus Christ I cast you out. It is He who commands you. Begone, then, in the name of the Father." Garcia gave the sign of the cross on Azra's brow. "And of the Son." He repeated the sign. "And of the Holy Spirit." He completed the signage. "Give place to the Holy Spirit by this sign of the holy cross of our Lord Jesus Christ, who lives and reigns with the Father and the Holy Spirit, forever and ever."

The group replied, "Amen."

Garcia again gave the sign of the cross on Azra's brow. This time, her face turned almost purple, and her skin smoldered. The room's shaking decreased. *Yes! I can see your pain. Get out!*

"Let Your servant be protected in mind and body. Keep watch over the inmost recesses of her heart." Garcia switched to signing over her heart. "Rule over her emotions. Strengthen her will. Let vanish from her soul the temptings of the mighty adversary. Through Christ our Lord."

The responders replied, but with less conviction in their voices. "Amen."

Garcia stepped back and wiped his brow. *One pass complete. We definitely hurt it.* "Father Sebastian, please start from the beginning. I'll back you up this round."

Azra growled. "Put that book down, Father Sebastian. Father Chancho and the Arrogant Loser are going to die soon. But I can still spare you. Unlike the rest of your family who died trying to fight me. Martyrdom is so overrated, don't you agree?"

Garcia could see the stress on Sebastian's face. "Don't listen to it, Father Sebastian! Start the ritual!"

A deep Palestinian voice upstairs called Father Sebastain's name in marginal English. Sebastian dropped the book. His face glazed over. "That's the security detail."

CHAPTER 53

Silt continued to fall from the ceiling, masking the minimal light provided by the candles.

"Ignore him," Morgan told .

"Be right there," Father Sebastian called upstairs. He met Morgan's glare. "He won't stop until he finds me. And he'll call for backup if he suspects anything is wrong. The local police are mostly worthless, but they have a whole task force dedicated to terrorist threats, and those guys mean business. What if he walks in on *this*?"

Morgan remembered the syringes in his pocket. *I was saving these for Lilith, but maybe I don't have that luxury.* "All right. New plan. Father Sebastian, I'll come with you. If he won't leave, I'll tranquilize him."

"Richard!" Linda exclaimed. "Think about what you're doing."

"It'll just put him out for a while. We can tie him up."

"The other one will call it in if his partner doesn't return from his rounds," Sebastian said.

Morgan shoved Sebastian to the stairs. "Try to get rid of him. If he comes down, distract him. I'll handle the rest."

Sebastian called out, "Coming," then looped up the staircase. Morgan stood at the bottom, with a vantage point that allowed him to see the guard.

A guard stood just outside the chain. He held his automatic rifle in a horizontal, shooting position. "What's going on, Father?"

"Just helping a fellow priest," Sebastian said. "I'll be in here for a few hours. My tour assistant should be here any minute. Can you help her with the tourists until I finish?"

"Not my job," the guard said.

Sebastian fidgeted. "I know. I just need a little time."

The guard made eye contact with Morgan. The look made it clear the guard wasn't buying any of this. "You there. Who are you?"

Morgan removed the protective caps from one needle. "Just a parishioner."

"Where is priest?" The guard asked Sebastian. "You said you're with priest."

"He's in the grotto," Morgan said. "Come check it out if it'll make you feel better."

The guard studied Sebastian, who glistened in sweat. "Something is wrong."

Sebastian's shoulder's sagged. The priest moved to the side and signaled for the guard to come down the stairs. "Of course you're welcome to come check."

The guard passed Sebastian and traversed the stairs two at a time, keeping his rifle in a defensive position. When he reached the bottom Morgan pounced.

Morgan dosed the guard with the sedative. The guard's eyes burst wide open, then drooped as his muscles relaxed. Morgan plucked the guard's rifle and eased him to the floor. He set his body up against the wall, put the rifle's safety back on, and moved the rifle to the other side of the chamber.

"Get back to the exorcism," Morgan said. "I'll tie him up."

Azra cackled. "You're all morons. I'll leave on my terms, not yours." She glanced at the silver box on a side table. "I know what you have there. A rat. Hoping I'll bail into it and you can close me in again. You underestimate me, stupid humans."

Morgan's chest tightened. *Not good. Can Lilith control its natural urge to get into a creature it can use to escape? Are we wasting our time?*

"You *are* wasting your time," Azra said. "I have all the power." She glared at Garcia. "You have nothing."

Morgan closed his eyes and covered his ears. *Stay out of my head!*

I will go wherever I please. Knowing the demon could communicate telepathically with him jarred Morgan. He opened his eyes. The world fell away into a mirage of fire and beasts flogging humans.

"I will kill you," Morgan said.

"No, you won't." Azra's body levitated inches off the marble, straining against the rope. "I will kill all of you before you leave this room. Then, I'll go to *my* Taylor."

Sebastian crossed himself and whimpered, "Help me, God. I thought I could do this, avenge my family, but I'm not strong enough. Help me get far away from this evil."

"Steady," Garcia said. "God is with us."

Azra shrieked. The room shook as if a powerful earthquake rumbled through. The lone light bulb exploded, leaving the room in almost total darkness.

"I can't do this." Sebastian broke for the staircase.

Morgan's gaze followed Sebastian's shadow and he drew the pistol. "Stop! I *will* shoot you."

A dim light emanated from the upper church via the stairwell. Sebastian stood with a foot on the first step. "Please. We must escape while we still can."

Before Morgan could respond, Sebastian was thrown from the stairs against the wall by an invisible force. He collapsed onto the floor and blood pooled around his head.

"Nobody leaves," Azra said. "Not until I'm through with each of you."

A chill rushed up Morgan's spine. *Lilith can do that?*

"I'm just getting started," Azra replied. "Watch this."

Morgan's right hand involuntarily aimed the weapon at Garcia. "Javi, I can't control my arm. The pistol." His trigger finger tightened. "Move!"

The pistol's discharge echoed through the chamber, all the way to Hell and back.

CHAPTER 54

The bullet ricocheted around the room, at one point whistling past Morgan's ear. "Javi? You okay?"

Garcia answered from floor level. "Yeah. Ducked just in time."

Linda stumbled to Morgan. "The demon did that?"

"I had no control," Morgan said.

Azra hissed. "I told you. *I'm* in control."

Morgan's arm tingled, and he shifted until he was facing Linda. "I can't stop it, Linda. Get down!"

He fired another shot. *Please, no.* The bullet ricocheted from wall to wall. "Linda?"

"I'm okay."

Morgan's arm relaxed, and he had control again. His first instinct was to eject the pistol's magazine to the floor. He fumbled at that, then felt a chill and froze. *Something's happening. Something bad.*

Linda rose and growled at him. "You want possession, I'll show you possession." Her voice was deep and demonic, her breath a foul stench, knocking him back. She snatched the pistol from him. "Say goodbye, Arrogant Loser. Give my regards to Satan."

Morgan lunged at Linda, trying to pry the weapon away, but she was too strong. The barrel of the pistol dug into his ribs. "Get out of her! We both know it's me you want."

The pistol pressure eased.

"That's right," Morgan said. "Come and get me! *Me!*"

Morgan's world blurred in a way he didn't comprehend. His final thought was of Taylor as a young girl. With Michelle. The three of them sitting around a Christmas tree. Laughing. Childhood bliss. Then, nothing.

* * *

Lilith seized Morgan's psyche. *Let's see. Where shall I begin? Yes. Your parents.*

Lilith pushed the vision of Morgan's father executing his mother in front of him, then committing suicide, into Morgan's thoughts. Morgan's body jerked in response. Lilith kept pushing. *I so enjoy toying with you humans.*

Lilith sent an impulse along Morgan's arm. *I should kill someone.* The arm raised while Lilith searched for Linda. *There you are. It was a thrill being inside you.*

But before pulling the trigger, Lilith wanted Morgan to know something. *Arrogant Loser! Pay attention! Did you know Linda thinks you're a terrible lover, and a worse father? She's been planning her breakup with you for weeks. Only her delusional sense of duty to save the world from the lamia has kept her with you.*

Morgan's body shook.

That's right. And, as for Azra, she never loved you. You and Taylor's condition were her ticket to fame and fortune. That's why she pretended to love you. She even let Michelle die. Could have saved her but didn't.

Lilith sensed Morgan's knees buckling and propped him up. *Not yet. First, you need to kill them both. Make them pay for what they've done to you.*

Despite the lower church's diminished lighting, Lilith saw everyone in perfect clarity. Linda was kneeling before Morgan, dazed from her brief encounter. Azra was awake now, and trying to free herself from the ropes, to no avail. Father Chancho cowered on the floor.

How lame to be human. I almost feel sorry for them.

Lilith forced Morgan to laugh. *Sometimes I crack myself up.*

And Taylor, she still believes you killed her mother. She wants you to pay for that. Father Chancho believes her and wants you to burn in Hell. After you kill Linda and Azra, you will kill Father Chancho and yourself. It's the only way to stop the pain. To give and receive justice.

With the pistol aimed at Linda, Lilith squeezed Morgan's trigger finger.

CHAPTER 55

Garcia steeled himself and crawled to Father Sebastian.. He found a faint pulse. He looked back into the lower church at Morgan raising the gun toward Linda. *What were we thinking?* "Pennywise?" His voice sounded like violin strings vibrating off-key.

Morgan's voice sounded demonic. "Busy killing Linda. Don't fret. I'll get to you next."

Oh, Lord. It's moved into Richard. I have to stop this.

He lunged at Morgan, making contact just as the gun fired. This time, the bullet slammed into a statue of Christ in the alcove, scarring His head.

Garcia held onto Morgan and wrestled with him, trying to get the gun away. But Morgan had a demon's strength and tossed Garcia aside.

Azra screamed. She had untied herself. Morgan had the gun pointed at her.

"Pennywise, no!"

But Morgan put a red hole in the center of Azra's forehead. The sound of a crushed skull reverberated throughout the grotto. Azra crumpled to the ground, landing at the base of the table, and sitting against it, her open eyes accusing Morgan of murder.

"No!" Garcia dove at Morgan's legs and pulled. Morgan crashed to the floor. The gun flew out of his hand, landing near the security guard's rifle.

Garcia straddled him. "In the name of our Lord Jesus Christ I cast you out! It is He who commands you! Do you hear me? It is Almighty God Himself who commands you!"

Morgan writhed. *It's working! Keep going!* He pounded Morgan's chest "I cast you out! God Himself casts you out!"

Morgan spit in his face. Garcia snatched the vial of holy water in his robe and dumped the last of it on Morgan. Morgan's skin sizzled like bacon in a greasy pan. "I cast you out, vile demon!"

Morgan wilted. His skin stopped smoldering. Steam exited his open mouth.

I did it! Didn't I? Make sure. "Richard. Talk to me."

Morgan groaned. A human groan.

Garcia sat over Morgan's body, stunned. *I did do it.* Then, a new concern. *But where'd Lilith go? We didn't have the silver box ready.*

Azra spoke, her face unidentifiable. "Looking for me?"

Garcia couldn't move. He stared into the abyss of Hell, and Hell stared back. "Azra's dead."

"You think I can't possess the dead? More evidence you are a fool."

"I'll kill you, if it's the only thing I ever do." Garcia remembered the gun and the rifle.

"You'll never reach it in time," Azra said. Blood gurgled out of her mouth when she spoke, and the words were almost indecipherable.

But I understand her perfectly. She's planting her thoughts in my mind.

"I haven't had a turn in you yet," Azra said. "Go for the gun and see what happens."

Garcia thought he saw Azra wink, but couldn't tell through the red glop that used to be her face.

A new noise, from the stairs leading to Mary's Kitchen, caused his attention to shift. Scratching noises. Loud ones. *What's up those stairs?*

The noise stopped. Garcia cocked sideways, trying to glimpse what was making the sound. He thought he might see a shadow on the wall, but saw nothing. *Maybe it's Lilith, messing with me.*

He returned his attention to Azra.

Her black eyes leered at him through a slick, oozing red mask. She laughed, a demonic cackle, and grinned. "Scared, Chancho?"

"No. The exorcism is working, and you're the one who's scared. Scared to be cast adrift again."

"We'll see." The beast's head rotated to the stairs. The noise returned.

Then, rats scurried down the stairs.

Garcia cowered and covered up as the rats assaulted him. Teeth tore into him. Nails scratched him. He shielded his eyes with his arms, but his ears were defenseless, and they gnawed at them in a frenzy. The pain and revulsion shook him to his soul.

He tried to cry out, but a rat burrowed into his mouth. He spit it out, clenching his lips tight. He chanced a squint at his friends. They were also under siege.

Azra laughed, such as she could through the blood. "It looks like my ride is here. I'll leave you and the Arrogant Loser to be eaten alive. I'm off to find *my* Taylor. I have an Antichrist to create."

CHAPTER 56

Morgan stirred. A nightmare of scenes flashed by. *Snap out of it. Save Taylor!* He chased the horrifying images of his father killing his mother and of Michelle drowning from his mind and opened his eyes.

Rats. Everywhere. Not New York City sized, but still.

Two pounced on his face, their claws scratching their way up his cheek. Their furry bodies were like wet towels against his skin, and they smelled like the sewer. Morgan closed his eyes just as they dug into his lids. He gagged, then grabbed the rats by the tails and flung them away.

Morgan sat up and opened his eyes a crack. Garcia was writhing on the ground, his body covered in vermin. The rats also covered the security guard and Sebastian, and blood trickled from their inert bodies. Linda stood in the corner of the elevated altar, surrounded. Azra sat against the altar, her face a bloody mess. A handful of rats dug into the fresh meat.

You did that to Azra. You killed her.

No! It was Lilith!

Lilith. Where is she?

The ocean of rats turned to him as if to answer his question.

Lilith's in one of the rats. I have to stop her from getting out of here.

All but one of the swarm stampeded Morgan. The largest rat stood upright on the marble altar, next to the silver box. Morgan swore it smiled.

Morgan jumped to his feet before the rats reached him. He kicked at the first attackers, but dozens more followed until they covered his pant legs. They crept up, toward Morgan's face.

Repulsion overwhelmed him. Shooting pain as the rats nipped at his flesh. The world spun, and he knew he was about to collapse. And succumb. *Lilith wins. I lose. Taylor's soul is lost.*

No!

Morgan grasped the first rat to reach his face by the tail and tossed it away. Rats continued climbing, but Morgan found the will to keep pace, discarding one after another. When he saw the thrown rats return to him, he changed his strategy. He gripped the next rat and twisted its head. The rat bit into the flesh between his thumb and forefinger, piercing his skin.

But Morgan was full of adrenaline now, and he snapped the rat's neck and tossed it aside.

The rats climbing up his torso whined, and the king rat on the altar hissed.

"Come on!" Morgan yelled as he captured the next rat. He killed it and threw it across the room, barely missing Lilith's host. "Come and get me!"

The king rat rose on its haunches. The rats around Garcia, Sebastian, and Linda abandoned them, and scurried toward Morgan. Once at Morgan's feet they bolted up his legs.

Morgan's bravado turned to fear. *They're too many of them. They'll dig out my eyes before I can kill them all.*

Garcia's voice broke through the high-pitched rat noises. "Hang on, Pennywise. We're coming."

The rats reached Morgan's face, and he clenched his mouth and eyes just after seeing Linda and Garcia storm toward him.

Rats tore at his ears and cheeks. One got its tail between Morgan's lips. He bit it and heard an eerie screech.

One by one, rats were pulled from his face. He braved a peek. Dead rats piled up at Garcia and Linda's feet. Both of their hands were bleeding.

"They're so many of them," Linda said.

"Keep going," Garcia said. "Every one we kill is one less to attack."

His face clear, Morgan went back to slaughtering them as they crawled up his body. With each rat came a new bite, and the blood made handling the rats a slippery mess, but the three of them were able to keep pace, until they'd eliminated all but the large rat.

A smug grimace replaced the king rat's smile.

"You're next, Lilith" Morgan growled.

Lilith's host bolted up the stairway that led to Mary's kitchen, and the outdoors beyond.

Linda fell to her knees, but landed on a dead rat and jumped back to her feet. "Jesus. I can't believe we survived that."

"God did it," Garcia said. "He gave us the strength."

Morgan turned on his friend. "Lilith got away. I don't see His hand in any of this."

Garcia stared at the altar. "Poor Azra."

"I shot her," Morgan said.

"That was Lilith, not you," Garcia said.

Linda stepped over the sea of rats and checked Sebastian for signs of life. "He didn't make it." She moved to the security guard. "Neither did he."

Morgan's eyes teared up and a river of saltwater streamed down his face, which stung like hell. "I forced Father Sebastian to do this. I killed him, too. And the guard."

"Stop it," Garcia said. "There will be time for regret later. Right now, we need to chase Lilith."

Morgan's head pounded. "To what end? Our best chance to save Taylor, *your* exorcism, failed."

Garcia withdrew. "We did our best, Richard."

"Yeah, well, your best sucked. God's best sucked. Why did I let you talk me into this exorcism nonsense?"

"You don't mean that," Garcia said.

"The hell I don't. Right now I'd trade all of your prayers and rituals for making a deal with that demon to spare my child."

"Demons aren't in the sparing business," Garcia said.

Morgan poked Garcia in the chest. "And God isn't in the saving business. So I guess I'm just screwed. Taylor's screwed."

Linda came to Morgan and tried to hug him, but he wanted no part of her empathy.

"Leave me alone, both of you. I killed Smokey. I killed Azra, I killed Father Sebastian. I killed this guard. For all I know I killed Riki. And Taylor will die. Because I trusted God, and He shit all over me."

CHAPTER 57

Taylor could not remember how she got from the car to the bed in the dark, damp, closet-sized room she was in. She screamed for help. No one answered.

If Cardinal Drakul was to be believed, Lilith had escaped from her father again and was only days away. Her skin crawled at the thought.

The lone door creaked open, and Cardinal Drakul entered, carrying a tray of food. Light streaked onto the floor, exposing black mold and dried blood stains. "No one can hear you. Save your strength. You have a long road ahead of you."

She screeched louder.

He looked at her in a lustful way that terrified her. Drool squeezed out of his mouth. "You are very feisty. I like that. It's no wonder Lilith chose you."

Taylor withdrew into a curled-up ball. "Stay away from me."

Drakul grunted. "You are not for me. You are for Lilith. Eat."

"I'm not hungry, you sicko."

Drakul set the tray on the bed. A single piece of bread, a bowl of broth, and a glass of water. Like the last four meals. "You must be strong for Lilith. Eat."

Taylor kicked the tray to the floor, splashing Drakul's feet in liquid.

"You stupid bitch. Do you know what will happen to you if you disobey?"

Taylor smirked. "You aren't worried about what Lilith will do to *me*. You're worried about what it'll do to *you*. You've been one big screw-up."

One of Drakul's minions appeared and swept away the tray.

"And, yet, here you are," Drakul said. "Trapped, with no way to escape. Eat. Don't eat. I don't care. My journey is almost done. But yours is just beginning."

Taylor slammed herself back onto the scratchy sheets. "Leave me alone."

Drakul exited and locked the door.

Taylor stared at the cracked ceiling. *I need to get out of here.* She once again felt along the wall along her bed, desperately searching for an escape route. As before, the wood panels were solid.

Wood can be cut. Can I get a knife?

But, deep in her heart, she knew that wouldn't happen. *Dad, help me. I'm fresh out of miracles, and Lilith will be here any moment.*

CHAPTER 58

Morgan closed Azra's eyelids. "I told you I was bad for you."

"I'll give her last rites," Garcia said.

"You know she wasn't a believer," Morgan said.

"That's irrelevant," Garcia said.

"If you say so." Morgan stepped aside. "But if you run into her in the afterlife, she'll give you shit about it."

Garcia ignored him and administered last rites, first to Azra, then to Father Sebastian, and finally to the security guard.

When Garcia finished the security guard's walkie-talkie came to life. "Abdulhadi, 'ayn 'ant?"

"My Arabic's a little rusty, but I'm pretty sure he's looking for his partner," Linda said. "What do we do?"

Morgan walked toward the exit leading to the church upstairs. "He must have heard the gunshots. Go to the hospital and get a shot of Rocephin, an antibiotic. And a tetanus booster if it's been a few years since your last shot."

"What about rabies?" Garcia said.

"You have six days to get a rabies vaccine. You'll want one, but it's less urgent."

"What about you?" Linda asked.

"I'm finding Taylor. Alone."

"What are you talking about?" Garcia asked. "We need to stick together."

Morgan turned back on them. The adrenaline rush had passed, and exhaustion slammed him hard. "The exorcism didn't work. Nothing you two have tried has worked. Go home. I'll solve this myself."

Linda fronted him and clutched his arm. "Just like that? You're leaving me behind?"

"I'm not leaving you. I'm releasing you of your obligation."

"Obligation? Seriously? You think I'm with you out of *obligation*?"

Morgan shook her hand off. "Whatever it is, it's over. I appreciate your help in Costa Rica. You helped save Taylor once. But there's nothing you can do for her here."

Footsteps approached from the spiral staircase leading to the upper church. Morgan tensed. *Shit. We're too late.*

But instead of the security guard, Dr. Hollister descended and stepped into the lower church.

Her first step landed on a dead rat, and the squish could be heard by everyone. She almost toppled over, but regained her balance. "What the hell?"

She stared at the dead rats littering the floor. Her face turned ghostly white. "Where'd these rats come from?"

"The demon summoned them," Linda said. "We had to kill them." She held her stomach. "All of them." She blew out a jittery breath. "Riki?"

Hollister sidestepped a pile of rats and joined the others. "He came through surgery okay. Should make a full recovery."

Temporary relief doused Morgan. "Thank God for that." *I mean, thank goodness.*

Garcia kissed his cross. "Praise God. Is the security guard still up there?"

"In the patio," Hollister said. "Tourists are lining up to get in. Should we call the guard?"

Morgan walked past the altar to the back stairs. "Not unless you want to have to explain this. Me, I'm leaving."

"Where to?" Hollister asked.

"I'm going to search for Taylor." Morgan started up the stairs, ducking in the tight space. He reached the small cave, and then a padlocked door. When the lock wouldn't give, he pulled out the pistol and, with one shot, destroyed the lock.

He shoved the door open and stepped into a garden. Beyond that, an exit near the convent. The glare hurt his eyes, and his head immediately ached. The smell of diesel fuel and rotten food assaulted him. *Now what? You have no idea where to search for Taylor.*

Garcia, Linda, and Hollister stepped out next to him. They departed the garden and passed through the exit, only to be met by a different security guard speaking into a walkie-talkie.

"Abdulhani, ajb." The guard noticed Morgan and company for the first time. His eyes grew bigger, and he stepped back. "Stop!" He shifted his rifle to a threatening position. "You are not allowed in there. Why is there blood?"

Morgan felt for the last syringe in his pocket and removed the safety cap.

When nobody responded the guard switched to his phone. "Mahzir at the Basilica. Abdulhani la tastajib. Send backup."

"Are you looking for Father Sebastian?" Morgan improvised. "He's helping an old woman who fainted."

The guard raised his rifle and aimed. "Stay where you are." In the distance, a siren went off. A handful of tourists wandered by, saw the rifle, and ran toward the upper church's patio.

Garcia made eye contact with Morgan, then seized his chest and fell to his knees.

The guard saw the priest in distress. "Are you okay, Father?"

Morgan used the diversion to inject a full dose of the sedative into the guard, who stammered, then lost consciousness.

"I'm so going to Hell," Garcia muttered as he returned to his feet.

"We need to hustle." Morgan found the van keys and tossed them to Linda. "You take the van. I'll find another way out."

"I'm going with you," Linda said.

"No, you're not."

Hollister interrupted. "I don't know what's going on between you two, but there's been another outbreak. In Pisa."

The sirens got louder.

"Lamias?" Garcia asked.

"Looks like it," Hollister said. "Apparently an infected girl got off that cruise ship before the quarantine took effect. We have to stop the plague while we still can."

Morgan exhaled. *Lilith wasn't lying. The plague is spreading.* "Then you all go deal with the plague. I'm looking for Taylor."

The sirens sounded like they were only blocks away.

Linda handed Morgan the car keys. "First, let's get out of here. Then we can decide a course of action, a plan."

Morgan stood his ground until Garcia shoved him in the back. "You won't find her in jail. And you need medical attention. Move!"

They rushed to the van and sped away before being seen by the approaching cars.

* * *

They pulled into the hospital parking lot. Hollister got out. "Probably best you three stay here. There'd be too many questions we don't want to answer. Fortunately, my WHO credentials give me some leeway on hospital privileges. I can administer first aid in the van before we drive to the airport. Strip to your undies."

Garcia blushed. "I beg your pardon."

Hollister smiled. "I should check the cuts. Just in case. Right, Doc?"

Morgan's breathing momentarily stopped at the term Smokey had used for him. *Doc. I sure miss you calling me that, Lieutenant.*

And we could really use you right now. "She's right. Suck it up, Javi. It's time you saw a girl in her skivvies."

"Suck it up, Javi?" Linda said. "What about me? Stripping in front of a priest?"

Morgan would have found that funny in another situation. "He promises not to look."

Garcia lifted his shirt over his head. "I'm the one you shouldn't be looking at. Too many tamales, not enough exercise."

Two nurses walked past the van. They stared inside, then hustled toward the hospital.

"Hurry up," Morgan said to Hollister. "We don't need the scrutiny."

Hollister nodded and closed the van door. She jogged to the ER entrance.

After the partial disrobing, Morgan checked the wounds on Linda and Garcia. "You're both fine. The antibiotic shots will take care of these wounds. After that, I'll take you to the airport. You'll need fresh clothes. These will draw too much attention."

"And you?" Garcia asked.

"I'm staying. Taylor's in Israel. I know it."

"How do you know?" Linda asked.

"Lilith wanted the impregnation in Nazareth. It will want the birth in Bethlehem."

Garcia nodded. "Makes sense. So you think Taylor is still in Nazareth?"

"I don't know. Maybe."

"But we can't let the plague spread," Linda said. "If we let the outbreak in Pisa get out of control, the entire world population is doomed, including us."

Morgan grunted. "Taylor is the only cause I'm fighting for. You three can go save the world."

Hollister returned and started treating Linda. "What'd I miss?"

"I did a cursory exam," Morgan said. "We were lucky. Mostly superficial wounds."

"What if we can save Taylor *and* kill the lamias?" Garcia asked.

"I don't see how," Morgan said.

"When Lilith was in my head," Garcia said, "I saw something."

Morgan recalled Lilith in his head, and the horrors he saw. "Yeah?"

"I saw Lilith's plan. How it impregnates Taylor."

"What do you mean?" Morgan asked.

Garcia became animated, waving his arms in gyrating circles. "Lilith's a demon, and a female. Haven't you wondered how she plans to do it?"

Morgan didn't know whether to laugh or cry. *I'm getting the sex talk from a priest. Oh, the irony.* "It's not an image I'm anxious to think about."

"The demon has to be *integrated*," Garcia said.

Hollister finished up with Linda and moved to Garcia. "What's that?"

Linda finished getting dressed. "That makes a difference."

Hollister frowned. "Will someone please explain what integration is, and why it matters?"

"Integration," Garcia said, "is when the demon becomes integrated with the host. The possession is complete, and can't be reversed. The demon can't be exorcised, and the host is lost."

"Forever?" Hollister asked.

"And ever." Garcia looked into Morgan's eyes. "But integration typically takes weeks."

"So," Linda said, "does that mean we have time to go stop the plague, and return to Israel to find Taylor before the integration can happen?"

"That's absurd," Morgan said. "Even if he's right about the integration being required, we don't know how long it will take. Javi's just guessing."

"It's more than a guess," Garcia said. "It's based on previous exorcisms."

"But you can't guarantee it," Morgan said.

"Well, no."

Morgan narrowed his eyes. "And isn't it true that the longer a demon is in possession of a host, the harder it is to eradicate it?"

Garcia hesitated, then nodded.

"Then you have your answer." Morgan opened the driver's side door.

"Hang on," Hollister said. "At least let me treat those cuts and give you an antibiotic."

Morgan closed the door. "Okay. But I'm staying in Nazareth."

"Then I'm staying, too," Garcia said.

"Me, too," Linda said.

Morgan squinted at them. "I know what you're doing. You think I won't allow the plague to spread. That I'll change my mind if it's the only way to stop it. Well, you're wrong. I told you. Taylor is my only concern."

Hollister moved on to Morgan. "So, you expect me to go stop a worldwide pandemic by myself? Thanks a lot."

"Call your WHO buddies," Morgan said.

"Yeah, I can see how that conversation will go. 'Hey, boss, we have a coven of vampires on the loose in Pisa. Can I get the cure for that out of our reserves? What? We have no medicine for that? How about crucifixes, stakes, and garlic? Maybe a few volunteers who have experience with vampires?' That'll get me locked up in the loony bin."

"Not my problem," Morgan said.

Hollister jabbed him hard with a needle.

"You did that on purpose," he said.

"Somebody has to get your head out of your ass." She completed the injection. "At least you won't die of infection. Guilt from letting the human race be overrun? Maybe."

Morgan's face flushed. "I tried. Can't you understand? I need to save my daughter."

"Sounds like you might be able to accomplish both," Hollister said.

"We don't know that," Morgan said. "I can't take the risk."

"Pennywise, we don't know anything. We don't know where Taylor is. We don't know if we'll ever find her. We don't even know where to start looking."

"She's still here," Morgan said.

"The only thing we know for sure is we can stop the pandemic," Linda said. "If we act quickly enough. We *know* where that is. We *know* how to stop it. I say we take the sure thing."

"And how is allowing the birth of the Antichrist better than a world full of lamias?" Morgan countered. "We're finished no matter which I choose."

"We're not finished yet," Garcia said. "We have to keep fighting."

"Save it, Javi. I've seen the future, and it's not anything I want to be a part of."

Linda looked at the ground. "You know I haven't given up on Taylor."

He saw the hurt in Linda's eyes, and his stomach broiled again. "I won't be responsible for killing anybody else. After what I've done, and who I've hurt, I can accept that my life is over. But you can still have a life. You can be free of me, and the curse that comes with it. Go live your lives. Leave me to rot in Hell like I deserve."

"So this is it for us, then," Linda murmured. She handed Morgan the silver box. "I guess you'll need this."

Morgan shook it and felt the weight of the frightened rat. "May I suggest one thing?"

"What?" Linda said, her heart not in it.

"Call Vitelli and have him reach out to *La Contención de la Plaga* in Costa Rica. I bet Margarita would help."

"You think she'd come all this way?" Linda asked.

Morgan nodded. "I think she'll do anything to keep the lamia plague from spreading."

"That's a good idea," Linda said. "I'll call Cardinal Vitelli from the airport."

"Since we're making deals, I'll make you another one," Garcia said. "We'll buy you a ticket for our flight to Rome. In case you change your mind."

Morgan opened the door again. "Don't hold your breath." He noted Linda's teary glare, cringed, and walked away.

CHAPTER 59

Morgan wandered the streets of Nazareth, circling wide enough to avoid the Basilica, trying to stay in the shadows. Listening, watching, desperately trying to find clues to Taylor's whereabouts.

A rat ran across the street, dodging the late morning traffic, catching his attention. But it scurried into a gutter, and Morgan sensed no evil there.

Come on, Taylor. Give me a sign.

But Taylor, if she was nearby, wasn't on the same frequency.

How about you, Lilith? You know you want a piece of me. It must piss you off not to finish the job back at the Basilica. Show yourself. I promise I'll come right over, and you can take care of me in front of Taylor. You'd like that, wouldn't you?

The wind chased plastic bottles scraping across the road. But no Lilith.

Why did I bring Taylor with me? We should have hunkered down in Salem.

He thought back to what Javi had said. *Integration takes weeks.* Did he really have that much time? Or was that another tease from God, intended to drag out his torture?

He sat on a street bench, set his face in his hands, and closed his eyes. *This is worse than losing Michelle on the beach.*

The crunch of a plastic bottle being stepped on startled him. He looked up into the sunlight and saw a blurred vision in front of him. A girl, maybe ten. When she didn't pass by, he barked, "What are you looking at?"

In a deep voice, the child responded. "An arrogant loser."

Morgan reached for her, his rage rising. *I'm going to kill you, Lilith.*

But she shifted away and laughed. "Save your strength, Doc."

That voice. She sounds like Smokey.

"Very good, Doc. Who else would you like to hear from?" She grinned. "Richard. Why did you kill me?"

Morgan dropped to his knees. *Azra.* He cried. "You bastard."

"Technically, I'm a bitch, but I feel you."

"Why don't you come closer?" Morgan said. "I have something for you."

"I bet you do. Sadly for you, I have another engagement. It's been fun playing with you."

"I'll find Taylor."

The girl guffawed. "Even you know that's not going to happen. It's a big world out there, and you have no idea where she is. None. Face it. She's mine now."

"She's still here."

"She's not."

"I don't believe you."

"Let me ask you this. If she's here, why am I bothering talking to you? Why am I not with her?"

Morgan stared at the ground. "Then, where?"

"Oh, no. I'm willing to play, but I'm not going to just *give* you the answers."

Morgan braced himself, then lunged again at the girl. But she vanished as quickly as she'd appeared. *Come back. I need you to do something for me.*

What's that? came Azra's voice in his head.

231

Morgan swallowed. "You win, okay? Just end it. Put me out of my misery. Like you planned to do at the Basilica."

Azra's voice responded again. *I've reconsidered. Seeing you suffer as Taylor gives birth to the Antichrist will be too delicious to pass up. And watching helplessly as my lamia children infect the world? I wouldn't miss that for anything. For that's the ultimate pain I can inflict on you. Punishment for all of your sins against me.*

"Sins against *you*? You're an evil abomination. You'll piss God off talking like that."

I'm counting on it, Azra's voice responded.

Morgan scanned the area, but didn't see the girl. "If you won't end me, I'll do it myself."

Still Azra. *No, you won't. You pretend you've abandoned God, but we both know you're not strong enough to go it alone. And, as a practicing Catholic, you can no more take your own life as I could deny myself the pleasure of possessing girls and turning them into lamias. And now, I bid you a final adieu. Enjoy the tortuous hell I've damned you to.*

A sour breeze blew by, and Morgan knew Lilith was gone. He shivered as if one of the church rats was scrambling along his spine. He dropped to his knees.

The bitch is right. I won't be fortunate enough to miss the carnage.

Then another thought trickled in. *Why would Lilith bother to come here?*

Playing with its food. That's what.

A new realization struck him and he bolted to his feet. *That wouldn't keep it from Taylor. A long journey makes more sense. One it needs a human host to traverse?*

He closed his eyes and paced back and forth in front of the bench. A scene from when he'd been possessed flashed momentarily into his consciousness.

The lamias. Lilith loves the lamias. Like a mother loves a child.

"Lilith's flying to Rome. And from there, to Pisa." A surge of hope ran through Morgan. "Taylor and Drakul must be in Pisa, too."

He huddled with his thoughts. *Am I sure? If I leave, and she's still here, I'll lose my chance to find her.*

A stiff breeze blew by, sending leaves and trash scraping along the street. He followed the noise and found the little girl standing a block away. She smiled at him.

Lilith. Fuck you and your mind games.

The girl scampered away.

But if I stay, and she's there, I also lose.

The girl met up with two adults and, after some scolding, they loaded into their rental car and drove off.

Rental car. Maybe going to the airport. Maybe the same flight Linda is on. He checked the time. *If I hurry, I can still catch it.*

He took out the silver box. *I'll never get a rat through security. I'll need to find a new one in Pisa.* He dumped the rat in the gutter, watched it scurry away, and hailed a cab.

CHAPTER 60

Morgan boarded a full EL AL flight to Rome. Several toddlers screaming in protest magnified the typical pre-flight hustle and bustle. Morgan rechecked his boarding pass, hoping it had magically morphed into a first-class seat, where the passengers were quiet and the cocktails strong. No luck.

Linda saw him first from her aisle seat in the last row. She furrowed her brow, then elbowed Garcia, who had Father Sebastian's ancient scripts spread out in his lap. He reacted with surprise and a smile. Dr. Hollister, across the aisle and with an empty middle seat next to her, looked up and gave him a quizzical expression.

A flight attendant rushed him toward the empty seat, but not before Morgan recognized the girl from the streets of Nazareth. His pace surged with a temporary elation. *I was right. Lilith is going to her lamias. That's where I'll find Taylor.*

The girl's lip turned up at the sight of Morgan. Her all-black eyes bore into him as he passed. His muscles clenched in unison, and he slowed to a crawl.

Hollister moved over so he could sit on the aisle, across from Linda.

Morgan buckled in. He tried to take Linda's hand, but she pulled it away. "I was an idiot. Can you forgive me?"

She refused to make eye contact. "What are you doing here?"

"Taylor's near the lamias. And Lilith's on this flight."

Garcia gulped. "Man, that's not good. Where?"

"In a little girl near the emergency exit. Lilith was taunting me through her. You see what this means? We'll find Taylor where the outbreak's been reported. In Pisa."

Linda strained against her seatbelt to see ahead. "Which girl?" Her voice hitched as she spoke, and she trembled.

"Blonde in the green dress. Middle seat."

"You're sure?" Garcia asked.

"Oh, yeah. I'm telling you, we know where to look for Taylor now."

Hollister shook. "Um, I don't want to be a buzz kill, but is anyone else worried about having a demon with a grudge on this flight?"

Morgan refused to allow that reality to dampen his enthusiasm. *I can find Taylor. I will find Taylor.*

But deep in his mind, he wondered. *Should I worry about Lilith doing something to us on the flight?* He addressed Garcia. "Anything useful in there?"

"Listen to this," Garcia said. "From *Zohar* 3:19. 'There is a female, a spirit of all spirits, and her name is Lilith, and she was at first with Adam.' Then, later, 'when Lilith saw Eve created, she fled. And she is in the sea and is trying to harm the world.'"

"But is there anything about how to destroy her?" Morgan asked.

"Father Sebastian marked several pages." Garcia flipped pages of the notes. "I think he was on to something. When I merge passages in *The Zohar* with the Book of Revelation, I get puzzle pieces I'm convinced will give us the solution."

"That's great," Morgan said.

Garcia frowned. "It's not great yet. I'm still working through it. I need more time."

"Time's something we don't have, Javi. Taylor's life depends on stopping this demon. For good."

Garcia went back to work. Sweat leaked from his forehead. "All of humanity does. Let me tell you what I've found, Maybe you can figure out how to put it all together."

"Go for it," Morgan said.

Garcia nodded. "I believe God gave us the blueprint on banishing demons in Holy Scripture. We are all aware of the writings of John of Patmos. 'And the devil that deceived them was cast into a lake of fire and brimstone, where the beast and the false prophets are, and shall be tormented evermore.'"

"The last judgment," Linda said. "You think we can use that, even before the final judgment? To destroy just one demon?"

"Maybe," Garcia said. "The original text has pieces missing from modern translations that gives me hope. Backed up by *The Zohar*. They refer to destroying the brazen serpent at the First Temple. The Temple of Solomon. What if Lilith is this serpent?"

"What makes you think that?" Morgan asked.

Garcia switched to a different pile of papers. "*The* Zohar mentions Lilith in several passages. It places her with Adam, even before Eve. I think she's the serpent."

"And if she is?" Linda said.

"Then we can destroy her." Garcia let that sink in. "In ancient Armenian texts we see her as a creature who emerged from fire." He wiped his brow. "Fire created her. And I believe fire can destroy her. Specifically, the lake of fire and sulfur. But, there are still some questions."

Morgan's heart raced. "Like what?"

"There are references to 'wicked Rome' throughout the original text. You can imagine that the original translators, under the watch of the Roman Empire, weren't eager to include this translation. They excluded it."

"What's wicked Rome mean?" Linda asked.

"We assumed it was talking about Roman power being a great enemy of the Church," Garcia said. "And how the fall, often translated as overthrow, of wicked Rome is prophesied. 'Then will come the last judgment of the wicked, after which there will be no more death.'"

He paused. "But what if Drakul is the embodiment of wicked Rome? What if *he* is a necessary ingredient for destroying a demon?"

Morgan sat back in his seat. "That would explain why it's never been done before. There's never been Drakul's kind of wickedness in the Vatican."

"If you're right, what do we need to do?" Linda asked.

Garcia's face turned red. "We need Drakul and Lilith together. We need to burn them both in a lake of fire and sulfur."

"At the Temple of Solomon," Morgan said. "Which no longer exists. And no one knows for sure where it was located."

"It's more complicated than that," Garcia said. "We need to do it in the Sistine Chapel."

Morgan strained forward against his seat belt. "The Sistine Chapel? The most heavily guarded church on Earth? And the most visited?"

"Afraid so," Garcia said. "They published *The Zohar* after the Sistine Chapel was completed. And after Michelangelo finished his paintings. Some lost translations found by Father Sebastian make it clear. We need to do it there, under Michelangelo's 'The Last Judgment.' In front of 'The Brazen Serpent' at the Altar Wall."

"But it's the Pope's personal sanctuary," Morgan said. "How do you propose we get in there?"

"Cardinal Vitelli," Linda said. "We have to convince *him*."

"To build a lake of fire and sulfur," Morgan said, shaking his head. "To burn a fellow cardinal alive. To damage the Sistine Chapel, probably beyond repair. He'll never do it."

"First," Garcia said, "we have to find Drakul and Lilith. Without them both, we can't save Taylor."

Morgan sat back and closed his eyes. *We know where Lilith is. And we're heading straight for Drakul. Can we really pull this off?*

The plane began taxiing, and moments later they were airborne. Morgan kept his eyes closed, focusing on the task ahead.

Turbulence hit immediately. The plane jerked like a rag doll being tossed by an overzealous child. Morgan glanced at the flight attendant. Her facial expression made it clear this wasn't normal for this run. Morgan checked on his friends.

Garcia crossed himself. Linda took the priests's hand. Hollister gasped with each violent tumble.

The pilot's calm voice - everything's under control, you're in good hands, there's nothing to worry about - oozed over the loudspeaker. "Ladies and gentleman, we apologize for the rough ride. Please stay in your seat with your belt securely fastened."

Then, Morgan heard a deeper voice. "And assume a crash landing position." The pilot laughed, a wicked guffaw. Morgan's body convulsed. The blood drained from his face.

Linda glared at him. "What's wrong?"

"Didn't you hear that?" Morgan asked her in a hushed tone.

"The pilot? Sure. Routine stuff, right?"

Not routine. And, apparently, for my ears only. "I think Lilith's going to crash the plane." Hearing the words caused a chain reaction. His vision blurred and dizziness assaulted him.

Linda frowned at him, but her eyes evolved to panic as she studied Morgan's face. "You're serious." She strained against her lap belt. "Can you sedate the girl?"

He put his empty palms up. "I used them on the guards in Nazareth."

"Well, we can't just sit here and let it happen. Would Lilith even survive a crash?"

Morgan focused on the girl in the middle seat. "No clue. It must think so, or it wouldn't do it."

"Or it's just messing with you."

"You're right," Morgan said. "It's just trying to terrify me. It knows I'm on to Taylor's location, and it's panicking."

The plane suddenly dropped, and the overhead bin above Morgan flew open, dumping a carry-on atop his head. He covered up and rubbed the impact area. His dizziness stepped it up a notch.

"I'm so sorry, sir," the attendant said. She unbuckled and put the luggage back. When she slammed the bin shut, she glowered at Morgan.

With black eyes.

Morgan reached for her, but his seatbelt constrained him. The attendant shifted to the galley on the far side of the lavatories.

"What is it, Pennywise?"

"Lilith. In the flight attendant."

Garcia and Linda looked back. Hollister almost climbed over Morgan to see.

The flight attendant moved her arms like an orchestra leader, and the plane veered from side to side like a marionette.

Morgan undid his seatbelt and faced her. "You blew it, Lilith. In your arrogance you told me where you've taken Taylor. I'll never let you have her."

The plane tipped forward, and Morgan fell to his knees.

"You dare to call *me* arrogant?" The flight attendant growled. "*You* are the Arrogant Loser. I am a *god*. And your stupid plan won't work."

She heard us. And she's worried. Javi's on to something.

The plane sped up its fall. Hysteria erupted. Screams and panic accompanied the descent. But that was just the appetizer. The oxygen masks deployed, and previous chaos turned into every passenger for themselves. Mothers tried to follow directions and cover their children's face with masks, but the children were freaking out and fighting them. Some people pulled the masks so hard they became disengaged from their supports. Simultaneous cries of "we're going to die" reverberated through the main cabin.

Morgan struggled to his feet and confronted the flight attendant. He searched the galley for a knife, but everything was buttoned up.

"Still hoping to kill my host," the attendant cackled. "How tedious you are."

"You're not going to crash this airliner," Morgan said. "It will only delay you getting to Taylor. Every moment you delay risks someone finding her and ending your chance. Drakul's already proven to be unreliable. And who's to say you can survive a crash in any of us?"

The attendant winced. Morgan could almost see the gears moving in Lilith's mind. Her eyes, pitch black when possessed, returned to brown.

The plane regained its equilibrium.

The flight attendant gave Morgan a puzzled expression. "What happened?" She saw the bedlam and rushed past him, working to restore order.

The captain came back on the PA and assured everyone that the turbulence was over, and to please return to their seats. That didn't seem to impress anyone. But his offer of free drinks had the desired effect.

Morgan scanned the passengers. *You're in here somewhere. And I'll find Taylor before you can do her any harm.*

He sat in his seat.

"Are we going to make it?" Linda asked.

"Are you talking about the flight?" Morgan said.

"Of course I'm talking about the flight. You've made it clear you and I aren't." She folded her arms and melted into her seat, staring straight ahead.

Morgan wanted to reason with her, but decided to wait for her to cool off.

* * *

The plane landed in Rome late in the evening. People departed nervously. Morgan watched for a sign of where Lilith might be hosted, but nobody showed any.

"You think Lilith is back in that girl?" Linda asked.

"I don't know," Morgan said. "Whoever will get it to Taylor the fastest." He checked the gate for a security patrol and found none. "We get to Pisa as fast as we can. We'll find Taylor and Lilith there."

"Not to mention a bunch of lamias," Linda said, a shake in her voice.

"We'll need weapons," Garcia said. "For the lamias and Drakul's men, if we find them."

"I have an idea about that," Morgan said. "Linda, you need to ask Cardinal Vitelli for another favor. Both with weapons in Pisa, and later at the Vatican."

Linda cocked her head. "I already used a chit by asking for him to reach Margarita's team. He said he'll try. But getting inside the Sistine Chapel is another matter. You're wanted by the Swiss Guard."

"Vitelli should have convinced the Swiss Guard Drakul is up to no good," Morgan said. "He'll want to help you. Use your charm."

"Really?" She glared at Morgan. "Sarcasm? Now?"

"I'm serious."

Garcia put his arm around Linda. "Don't forget Cardinal Vitelli called on *you*. He sent Riki. Pennywise is right. He'll want to help." He stared at the ground. "At least with weapons in Pisa."

Hollister motioned toward the exit. "We should get moving." She lowered her voice. "Those vampires won't kill themselves."

He smiled until light from a nearby window streaked her neck. *Like blurred markings on the camera film in* The Omen. *Streaks that foretold of impending doom for those characters.*

Morgan shook off the thought and followed Hollister to the car rental counter.

CHAPTER 61

Pisa, Italy

Morgan drove the rental SUV along the two lane highway to Pisa. After Linda disconnected her call to Cardinal Vitelli he asked her, "Is Cardinal Vitelli sending the weapons we need?"

"The Swiss Guard will meet us there with the supplies we asked for," Linda replied. "Vitelli sounds good, by the way. Says he's healing nicely. Not that you asked."

Morgan felt a tinge of remorse for not inquiring. "That's great. Has he convinced them I didn't kill their Commandant?"

Linda continued to avoid eye contact with Morgan. "The cardinal assured me the Swiss Guard knows you didn't kill anyone at Vatican City. They're focusing on Drakul."

"Did they tell Interpol and the local police that?"

She feigned disinterest. "I didn't ask."

"Gee, thanks."

"The cardinal mentioned two other things," Linda said. "*La Contención de la Plaga* sent a team to Pisa. We'll get help."

Morgan looked at Garcia. "I'm not eager to run into that Margarita lady and her machete again. She did try to kill Taylor."

"Taylor's not spreading the plague now," Garcia said. "They have no reason to harm her."

"I hope you're right," Morgan said. "I'm not sure they see things clearly when it comes to the lamias."

"Have faith, Pennywise."

Morgan grunted. "I'll have faith when Taylor's safe."

"Fair enough." Garcia turned to Linda. "What's the other thing?"

Linda perked up. "Riki is fit to travel and is coming home."

Morgan smiled. "That's excellent news." *Maybe we've turned a corner.*

* * *

Darkness filled the night when they arrived in the tourist mecca of Pisa. Lights lit up building facades, and the white, leaning tower peeked over the surrounding walls. The street merchants had packed up for the night, and the town gave off an eerie, silent vibe.

A dark van pulled up at the appointed meeting spot.

"That's the Swiss Guard," Linda said. "Right where Cardinal Vitelli said they'd be."

Morgan watched the van with apprehension. "You sure they're not here for me?"

"Will they stay and help?" Garcia asked.

Linda shook her head. "This is foreign soil for them. They're already going above and beyond by providing us with unregistered weapons. And if we get caught, they'll disavow us."

"What about using the local police?" Hollister asked.

"We can't afford to get them involved," Morgan said. "Even if we're not on their radar, we need to kill the lamias without red tape."

The side door to the Vatican van opened, and a man in black stepped out with duffel bags. Morgan and Linda met him halfway.

"Doctor Morgan, Doctor Copeland, the weapons and drugs you asked for." The man dropped the duffels. "I was never here."

"Thanks," Morgan said, but the man was already retreating. He climbed back in the van and the driver sped away.

Morgan opened the two bags and checked on the gear. "Four

submachine guns with ammo. Four combat knives. Two syringes with the sedatives. Vitelli came through."

Linda stared off into the city. "It's dead out here. I expected more people."

Garcia grunted. "Dead? Can you please use a different word?"

"Sorry, Father."

"Thousands bus in and out every day," Hollister said, "but not much goes on once the sun sets." She shook. "Now, with the lamias, who knows what we'll find?"

"Remember," Morgan said, "our primary aim is to find Taylor. If we find the lamia nest, we're probably close. We stick together. Don't be a hero. Don't let yourself get isolated. We find our target, then attack. Shoot to kill. No mercy. *They* won't have any."

"There could be hundreds of lamias by now." Garcia reduced his voice to a whisper. "We saw what just a few of them did to Smokey."

Morgan thought back to Smokey's mutilated body, and his face flushed. *I'll make them all pay for that.* He looked at Linda and Hollister. "You two know how to use these?"

Linda took one. She checked the grip and scope like an expert. "Lots of target practice in Peru."

Hollister took hers and handled it uncomfortably. "I've never used a gun before. But I'll manage."

Morgan kept one rifle and tried to hand the final one to Garcia.

"I'm a priest. I don't do guns."

"Javi, it's dangerous out here."

Garcia raised his eyebrows. "No kidding. But I will decline. God will watch over me." He shrugged. "And, I'd appreciate it if you three are also by my side."

A girl's shriek in the distance interrupted their nods. Morgan's body erupted in uncontrollable shivers. He placed the spare rifle back in the bag. He passed out the knives. Garcia refused his.

"We better go," Garcia said. "Before I lose my nerve."

They marched in single file toward the direction of the screams, Morgan in the lead, with Garcia watching their flank. A layer of fog formed along the cobblestone street, nearly hiding their feet. The deeper they went into the town, the thicker the fog got, until they were waist deep in it, reminding Morgan of the ground fog in *Dracula*. But this was deeper. *And this isn't a movie.*

"This isn't normal," Hollister said. "A lamia could hide in this soup."

"Steady," Morgan said. "Remember, lamias aren't that clever. If they're here, we'll see them coming."

He reached an intersection and checked both ways. The glare from the street lamps bounced off the hip-deep fog, obscuring his view.

Another outburst, this time multiple voices straight ahead. Childish, high-pitched sounds. Much closer.

Morgan raised his rifle. "Guns up. Stay sharp."

He forced his feet to press on. After a half block, a sound from within the fog froze him. *What is that? Another rat?*

Morgan felt something brush against his feet. He jumped back, his hand over his pounding chest.

That was no rat.

"What happened?" Linda asked, her voice panicked.

"I felt something."

Garcia moved up next to him and kicked his foot out. "I don't feel anything."

"It was there." Morgan bent over, his face nearing the fog.

"Careful, Richard," Linda said.

Morgan swept his hand along the top layer of fog but felt nothing. "Maybe my imagination." *They might buy that, but I know better. Something's in there.*

The fog ten feet ahead swirled in the form of a miniature volcano. Morgan tried to swallow, but had nothing.

"Oh, Jesus," Hollister said. "What's happening?"

The tip of the fog-volcano rose until it reached Morgan's height.

When the fog drifted away, it exposed the body of a young girl. Her eyes glowed red, and her mouth displayed protruding incisors.

Morgan quaked. His palms perspired like they were crying, and he almost dropped his weapon.

"Pennywise, fall back. They can hide in this fog."

The girl cackled. "Nowhere to run."

CHAPTER 62

In a scene out of Morgan's childhood nightmares, the fog surrounding them swirled, and a dozen more lamias appeared. The lamias converged, fangs glistening in the night. Morgan backed into Garcia and pulled Hollister and Linda next to him. "Make a circle. Javi in the middle. Remember, they're not girls anymore. No mercy."

The lead lamia hissed and laughed. "No mercy. You right." She took a step forward. The others followed in sync.

Morgan set his sight on the leader. *Maybe if I take her out the others will get disoriented.*

Before he could pull the trigger the leader attacked him, driving sharp nails into his arms and pinning them to his sides. The rifle was stuck pointing at the ground. The lamia opened wide and exposed her fangs.

But Morgan improvised and drove his head forward, his head butt cracking into her teeth. His pain was horrendous, but he pulled his head back and checked out the damage he'd caused.

The lamia's incisors were chipped and her mouth bled. The fire in her eyes told him he'd hurt her.

He rammed again. This time, the lamia released him and stepped back. Blood drained from its mouth, and the other lamias picked up the scent and changed course, mindlessly targeting the red sustenance.

Morgan seized the momentum and raised his rifle. *I've got you, bitch.*

The injured lamia snatched the weapon before he could fire and tossed it aside. She clutched him by the neck with one hand and held him in place, her strength not something Morgan had bargained for. Even though he had longer arms, she was quicker, and every attempt to catch her came up with air. Behind him, shots fired.

The lamia cocked her head and jeered. Much to Morgan's astonishment, her incisors had grown back. She licked the blood from her lips and moved closer, her rancid breath an abomination.

The sounds of the struggle bounced off the buildings surrounding them. But no human sounds. Just the inhuman growls of an angry pack of animals.

Not animals. Monsters. Even stronger than before.

The lamia's teeth were inches from Morgan. She paused, as if savoring the moment. Then the lamia's teeth advanced, and her panting breath tickled him.

Morgan remembered the knife. *Hurry!* He reached to his waist and swung it wildly at the lamia's throat.

He connected, and the knife cut through neck muscles like a tender steak until he reached bone. The lamia's eyes shot wide open, and the red flickered. Morgan thought he saw a trace of humanity. It caused him to hesitate, but the red returned, ablaze with hatred.

Morgan finished the job, needing both hands and all of his strength to get through the bone. Blood exploded skyward in a fountain-like display, drenching him. The lamia dropped to the ground, head landing first, creating a gap in the fog.

The other twelve lamias screamed as one, a piercing, inhuman shrill. Morgan wiped his face, leaving Rambo-like streaks, and retrenched himself with his team. "Everyone okay?" He recalled his premonition at the airport. "Hollister?"

"I'm okay." Her voice was shaky.

"I'm not dead, either," Linda said. "In case you're interested."

"Not really the time," Morgan said. He searched for his rifle in the fog, but the muck was too thick, so he snatched the spare.

The lamias, still in a circle surrounding them, stopped whining and locked in on Morgan. "Here comes the next wave."

They charged. Morgan, Linda, and Hollister fired their rifles. A few lamias fell, but there were too many, and they dodged shots fired with freaky quickness.

The lamias laughed at the impotent threat. One by one, the lamias ripped the rifles out of their hands and discarded them.

"Your knives," Morgan yelled.

A lamia attacked Morgan's arms. It wrestled his knife away. A talon tore at his esophagus.

"No, you don't!" Morgan yelled as he twisted the lamia's arm. The lamia screamed. Morgan snapped the shoulder out of its socket and tossed the lamia aside.

Morgan turned to check on the others. Garcia crouched near Linda, who held off two lamias.

Dr. Hollister wasn't as fortunate. Three lamias surrounded her. There was no sign of her knife.

"Hollister, hang on!" Morgan reached her as a lamia clamped onto her trachea.

Morgan jumped on the lamia and wrung its larynx until he heard it crack. The lamia collapsed at his feet.

The other two left Linda and were on Hollister now, tearing at her throat. Her gullet opened up like a geyser, and the two lamias fought over her squirting blood. Morgan kicked at them, but he knew his premonition had come true. But there was no time to mourn.

"Richard," Linda called. "Help!"

She and Garcia had backed against a building. She shielded him from the lamias, but they were moving in.

Morgan rushed to them. A lamia swung back and forth in front of Linda, avoiding her knife's thrusts. Morgan reached for its windpipe when the lamia turned on him. It surprised him by kicking the knife out of his hand. He tensed, knowing the lamia had the advantage, and awaited its strike.

The sound of high winds brushed past him. The lamia collapsed, its head severed.

What the hell?

Morgan wiped the blood splatter from his eyes. More swooshing sounds were followed by childish cries.

The fog dissolved as if swept up by a vacuum cleaner. The remaining lamias were strewn across the ground, each one beheaded. Linda and Garcia were bloodied, but not seriously hurt.

Morgan spun around, searching for the source of their salvation. A face from the past stepped into the streetlamp's glow. "Margarita?"

The Costa Rican task force soldier poked at a dead lamia with her machete. She looked just as she had in the Costa Rican jungle. Beige khakis and a loosely fitting white shirt. And a big-ass machete. "*Bueno*, Dr. Morgan."

Morgan recalled the many times she'd tried to kill Taylor, and their bitter confrontations. "I can't believe it's you." Morgan checked again on his friends and saw another face he recognized from the Bribri village. "Valverde?"

The Bribri *Awá*, dressed in a heavy camouflage jacket and jeans, somberly hugged Garcia. "Father Garcia. How is my favorite exorcist?" He then hugged Linda. "Good to see all three of you." He looked at Dr. Hollister's mutilated body and shook his head. "Sorry it has to be under such tragic circumstances. Tell me about this one."

Morgan kneeled and shut Hollister's eyes. "Dr. Hollister of the World Health Organization." His chin shook with remorse. "She risked everything to help me, a complete stranger. To kill the lamias. A special person."

"She deserved better," Linda said. Her tears streamed. "Like Smokey, and so many others."

"*Lo Siento*," Margarita said. "We were not aware of the plague's spread sooner. The lamias are mature. The Cardinal told me this all started when the demon escaped from under their noses." She spit on the ground. "Did your daughter get infected again?"

"No," Morgan said. "Taylor's being held prisoner by a deranged cardinal who wants Lilith to impregnate her."

"Impregnate?" Margarita said. "How? Why?"

"To birth the Antichrist," Garcia said. "As for the how, it has to do with possession and integrating the demon with Taylor."

Margarita crossed herself.

Valverde pulled packs of wipes out of his backpack and tossed them to Morgan to clean up. "That is most disturbing. Do you know where Taylor is?"

Morgan passed the packs out to Garcia and Linda. "I believe Taylor's nearby. The lamias are Lilith's offspring, and the demon's maternal instincts are real. I sensed the deep connection while I was possessed."

"*You* were possessed?" Margarita asked Morgan, taking a step back.

"Yeah. Turns out Lilith is an equal opportunity demon."

Valverde helped Linda clean the blood off her arms and face. "In Costa Rica, I thought this demon only possessed young girls, to turn them."

"It can possess anyone," Linda said. "But it can only turn young girls into lamias."

"I see," Margarita said. She re-gripped her machete.

Garcia finished cleaning up, then administered last rites to Dr. Hollister as the others watched in reverent silence. "I've had to do way too many of these lately. I sure hope this is the last one."

Morgan covered Dr. Hollister's face with his jacket. "Not likely, Javi. I'll see that Drakul needs one. Not that his soul deserves it."

A tangential thought struck him. *I wonder if a demon gets last rites when you kill it?* He chose not to share.

In the distance, a police siren struck the night.

"We must move," Margarita said. "The police will not understand."

They hustled deeper into town, away from the siren.

"This lead lamia wasn't like Taylor, or the ones she created," Morgan said. "She had supernatural power and strength beyond anything we dealt with before."

"She was turned," Margarita said. "Decapitation is the only way to kill them once they're turned. Your guns will kill the immature ones, but once they turn, only taking their head off will do the trick. We caught Taylor before that happened." She kicked at the lead lamia's body. "But this is not the first. We have more to weed out and destroy."

"How can you be sure?" Garcia asked.

"If she was the first, the others would have died when she did," Margarita said. "The nest will continue to grow exponentially until we kill the original."

"Then let's go find it," Morgan said. "I'm betting they'll lead us right to Taylor."

"You cannot come with us," Margarita said. "Too risky that Lilith and the lamias have your scent." She pointed at Valverde. "We are another matter. We should be able to sneak up on them."

"Taylor's out there." Morgan exhaled. "I can't stop looking for her."

Valverde nodded. "Of course not. You are welcome to join us." Margarita started to protest, and he shushed her. "She is his daughter. Maybe his presence will provoke the lamias and we will find them quicker."

Margarita scowled but said nothing.

"Okay," Garcia said, "That's settled. Where to?"

"We must hurry," Margarita said. "Once the sun rises they will sleep, and it will be much more difficult."

Morgan, Garcia, and Linda retrieved their rifles.

"Do you and Valverde have more than machetes?" Morgan asked Margarita.

"Why?" She admired her weapon. "I have all we need."

Morgan addressed Valverde. "Did you bring those plants that slow the lamias down? Or the wonder drug that brought Taylor back to life?'

"I'm afraid not. Customs officials wouldn't look kindly on either."

"Right."

They continued side-by-side deeper into the city.

"I haven't forgotten you shot my friend," Margarita said.

Morgan studied the machete in her right hand. "You were going to kill my daughter. You'd have done the same thing in my position. Right?"

She wiped the blood off her machete blade with her sleeve. "She was a danger to all of us. Still is, from what I hear. But that is a discussion for another time. Tonight, we must find the lamia nest and destroy the carriers of the plague."

Morgan walked with her, worried about the risk she posed to Taylor.

CHAPTER 63

Morgan and Margarita led the way into Pisa's residential neighborhoods. Each new pocket of fog caused Morgan's heart to race faster until his chest could barely contain it. Street lights became scarcer, with only an occasional porch light to illuminate their path. The humming of crickets was all that broke the silence of the night.

Come on, Taylor. Show me a sign.

"It's been fifteen minutes," Linda said, following Morgan. "Maybe we got them all."

"No," Margarita said, her voice sharp. "We must find the nest and destroy the first lamia."

The cool breeze picked up, swirling paper cups across their path. Morgan kicked one ahead, and the wind pushed it back to him. He played this game for an entire block before the wind grew tired of it and sent the cup in another direction.

Valverde came up next to him. "I did not expect to see you again. I'm certain you felt the same way."

"I'm sure neither of us wanted to relive that experience," Morgan said. "How are things in your Bribri village now that Lilith is gone?"

"Much the same, actually," Valverde said. "Whether you refer to the demon as *Bé* or Lilith, the race of demons is a part of our culture. It will be back. Perhaps not in the same form, and hopefully not turning our young women into monsters, but *Bé* will emerge whenever our gods are angry about the way we treat the planet."

Morgan froze. Someone, some *thing*, approached from the shadows straight ahead. "Heads up." The pounding beneath his ribs became a crescendo. "Something's coming."

The team created a human barrier on the street. Mist formed ahead, then matured into a thick fog.

"Lamias," Margarita said.

"Weapons, everyone," Morgan said.

The fog rolled toward them in uneven patterns, like arms reaching out for them. A dog bayed.

"Any way to follow them back to their lair?" Garcia asked. "Killing them doesn't get us closer to Taylor."

"Javi's right. Use the rifles to maim and force a retreat. Margarita, that means no beheading."

"I don't answer to you," Margarita said.

Valverde addressed Morgan. "We will try to save one or two for you. But if we find the original lamia, we must kill it. We can't risk the plague spreading any more."

The fog edged closer. Soft whispers urged them to come nearer, like siren songs.

Morgan closed his eyes, a peace falling over him.

"Pennywise, stay with us."

Morgan forced his eyes open and found the fog within arm's distance. A voice in his head urged him to sleep. He slapped himself with his free hand. "Anyone else hear that?"

"They're talking to us," Margarita said. "Do not let your guard down."

"What are they waiting for?" Linda asked.

Morgan poked the fog with his rifle but hit nothing. "Trying to scare us."

"They're doing a good job," Garcia said. "What do we do now?"

Margarita pointed her machete at the haze. "We go straight at them." She stepped forward, her body vanishing in the mist.

Valverde followed her lead. Morgan, Garcia, and Linda stepped into the muck.

Once inside, the volume rose. What was a whisper now came through loud and clear. They were calling Morgan's name, sounding like the demon's gravelly voice in "The Exorcist." But instead of *Merrin, Morgan!*

Morgan's teeth chattered. He bit his tongue. Blood smeared his lips.

The voices stopped. But sniffing replaced by them. *They can smell the blood.* He aimed his rifle at the sound. *That's their weakness. They can't resist the blood.* He spit red gold toward the noises.

Something dropped to the ground where he'd spit. *Got you.* He fired one shot at it, and the calm erupted into screeching. At ground level, an inhuman scream rocked the night. Figures danced in the mist at eye level, like rudderless projectiles. The fog vaporized, leaving a clear view of a half-dozen lamias scrambling around the fallen beast.

Margarita pounced. She swung her machete in tight arcs, lopping heads off with her razor-sharp blade. Before Morgan could stop her, all six lamias were beheaded.

But the one Morgan had shot was writhing on the ground. Margarita straddled her, machete raised.

"No!" Morgan yelled. He grabbed Margarita's arm before she could strike. "We need her alive. She can lead us to Taylor."

"They took my daughter from me," Margarita said.

"I know," Morgan said. "And I know you don't want the same thing to happen to me."

Margarita yielded and pulled off her rope belt. "First, tie her wrists together. *Carefully*. I am not hopeful she will lead us back to them, but I will let you try." She held her machete against the lamia's neck. "If she attacks, I will kill her."

The gunshot had drilled through the lamia, and she was licking her own fresh blood off the wound on her shoulder. She paid no attention to Valverde and Garcia as they bound her wrists. Morgan took the other end of the line so he could keep the lamia in tow.

"She's strong," Linda said. "Will that hold her if she tries to run?"

"It'll have to," Morgan said.

Garcia grimaced. "I hope you know what you're doing."

"I stopped knowing what I was doing weeks ago."

"I hear you, Pennywise."

Margarita rolled her eyes at them. "You *imbécils* are worried about the wrong thing. She will not try to run. Her teeth and talons are the issue. When her own wound heals, she will come after the next available source. She will carve you up like Juan does his chickens."

Oh. Yeah. "What do we do about that?"

Margarita motioned for Valverde's backpack and retrieved a device right out of "Silence of the Lambs." A face guard that forced the lamia's mouth to stay securely closed. Valverde helped her place it around the lamia's head. The lamia could no longer get at her blood and she convulsed violently. But the ropes held.

Next, Valverde withdrew two boxing-style gloves, thick with padding. They placed these on the lamia's hands and tied them tight. Her talons would no longer be a problem.

"You make those contraptions yourself?" Morgan asked Margarita.

"I do. Comes in handy in my work."

"I bet it does." Morgan pulled the rope hard, and the lamia was forced to her feet. The monster glared at Morgan with bright red eyes. "Where's Taylor?"

The lamia lunged at him but had no way to harm him. Morgan stepped aside and yanked on the rope, which cut into the lamia's thorax, causing a new flow of blood. The lamia forgot all about Morgan and tried frantically and unsuccessfully to get to the blood.

"Is she the first?" Linda asked.

"Maybe," Margarita said. "The only way to know for sure is to kill it and see if the others die." She looked at the dead girls. "I guess we will not know for certain unless we find the nest."

"How do we get her to lead us there?" Linda asked. "She has no reason to help us. If she's the first, then Lilith is probably commanding her. If she's not the first, the first one is controlling her. Either way, they won't let her come home now."

The lamia contorted herself to reach the blood.

"We have all the motivation we need. Something even Lilith can't overcome." Morgan put his hand out in front of Margarita. "Cut me."

Margarita lit up like a Christmas tree.

"Pennywise, what are you doing?"

"Make me bleed. Find a container to save the blood. We'll use it as bait."

The lamia stood at attention.

"That could work." Valverde ruffled through his backpack and came out with a plastic water bottle. He poured the water out, and Morgan set his hand over it, palm up. Margarita poised the knife over the palm.

"Not *too* deep, now," Morgan said. "Just enough to get her attention."

Margarita smiled. "I do my work." Her eyes advertised her raw enthusiasm for the idea.

My work? What does that mean?

Margarita wasted no time. She sliced into Morgan's palm. The shock struck him harder than he expected. He winced, and his eyes watered. "Shit. I said not too deep."

"I barely scratched you." The enthusiasm in her voice echoed off the nearby apartments.

She's enjoying this.

Blood dripped into the bottle. Valverde had a rag ready, and once

258

the bottle had an inch of blood, he wrapped Morgan's hand. "Make a fist. Keep it clenched."

The lamia reacted to the smell of fresh blood. It bounced like a girl on a Pogo stick.

"I think you have her attention," Garcia said.

Morgan took the bottle and passed it under the lamia's nose. "You want? Take me to your nest and I'll let you drink. Take me to Taylor."

The lamia's brow furrowed. She shook her head.

Morgan poured a drop onto the ground.

The lamia whimpered.

"Take us to Taylor."

The lamia pouted, then nodded, and pulled Morgan the way she'd come. The rest of them followed.

"I'll be damned," Garcia said. "It's working."

"I hope that's true," Linda said. "The other option is Lilith is behind all of this, and we're walking into a trap."

Morgan's stomach lurched. *She's right. We could be playing right into Lilith's hands.*

His apprehension doubled when they reached the next block. Four Pisa police officers with drawn pistols stepped out of the shadows.

"Dr. Richard Morgan," the man in charge said. "I am Chief of Police Gazzaro. You need to come with us."

Gazzaro noticed the tied-up girl covered in blood. His hand morphed from steady to shaking, and his pistol wobbled in Morgan's direction. "*Dio mio.* Don't any of you move."

CHAPTER 64

A cloud passed over the moon, and the street darkened. Morgan stared down the barrels of four pistols. His teeth rattled. He choked out, "This isn't what it looks like."

Gazzaro stepped forward. It appeared he'd been awaked from a deep sleep. His hair was askew, and he hadn't shaved. "It looks like you're kidnapping a young girl. And she's hurt."

Okay. So it is what it looks like.

"Chief Gazzaro, I can explain." *I'm close to finding Taylor. I can't be locked up now.*

Margarita advanced to the front of the group. "Wait! The girl is infected with a dangerous plague. We are taking her to a place where she can't infect anyone."

Gazzaro took a step back. "Plague? *The* plague?"

"Worse," Garcia said, making sure they saw his collar. "We're on orders from the Vatican. You can check."

The chief grunted. "Is that so? Sounds like *una scusa* from a *penale*. Well, let me tell you, we run our own *Dipartimento di Polizia* here. This isn't Rome. The Vatican has no authority in Pisa."

Morgan stepped up. "You don't believe us? Look at this." He flashed the bottle of blood in front of the lamia.

She put on the display Morgan had hoped for. She groaned. Her eyes glowed a deeper red.

Gazzaro stumbled backwards into his men, who each took a step back. "*Che diavolo?*" One officer broke ranks and ran.

"That's the plague at work," Morgan said. "And it's incredibly contagious. You should keep your distance."

The remaining officers mumbled to each other. Gazzaro held his ground and aimed his pistol at Morgan's heart. "I have orders to bring you in. Interpol says you are the one spreading the disease."

"Call the Vatican," Linda said. "Speak with Cardinal Vitelli. He'll vouch for us."

The officer beyond the leader tapped his boss on the shoulder. His terrified face wouldn't leave the girl. "The Ministry of Health sent an alert tonight about a possible contagion in the area. Look at her. It wouldn't hurt to check."

Morgan thought about Dr. Hollister and a part of his soul bled. He decided against informing them about her body in the street a few blocks back. "You should hurry. We don't have much time." *To find Taylor before Lilith can start the possession, and integration.*

Gazzaro nodded to his partner to make the call. He waved his pistol at Morgan. "Nobody moves."

Given the hour, Morgan didn't expect the call to get through to Vitelli. But the officer stood at attention when the Cardinal came on.

Morgan held his breath. *If this doesn't work, we're screwed.*

The officer spoke in Italian, listened reverently, then handed the phone to the chief. "He wants to speak with you. He's conferencing in Interpol, the Italian Ministry of Health, and the World Health Organization."

The chief took the phone, ordered his men to watch the prisoners, and withdrew to confer in private. After several minutes, he turned and gave Morgan an astonished expression. He said some final words and hung up. He approached Morgan slowly, then shifted to face Linda. "Are you Linda Copeland?"

"Yes," Linda said. "Why?"

"You convinced the Cardinal that Dr. Morgan is innocent of all charges?"

Morgan's face flushed. *Why didn't she tell me?*

The officer continued, "And the Cardinal has convinced Interpol of your innocence. I've been ordered to stand down and discard the arrest warrant."

Morgan shivered with relief. *Thank God. At least that part's over.*

"*Inoltre,*" the officer continued, "the WHO says you are acting on their authority to contain the *malattia*, which they assure me is real, but not well understood. I am to offer any assistance I can to help you eradicate it."

Morgan turned to Linda. "You did all that?"

Linda didn't smile. "Just because you're a self-absorbed asshole doesn't make you a killer. I just told them the truth."

"Thank you."

She looked away.

Morgan addressed the chief. "What I need is for you to let us go with this infected girl. We hope she's taking us to the origin of the plague. Once we find it, we can handle it."

The chief looked puzzled. "I am offering you the full weight and force of the Pisa police. Surely you want our help."

Morgan wiped his lips with his tongue. *How do I explain I plan to kill a bunch of lamias, then a demon, and rescue my daughter? We have to do this on our own.* "Of course we do. But I don't want to put you and your men at risk of the plague. Best if you hang back and wait for us to contain it."

"I can not *hang back.* I am responsible for the welfare of the citizens on my watch. Besides, you are not wearing Hazmat suits. Why are *you* not worried?"

Morgan didn't know how to respond. He swallowed, desperately trying to think of an excuse.

"We've been inoculated," Linda said. "Until more serum arrives, it's best you stay away from us."

Morgan's eyes met Linda's. *That's my girl.*

The chief considered that. "The WHO has the serum? They will bring it?"

"Of course," Morgan said. "But they need till morning to get it to your Ministry of Health. As soon as you and your men get the shot, you can join us. Until then, if you'll provide me with one of your police radios, I'll keep you appraised every step of the way."

The chief pondered that, looked to his men, who nodded vigorously, and conceded. "Okay. We'll do it your way. I'll have my people coordinate with the WHO to expedite the delivery." He handed Morgan a radio. "You'll stay in constant contact."

Bureaucracies being what they were, Morgan hoped he had a few hours before anyone at the WHO would confess they had no such serum. "Of course. Now, if you'll excuse us, we have a disease to wipe out."

Morgan turned to the lamia. "Let's go. Show us where and you'll get your reward."

They rushed away from the police force. Once they were out of earshot, Morgan stepped next to Linda. "Thank you again."

"I didn't tell you earlier because I didn't know if they'd listen to Cardinal Vitelli, and I didn't know how long it would take them to act if they did. But it doesn't change anything about us. I'd have done it for my worst enemy." She drifted back to Garcia.

Margarita joined him in the lead. "Can we get back to work?"

"I'm all business."

Hang on, Taylor. I'm coming for you.

CHAPTER 65

Taylor, in pitch darkness, shifted on the bed, trying to find a spot where the mattress springs didn't jab at her. The constant poking resulted in indentations on her skin. A few of the jabs caused enough pain to make her cringe. *It's not enough to be held here, concubine for a demon. They have to torture me with this lame excuse of a bed.*

A new thought hit her like a ray of sunshine in a hurricane. *If I can get to those sharp coils inside, maybe I can make a knife or something.* With a new sense of purpose and hope she tore at the sturdy mattress with chipped nails. But the thick surface gave her nothing for free.

She exposed an opening in the fabric. *Yes.* Then scratching noises, like fingernails on wood, caught her attention. She squinted in the door's direction. She swallowed. *Drakul said Lilith would be here soon.*

The door creaked open, exposing a shadow framed in front of a floor lamp's light. *That's too small to be Drakul.* She quivered. *I don't know what Lilith will come as.*

The figure glided in as if on rails. As it neared, the shape of a girl materialized. A Mediterranean beauty. Young, maybe early teens. Slim. Dark hair. Smoldering eyes. No, not smoldering. Ablaze.

Taylor gasped. *Lamia*.

Then Drakul stepped into the doorway, blocking most of the light.

"I brought you a friend," Drakul said. "Orders from Lilith."

The lamia smiled, exposing lengthy incisors.

Taylor wiped a river of sweat from her brow. "Why is *she* here?"

"So you don't run." Drakul's voice reeked of bitterness. "It seems your near escape in Nazareth has Lilith on edge. Not that I need help with you."

"So Lilith doesn't trust you," Taylor said, searching for any weakness she could use.

"Shut up," Drakul said.

He's pissed. Keep attacking him. He might make a mistake.

The lamia stepped closer to Taylor. The beasts's eyes illuminated the room.

Taylor held her breath. *So that's what I looked like. A monster. No wonder Dad wouldn't tell me.* She teared up, forgetting about getting the upper hand with Drakul. "Is she going to bite me?"

"Not if you behave," Drakul said. "Lilith doesn't want you touched until she arrives. But she isn't taking any chances."

Not with either of us. "When will that be?"

"Tonight. There was a small delay. But soon she can begin."

"You don't have to do this, you know. It's not too late to do the right thing. The *Christian* thing."

"I am helping make the Biblical prophesies of Revelation come true. The Antichrist is inevitable. Nothing could be more Christian."

Taylor tried to stand, but her lack of nourishment over the last two days had weakened her. *I'll never have the strength to fight back. And Dad doesn't know where I am.* Tears fell like a faucet had ruptured. "I don't want to be possessed again. I don't want to be the mother of the Antichrist."

"Stop whining," Drakul said. "Your legacy will live forever. You will be the new Virgin Mary. Be thankful Lilith selected you." He took a huge breath. "I wish I had the right plumbing. It is a great honor."

"You're insane."

Drakul stiffened. "No, dear. You just haven't accepted the truth. Yet."

The lamia stepped over Taylor. Her breath reeked of death. Her legs were scarred, her fingernails long and sharp. Her face lacked any color. "So you the great Taylor." She snarled. "You not so special. Lilith should choose me."

"She's all yours," Taylor said. "If you kill Cardinal Drakul and let me go, you can have Lilith all to yourself."

The lamia flinched. Whatever wheels remained in there were spinning.

Taylor pressed. "He's a weak old man. You could kill him without breaking a sweat."

"You're wasting your time." Drakul's eyes revealed discomfort. "She is completely dedicated to her master. If you sit quietly, she won't harm you."

Taylor met the lamia's glowing eyes with her own shimmering ones. "Where'd you get her?"

"Lilith took possession of her boarding a cruise ship. She turned while at sea. Now she's the mother lamia of a spreading family."

"She made others?"

"Of course. Just as you tried to do, and would have done if they hadn't exorcised Lilith before you turned."

Taylor's mind swirled. *Dad told me when I was saved, all the girls I bit were saved, too.* "How many are there?"

"Hundreds. By tomorrow, thousands. Each capable of creating more. They'll grow exponentially."

Taylor held her head. "You're a monster. My dad will find you and kill you."

Drakul laughed. "We have a surprise for him. Just like in cards, where you let someone win early on, give them confidence. Then you raise the stakes and wipe them out. That's what awaits your father and his pitiful band of misfits."

CHAPTER 66

The fog returned as Morgan and his party advanced through the town. A single street light shown in the middle of each block. Eerie silence greeted them in every direction.

"Which way?" Morgan asked the lamia.

The lamia pointed right.

"No," Margarita said. "We go straight."

Morgan glowered at her. "Why straight?"

"I've been doing this a long time. One gets a sense of where the lamias are."

Garcia joined them. "Maybe we should listen to her. The lamia might be lying."

Morgan yanked on the chain holding the lamia's neck. "*Are* you lying?"

"I take you. Get reward." The lamia's eyes blazed at the thought of blood.

"I think it's telling the truth," Morgan said.

Margarita raised her machete in front of Morgan. Morgan took a step back. *Jesus. She's lost her mind.* "Hey, lower your weapon."

Margarita's lip slowly turned up at both corners, reminding Morgan of the Joker in a *Batman* movie. She raised the machete higher.

"What are you doing?" Linda said.

"We go straight." Margarita swung the machete.

Morgan ducked, expecting the worst.

But the machete whizzed past him and struck the lamia in the throat. The lamia gagged. Blood rushed from its gullet. In a pitiful gesture the lamia tried to capture her own blood in the cups of her hands and drink it. Margarita swung again and lopped off the lamia's head.

"What the hell?" Morgan cried.

"We do not need her," Margarita said. She wiped her blade with her pant leg. "I know where to go. She is only giving the enemy information about us."

Morgan shoved Margarita. "You considered using that on me. I saw it in your eyes."

Margarita didn't bother to deny his accusation. "I am your best chance to save your daughter."

"Do you even want to save her? You still see her as a threat, don't you?"

"If she is a threat, I will do what is necessary. I hope she is not. But the longer we argue, the worse her chances are."

Morgan's face turned crimson. "You're not in charge here. I decide what is necessary."

"I *am* in charge here." Margarita spit at Morgan's feet. "If you don't like it, leave. Valverde and I can handle the lamias without you."

"I knew I couldn't trust you," Morgan yelled.

Garcia stepped between them. "That's enough. What's done is done. We need to focus on finding the nest." He put his hand on Morgan's shoulder. "Right?"

Morgan shrugged it away. "We should split up. Cover twice as much ground and get this lunatic out of my face. It'll be daylight in another hour."

Linda stepped next to Margarita. "I don't think dividing us is a good idea. The nest will probably be swarming with lamias. We'll need everyone."

"She's right," Valverde said. "We should stick together."

Morgan folded his arms over his chest. His head drooped. "Lilith's got to be here by now. Taylor doesn't have much time."

"We'll find her," Garcia said. "And we'll exorcise Lilith before integration."

The fog thickened.

Margarita moved in front of the group. "We won't have to choose which direction to go to find them."

"Why's that?" Linda asked.

Margarita raised her machete. "Because *they've* found *us*." She glared at Morgan with an *I told you* dagger.

Morgan instinctively pulled Linda closer. "Stay by me." She surprised him by allowing herself to be held.

Some *things* howled, surrounding them.

"We're surrounded," Margarita said. "Form a circle."

After setting Linda up next to him, Morgan tightened his grip on his rifle. His hands, in need of a squeegee, lost their grip, and the rifle slipped, falling to the ground. "Shit." He reached to reclaim it.

But while he fumbled for it, Linda dug her nails into his back and screamed. "Look out!"

Morgan glanced up in time to see the attack before he felt it. Hundreds of lamias blitzed them from every angle. Gunshots pierced the night, maiming the front rows, but dozens more invaded, and Morgan braced for their attack.

CHAPTER 67

Taylor shifted on the bed. The darkness would mask much of her movement from Drakul, but the lamia was another matter. *She can see everything. I need a distraction.* She placed one hand behind her and continued her assault on the mattress. "My dad will beat whatever obstacles you put in front of him."

"You're such a child." Drakul snapped his fingers at the lamia. The sharp sound reverberated through the room. When the lamia stayed focused on Taylor, he clapped. "Hey. You. Pay attention."

The lamia sneered at him. "Lilith in charge."

Taylor took advantage. Still facing forward, she used her hidden hand to rip open the mattress fabric and wrapped her fingers around a metal coil within the stuffing. Neither the lamia nor Drakul noticed.

Drakul raised a finger toward the lamia. "*I* speak for Lilith." He reached into his belt and pulled out a butcher knife in a leather sheaf. "You *will* obey me." He unclasped the band holding the knife.

The lamia hissed.

Taylor pulled on the coil. The stuffing created too much resistance, and it barely budged.

"Do you sense anything from your offspring?" Drakul asked the lamia. "Have they killed Morgan yet?"

"They find. Soon."

"Tell them to hurry. Lilith won't be pleased to find they're still alive."

"Morgan no escape."

Taylor yanked on the coil. It gave enough that she lifted half above the mattress. She grunted with the effort, and the lamia's head rotated as if on a swivel. Drakul saw the reaction and turned to Taylor, his eyes condemning. And something else.

Is that lust? Taylor shook with a mixture of terror and disgust. But a thick goo formed on her fingers around the coil. *Blood. Use it.* She pulled her hand around in front and flung a red stream toward Drakul. Blood splattered on his shirt.

The lamia followed the river of nourishment, its eyes turning brighter. It lunged at Drakul, who couldn't retreat fast enough. She knocked him into the wall where she lapped at his torso.

Drakul pulled the knife out of its cover, but fumbled it to the floor.

Taylor twisted and clutched the coil with both hands. Two tugs did the job. She spun around and confirmed the coil had the point she needed. *This is going to work.*

The lamia had Drakul pinned, licking at the splattered blood. He cried out for it to stop, but the lamia was all in now. She clawed at his face, opening new wounds. With each new food source, she became more fanatical.

Taylor edged toward the lamia. *Do I attack it now, or wait for her to kill Drakul?* She considered only a moment, feeling a surge of adrenaline. *Kill the lamia. I can take the Cardinal bastard.*

The lamia, focused on the lure of the blood, paid her no mind. Taylor sneaked up and poised the tip of the coil to assault the beast.

The lamia stopped slurping and stood up straight.

Taylor tensed. *It knows.* She lunged at it, planting the razor edge of the coil against the lamia's esophagus.

But the lamia spun and glared at Taylor. Drakul slid down the wall, leaving a red smear.

The spin gave Taylor a better angle at the lamia's larynx and she drove in the coil, slicing above the collarbone.

The lamia squeezed Taylor's wrist. Taylor thought her bones would snap. She dropped the coil.

The gash in the lamia's throat closed until only a scratch remained. "You fail. Now I feed."

Taylor's knees buckled. *Why did I think that would work?* She dropped to her knees and lowered her head.

Drakul's knife lay directly in front of her. She retrieved it and looked up.

The lamia had settled over Drakul. His breathing was labored, but he was alive. The lamia seemed to forget about Taylor and resumed drinking.

Taylor moved quickly. She slipped the knife in front of the lamia's trachea and pulled it toward her with every ounce of strength remaining in her body and soul.

The knife cut deep, reaching resistance at the girl's spinal cord. That coincided with an overpowering feeling of remorse, and uncertainty. *Can I really kill someone?*

This is survival. It's her or me. Taylor pulled harder, but cutting through bone wasn't like slicing through flesh and muscle.

The lamia growled and turned to face Taylor. The head wobbled. Blood poured from its windpipe, but the wound was already closing. A talon ripped a hole in Taylor's cheek.

Last chance. Her or me. Taylor drove herself into the lamia, using her weight as extra leverage. The knife crashed into the lamia's spinal cord.

The lamia's eyes faded. It grasped at its throat.

With shaking hands, Taylor kept sawing, like trying to cut through a T-Bone. She gave one last violent thrust and heard the spinal cord snap. The knife embedded itself into the wall, having severed the monster's head.

The lamia dropped to the floor in a lake of blood.

Drakul stirred. "You killed it. Lilith will be pleased to mate with such a strong child. Now, help me up." He gasped for breath, fighting to stop the bleeding along his face and torso.

Taylor stood over him. "I guess you were right. My dad won't kill you." She picked up the coil at her feet and drove the bloody tip into his right eye. "But *I* will."

Everything slowed. Drakul screamed, a shriek worthy of a banishment to Hell. Blood squirted out of his eye socket, and then from his nose. Taylor froze, feeling nauseated and weak. She let up on the pressure to Drakul's eye.

Drakul gripped her wrist and ripped it away from the coil. Screaming louder with each twist, he unscrewed the coil, and his eyeball with it. He tossed them aside and glared at Taylor with one eye open, the other a crimson crater.

"You bitch. You childish whore."

Taylor dug her knee into Drakul's throat. Drakul's face turned white as he gasped for air.

Don't kill him, a voice admonished. *Your dad wouldn't want you to. Father Garcia wouldn't want you to.*

Drakul lost consciousness.

She let up. "Don't call me a child. I'm a woman, you sick bastard."

"You certainly are," came a voice from the next room.

Taylor stood and came face to face with another young woman. One with dead black eyes.

CHAPTER 68

A horde of lamias reached Morgan as rifle shot-after- shot failed to deter them. In between the booming gunshots, sounds of despair circled Morgan. Valverde yelled in Spanish, "*Sibú, sálvanos de este mal.*" Linda whimpered, "They're too many of them." Margarita cursed, "*Vete a la mierda, zorra.*" Garcia muttered, "Holy God, forgive us our sins."

Nails grasped Morgan's neck. The familiar stench of the lamia's breath sickened him. *This must be what a spider feels like trapped in a swirling toilet. Nothing to grasp while life spins out of control.*

Morgan shot into the lamia and blew its chest open. Another took its place. And another as he repeated his feeble attempt at defense. And then his next shot clicked instead of roared. *Out of ammo. That's it.*

The next lamia reached him. Morgan rammed it with the butt of the rifle, trying to beat it to death. Another took its place. And another. The ones Morgan had knocked down all got back up. *It's no use.*

A lamia pulled the rifle away from Morgan. The gunfire from his compatriots all subsided, replaced by machetes and knives. Morgan followed suit, pulling out his knife and waving it at the pack. *What's that saying? Don't bring a knife to a gunfight. Well, I brought one to a vampire fight. Clever.*

He jabbed at the nearest lamia, who easily dodged the thrust. The next thing Morgan knew, the knife was wrestled away, tossed aside, and he was surrounded by drooling monsters.

The lamia facing him put a talon under his chin. "Lilith says I kill you now."

At the mention of Lilith's name, Morgan surged with fresh resolve. He took the lamia's arm, and they wrestled for control. The lamia seemed puzzled by Morgan's strength, and its eyes dimmed slightly. Morgan screamed and used the lamia's talon against itself, jamming it into the lamia's windpipe. The lamia shrieked in a high-pitched wail, then collapsed.

The other lamias surrounding him closed the circle. Morgan braced for the next wave.

But the lamias froze, confused looks on their faces. They gripped their own throats, then fell at Morgan's feet.

What the hell? Morgan checked on Linda, who was bleeding but standing, then Garcia. Several fallen lamias at their feet. Around the circle, a pile of lamias. All lifeless. Morgan verified they were lifeless, then counted by fives. *Over a hundred. Dead. But neither decapitated nor shot to death.*

"What happened?" Linda said. "Don't get me wrong, I'm relieved. But why?" She turned to Garcia. "Did you make some kind of deal with God?"

"I prayed for our salvation, but I never imagined this. It's a miracle."

Margarita scoffed. "It is no miracle. The queen lamia must be dead. It is the only explanation."

Valverde raised his hands to the heavens. "*Alabado sea Sibú.*"

"I'll second that," Garcia said. "People ask for miracles to justify their faith. Well, I challenge anyone not to see God's hand in this." He gulped and pulled the lips back on the nearest lamia. "Their teeth are returning to normal. You think the police found the nest?"

Morgan kicked at a few, and they stayed dead. "No. Not the police. Taylor."

"How do you know?" Linda said.

"I just know. She's near. She's still fighting. Lilith doesn't have her yet. We can do this."

A light went on at a residence nearby. A shadow appeared in the window.

"I think we've attracted some unwanted attention," Morgan said. "We better move."

Margarita sheathed her machete. She motioned for Valverde to follow her.

"Where are you going?" Morgan said.

"Our work here is done," Margarita said. "We destroyed this lamia nest. Now we go home and wait for the next to arise."

Valverde stood his ground. "Our work is not done. This man's daughter is still in danger. As is the world if we allow Lilith to complete its plan."

"We are lamia killers," Margarita said. "The demon can't be killed. It is futile to try."

Morgan raced to cut off her retreat. "You listen. Taylor is still alive, and free of the demon. We *will* save her and defeat the demon once and for all."

Margarita grunted. "I hope you find your daughter and escape Lilith's clutches. But you delude yourself if you think you can defeat it. People have tried for centuries. You had it locked up in the Vatican, *Madre de dios*. What makes you think you can do better?"

"You're afraid," Morgan said, his voice rising. "You're a hypocritical coward. You talk a big game, but, in the end, you have no heart."

Margarita unsheathed her machete. "How dare you? I lost my daughter to that evil. I have spent my life trying to stop it. Never once did I put my safety ahead of the cause."

"Prove it," Morgan said. "Help me save Taylor and kill it."

"Did you not hear me?" she said. "It *can not* be killed."

"We know how to kill it," Morgan said. *Getting all the necessary pieces in place is another story.* "Now, which way?"

Margarita glanced at Valverde, who nodded to her. She sheathed the machete and sighed. "Straight, as before."

"Good." Morgan started in that direction. "Try to keep up. We don't have much time."

Linda caught up to him. "Look at you. All bad boy, talking smack to the most dangerous lady on the planet."

Morgan couldn't help but smile. "Can I tell you a secret? I was scared shitless the whole time."

Linda stopped him and wrapped her arms around his torso. "You put my well-being ahead of your own. Thank you. Can we start fresh?"

Morgan held her tight. *God, you feel good.* "I'm sorry about before. I'm such an idiot. I don't know what I would have done without you. I know I don't deserve you."

"It's okay. I forgive you, and I beg you for your forgiveness. But you have more forgiving to do if we're going to have a real shot."

"What's that?"

"You have to forgive yourself."

Morgan looked at her askance.

"For Azra. And for Michelle in Costa Rica. It wasn't you. There wasn't anything you could have done. For either of them. Until you forgive yourself, you'll never be free of doling out your own punishment. And free to love again."

Morgan closed his eyes and pictured Michelle lying on the beach, drowned. Of Azra, up against the altar, a bullet in her brain. His bullet. "It's hard."

"I know. And I also know a good person you can confide in." She waved Garcia over. "Trust your friend. He knows a little something about forgiveness. And salvation."

Garcia stepped between them and put his arms around them both. "Good to see you two back. And, Pennywise, we *will* talk. But first, let's go get Taylor. By now, Lilith can't be far away, and we have precious little time."

CHAPTER 69

Lilith's host glided into the bedroom from the living area in the basement. The girl's black eyes had a pronounced effect on the lighting. Without the lamina's red glow, Taylor was almost completely in the dark.

But Taylor could smell the approach. A rotten, sour scent, a bouquet of death.

The girl waltzed up to Taylor. "You wish to see what you'll look like?"

A subdued glow emanated from the host's eyes, and Taylor could see the decay on the girl's face. Open wounds like lighting bolts on her cheek. Cracked, bleeding lips. Her skin parched.

"This is what you'll look like." Lilith cackled.

Taylor's leg muscles involuntarily cramped. She fell to her knees.

"*My* Taylor. You put up a valiant fight. You will be a worthy mother for my offspring."

Taylor couldn't form any response. She squinted toward the demonic voice.

"Here's what will happen," Lilith said. "First, I will take my rightful possession of you. You remember what that was like, don't you?"

Taylor shivered.

"The lack of control as your body degrades. The helplessness to stop me. The terror as you realize you belong to a demon."

"Please, don't." Taylor sobbed. *Dad, where are you?*

"Then, I will impregnate you with my seed, the Antichrist. You may find that confusing, but, trust me, I can do it once my spirit is inside you."

"My Dad will stop you."

Lilith's eyes dimmed momentarily. "I've been here since time began. Better men than your father have tried. But nobody has defeated me. And nobody will."

Taylor covered her ears. *Somebody, end this horror.*

"You will give birth to the Antichrist, and he will rule. I will, of course, be at his side. You won't be so fortunate."

Lilith stepped closer.

Taylor screamed.

CHAPTER 70

The threat of dawn approached. The night sky morphed into a grayish canvas. Impressionist versions of angels and demons hovered within the clouds in the hint of daylight. Morgan recognized the onset of vertigo. The world spun. Nausea invaded. *Stay calm. Keep your head steady. It's just your imagination.*

The wind picked up, slicing through Morgan's light jacket. He stuffed his hands in his pockets, bumping two sedative syringes given to him by the Swiss Guard. *What do I do if I'm too late? What if Lilith has Taylor, and she's pregnant? Do I use these against her? Kill the fetus?* He shuddered. *Kill Taylor?*

"Stop it!" Morgan yelled at himself.

"What's wrong?" Linda asked.

He rattled his head. "Nothing." But his frustration mounted with each step. "Anybody have any ideas where the nest could have been?"

"With the lamias dead, maybe now's the time to split up," Garcia said. "Get the police involved."

"No." Morgan said. "They'll impede dealing with Lilith."

"I told you I know where the nest is," Margarita said. "We are close."

Morgan eyed her. "You said that before. Prove it."

Valverde whispered something into Margarita's ear.

She grunted. "My shaman tells me to trust you. I am not so sure. You will do anything to save your daughter. I am more committed to stopping the spread of lamias."

"Of course I'll do anything to save her," Morgan said. "Any parent would."

Margarita narrowed her eyes. "Perhaps you forget the sacrifice I made to stop the plague."

Morgan's breath hitched. "Of course I remember. You killed your own daughter. Something I was prepared to do back in Salem until Linda convinced me she had a solution."

"Are you prepared to sacrifice her once more to save the world?" Margarita said.

"No parent can answer that until they have to decide," Morgan said.

Margarita looked at Valverde, who nodded. "Fair enough. I will take you. But do not get in my way. Just like before, if I decide I must destroy your daughter, I will give you first chance to do it. But if you cannot, I will."

Margarita rushed ahead. The other four of them raced to keep up.

After reaching the outskirts of town, Margarita stopped. She sniffed. She pulled out her machete.

Morgan tried to smell what she smelled, but all he came up with was the sweet aroma of a nearby bakery.

Margarita indicated a small home with broken shutters. "The lamias were here."

"Taylor?" Morgan asked.

"I do not know."

Morgan passed her and approached the building. Single story. Yellow plaster. Red brick pathway through a yard of dust and dead grass. Tile roof. Innocuous, yet somehow ominous. "Looks deserted. You sure?"

"Positive. You cannot smell it? Feel it?"

Morgan tried again, to no avail. "I do sense *something*. Can't put my finger on it. We better get in there."

"Shouldn't we discuss our plan?" Linda asked. "What are we trying to accomplish?"

"Kill Lilith," Morgan said. "Save Taylor."

"Duh," Linda said. "But how? What if Lilith is already inside Taylor?"

Morgan pulled out the silver box. "Are we going to need this? And another rat?"

Garcia pulled rumpled sheets of paper from his pocket. "If I'm interpreting the clues correctly we're not going to trap it. We're going to *kill* the demon. So, no, you can toss that."

Morgan pitched the box into a bed of dead flowers. "I hope you know what you're doing."

"You have the sedative, right?" Garcia asked.

"Two doses," Morgan said. "We can sedate whoever Lilith is in, which will sedate Lilith."

"Good," Garcia said. "If Drakul's in the house with Lilith, we'll want to knock them both out."

"Then we better get in there," Morgan said.

Linda joined Morgan at the front door. "What if Margarita's wrong? We could barge in on an innocent family."

"I think Margarita's right," Morgan said. "The air feels heavy. Moldy, even."

Margarita made their debate meaningless. She pried her way between them and kicked open the door, splintering the wood. She crept in like a tiger on the prowl.

CHAPTER 71

Using its host's hand, Lilith clutched Taylor's neck. She gazed at the decapitated mother lamia. "You shouldn't have done that. She belonged to *me*."

"Bite me," Taylor said.

Lilith dug the girl's fingernails into Taylor's larynx, drawing blood. "Drakul was a fool. But the lamia was family." *Should I punish her? Toy with her? Or take possession and get on with the show?*

Lilith let up on Taylor when the front door came crashing down. *Morgan. Again. What do I have to do to kill that pest? And he brought his friends. Good. I can slaughter them all.*

She looked at Taylor. *I can't take her now. They will attack whichever human I'm in. I can't risk my Taylor being hurt. I'll kill them from this host.*

"Taylor, I can make your possession easy on you, or I can torment you in ways that will drive you insane. Pain like you can't imagine. Be silent while I take care of your father and his band of pathetic followers. Understand?"

Taylor didn't make eye contact.

"I'll take that as a yes. Don't disappoint me." Lilith picked up the bloody knife Taylor had used on the lamia. "You cannot save your father."

Drakul gasped and Lilith gaped at the cardinal. His breathing was labored but constant. *The old goat's alive. Interesting. Another host option for the battle.* She marooned Taylor within her bedroom prison and locked the door. Footsteps rattled the floorboards above. She poised the knife blade forward.

With the electricity off, she would be the only one able to see in the dark. She smiled.

CHAPTER 72

Morgan followed Margarita into the dark, gloomy house. An eerie wind whistled through. The stench made him gag. *Like dead bodies are piled up in here.* Out of nowhere, as if called by Lillith, flies launched toward him from every part of the room. They hovered around him. His heart skipped a beat.

His first move, turning on the lights, didn't work. *Electricity must be out.* With the early morning backlight assisting, his eyes adjusted enough through the blur of flies to see a small living area, with a kitchen straight ahead through the hall.

"Taylor," he yelled. Two flies flew his mouth. He spit them out. "It's Dad."

A muffled response from behind a door in the hallway. "Here! I'm in here!"

She's not possessed! Morgan raced toward her voice, followed by the rest of his party. "Hang on, Sweetie. I'm coming." He had his last weapon, the combat knife, poised in his hand.

"Lilith's the girl," Taylor yelled from below. Her voice quivered. "She's got a knife."

Morgan yanked the doorknob. The door creaked open, revealing nothing but pitch blackness and a fresh wave of flies. He clenched his mouth tight.

A burst of wind blew across him, almost knocking him into the dark space. His hand caught a guard rail. *Stairs.* "Taylor?" He took a hesitant step. The top stair moaned under his weight. A chill ran up his spine. "I know you're in here, Lilith. I've come for my daughter. Your lamias are dead. It's over."

The wind gusted. In the basement below, leaves rattled. Their buzzing assaulted his ears, and his nerves. A low voice cackled.

"Taylor, where are you?" Morgan called out.

"Small bedroom."

Morgan exhaled. "Okay. I'm coming down."

"Hurry, Dad. Be *careful.*"

The desperation in Taylor's voice unnerved Morgan. He took one step, his knife aimed ahead. The step creaked.

A piece of the handrail came loose. Morgan caught himself just in time. *Christ. Even the stairs are trying to kill me.*

Something flashed by at the base of the stairs. Perspiration covered his arm. Morgan re-gripped the knife.

Another stair creaked. He turned, expecting to see the girl materializing out of thin air.

But it was only Margarita, followed by Valverde. She had her machete ready.

"Jesus." Morgan said. "You scared me."

"Go," she said. "I am at your back."

Morgan envisioned her machete in his back but chased the thought away. He faced forward and took another step. *This is madness. Even if I trap the girl, Lilith can always hop into another person. Maybe me again. It'll make me do horrible things.*

He traversed two more steps. The basement floor came into fuzzy focus. *Five stairs left. Then what? I don't see the girl.*

"Pennywise," Garcia said from beyond the doorway. "Remember, we need both Cardinal Drakul and Lilith alive and sedated."

"I understand."

"Dad?" From beyond the closed door on the far end of the room. "What's happening?"

"Almost there. I love you, Taylor." He reached the dirt floor. Sweat leaked from his face. He turned in every direction, searching for the demon.

The door at the top of the stairs slammed shut. A gale blasted Valverde and Margarita, sending them crashing into Morgan. The three of them toppled onto the ground. An invisible force ripped Morgan's knife from his hand and slammed it, blade first, into the wood wall where it stuck like a dart in a cork board. Margarita's machete met the same fate.

We're defenseless. Morgan scrambled to his feet and lunged for the knife. But a blizzard of dust met him and shoved him backwards. He covered his nose and mouth with his sleeve, fighting to breathe.

Lilith's voice rattled in his mind. *Welcome to Hell, Arrogant Loser.*

Beyond the entrance to the stairs, Linda cried out. "Richard! I can't open the door!"

The door above rattled. "It's stuck!" Garcia yelled.

It's not stuck. Lilith's holding it closed. Morgan scanned the room, looking for the girl, but the debris swirling around made it impossible to see more than a few inches.

"Lilith, are you afraid to face me?" Morgan yelled.

The wind stopped as if someone flipped off the power switch.

A girl appeared from the shadows. Even in the basement's darkness, her black eyes glimmered. "Afraid? Of you? A mere mortal? Be serious."

Valverde jumped up. "Demon, I command you to abandon the girl."

But the girl laughed. "Silence, *Awá*. This does not concern you." Her demon voice shook the walls.

"All matters of *Bé* concern me," Valverde said. "My life's purpose is to protect *Sibú's* realm from you."

Linda and Garcia pounded on the door, but it held firm.

Margarita made a move for her machete. Again, Lilith had an answer. Margarita froze two steps from the wall. Her machete wiggled its way out of the wall, levitated and turned its blade toward Margarita's face, poised at eye level.

"No!" Morgan yelled. "You don't want her. You want me."

"Whatever you say." The girl's voice came low and menacing. The machete rose, still levitating, until it cleared the top of Margarita's head. It tilted to point at Morgan.

God, please spare Taylor. Don't let that monster get her again.

Before the machete could strike, the door at the top of the stairs burst open. Linda and Garcia tumbled down the steps, screaming. They landed in a heap.

"No, no, no." Morgan forgot about the machete and rushed to them. Each had a faint pulse, but both were out cold. He didn't dare move them. *They could've broken their necks or suffered internal injury.* He brushed Linda's hair back from her cut and bruised face. "Stay with me."

He glowered at Lilith. "You bitch. Always afraid to take me on. Instead, you pick on my daughter, my girl, my best friend. You're a coward."

The girl's eyes flared a shinier black. "Big words for a little man. Prepare to die."

But before Lilith could drive the machete into Morgan, Valverde stepped between them. "I will not let you hurt any more people."

"Be still," Lilith commanded. "I am gone from your irrelevant village. From you and your false gods. You've been a problem long enough."

Lilith shifted the machete like a marionette master. With a flick of her wrist the machete launched toward Valverde. "Take that, *Awá*."

Valverde took the machete in the chest. The sound of cracking bone filled the room.

Morgan's vertigo sent him spiraling in a swirling haze. He closed his eyes and tried to gain his equilibrium. That worked, and he opened them again.

Valverde lay at Morgan's feet, blood swilling. With his last words, he mouthed, "Kill it. For *Sibú*. For me."

Anger overwhelmed Morgan, and he discarded his instructions from Garcia. *Forget sedation. Kill it now. Save Taylor.* Morgan pulled the machete out of Valverde's chest with a mighty heave. His army training muscle memory kicked in. He threw it overhand at the girl, point forward. It rotated in a tight spiral and landed in the girl's chest.

The girl tried to pry out the machete, but it didn't budge. Shock replaced condescending arrogance. She collapsed. Her eyes returned to human.

Morgan raced to the girl's side. No pulse. *Where are you now?* He checked on Margarita and Linda, the most likely escape routes for Lilith. One at a time, he pried their eyes open. Neither's showed signs of the demon. His heart skipped a few beats. *No. Not Taylor.* "Taylor?" His palms wept.

"I'm here," she yelled in a loud, but human, voice. "But Drakul's waking up. He's growling."

Lilith found refuge in Drakul. I can sedate them both. "I'm almost there."

Morgan yanked the machete out of the dead girl—*I'll grieve for you later, I promise*—and hacked at the lock on the door. He broke it on his second try and the door swung open, its rusted hinges complaining.

Drakul stood in the center of the room. He held Taylor by the throat. "One more step and I crush her windpipe." Lilith's voice. His bloody eye socket glared back at Morgan. The other eye was pitch black. The revulsion from staring at that eye caused his stomach to cramp.

Morgan shifted his attention to Taylor. *My God. Taylor's been in a war.* But reality sturdied him. *Lilith won't hurt Taylor. She needs her.* He reached into his pocket and flipped off the tip of a syringe.

Margarita joined Morgan at the door. She had Morgan's knife. She forced her way in and squared off against Drakul. "This is for my daughter." She lunged at Drakul, knife first.

Drakul dragged Taylor in front of him, exposing her to Margarita's attack.

"No!" Morgan yelled. "You'll kill Taylor."

Margarita flinched and stopped the knife's thrust inches from Taylor's thorax.

Drakul used his free hand to wave the knife out of Margarita's hand. He then made a fist. Margarita's eyes bugged out. She grasped at her throat. Her face turned blue.

Morgan leapt at him. He caught Drakul in the arm and injected the sedative.

Drakul screamed. He let go of Taylor and fell against the bed. He pulled the syringe out and tossed it aside. But too much had gotten in his system, and he drooped.

Morgan seized Taylor and pulled her away from Drakul. A swift kick to Drakul's stomach toppled him onto the floor.

He turned to Taylor. "You okay?" he whispered.

She hugged him hard. "I knew you'd come."

"We need to get you out of here. Far away from the demon before it wakes up. Let me make sure he's out and we'll go."

Morgan checked on Drakul. His one eye was open, and still black. The sedative had done its job. *And I've got them both in the same body. Step one of destroying the demon. For good.*

Garcia entered, holding his head. "Holy Mother of God. Did you?"

"Capture Lilith?" Morgan said. "Yes. It's in Drakul and sedated. We should have a few hours. Is Linda okay?"

"She's unconscious, but breathing." Garcia hugged Taylor. "Nice to have you back."

"Grateful to be back. Can we go now?"

"In a sec." Garcia checked Margarita's pulse. "She's alive. But Valverde didn't make it."

"I know. He saved my life." Morgan took Taylor back into his arms. "And saved Taylor." Morgan stared at Drakul. "Valverde dedicated his life to fighting this wicked beast."

Garcia scratched the top of his head. "We need to take Drakul back to the Vatican. Before Lilith wakes up and moves to someone else." He paused. "Then we have to convince Cardinal Vitelli I'm not insane."

CHAPTER 73

Vatican City State

Morgan pulled the van through a private gate in the Vatican wall shortly after 8a.m.. They parked on a private road near St. Peter's Cathedral. The crisp morning air was conflicted with the smell of pastries from nearby bakeries and sausages from street vendors outside the Vatican.

Off to the side of the road, Vitelli sat on a stool, accompanied by two Swiss Guards. With a surprise.

Taylor saw him first. "Riki!"

"Hang on," Morgan said. He stopped the van and checked Riki out. His blue checkered hospital gown hung below his overcoat. He was also seated on a stool. With a wide grin.

Taylor ignored Morgan and raced to Riki. "Dad told me what happened. When did you get back?"

"Less than an hour ago." He hugged her gently, with a hint of a wince at the effort and contact. "They could not keep me away. I am an expert at healing."

Taylor laughed. Morgan caught up with them and shook Riki's hand. "Good to see you up and around. We missed you."

Riki turned red. "My uncle told me what happened after they hospitalized me. I owe you my life."

"You owe me nothing. I put you in serious danger, time and again."

Swiss Guards confiscated all of their weapons. Medics took Linda and Margarita from the van. Both were conscious, but groggy and disoriented. They were placed on gurneys.

Morgan settled next to Linda. "You okay?"

"I'm fine."

"The medics will take you, Margarita, and Taylor to the infirmary. Javi and I will go with the Cardinal and vanquish the demon."

Taylor overheard. "Like hell. I'm going with you."

Morgan balked. "We need to keep you away from Lilith."

"Bullshit. My being in the infirmary won't protect me if you don't destroy it. It will always find me, no matter where I try to hide." Taylor stamped her foot on the cobblestones. "I'm going with you."

"But?"

Linda took Morgan's hand. "She's right. The only way to protect her is to kill it. Besides, we all need to see this. We've earned being there."

Morgan agreed and kissed her. Even after all she'd been through she smelled like orchids. "Okay. We'll do it your way." He frowned at his daughter. "And, young lady, watch your language. We're in the Vatican, for Christ's, um, goodness' sake."

Morgan shifted to Margarita's side. "I suspect you have a concussion. You probably should get it checked."

"Please take me in with you. I need to see this through, like your daughter."

Morgan nodded. "Would you have really killed my daughter back there?"

"You know the answer to that."

"Right. Okay. You can witness it."

Valverde's body was taken off next. Then, the dead girl.

"He gave his life to save ours," Morgan whispered to Vitelli. "Like so many other heroes. Please see he is recognized appropriately. He's a saint."

"Well," Vitelli said, "we have a different interpretation for the word 'saint,' but I promise he'll be treated with honor and respect."

"Fair enough," Morgan said. "The girl was possessed. I trust God won't hold that against her."

"Of course not. We'll contact her family."

Garcia climbed off. He walked gingerly to Vitelli and kissed the cardinal's ring. "Your Eminence. Thank you for believing me about this. Were you able to get the materials I asked for?"

Vitelli motioned toward the Sistine Chapel. "They are inside, laid out on the Altar as you described. I must confess, as compelling as your argument is, I am still saddened that we will ruin one of the holiest landmarks on earth."

Garcia bowed. "I share your remorse. But, as I explained on the way here, it's necessary to destroy the demon."

"There will be other demons," Vitelli said. "But there is only one Sistine Chapel."

Morgan stepped in. "But there's only one demon who wants to create the Antichrist."

"The Antichrist is a certainty," Vitelli said.

"Of course," Garcia said. "But that should happen on God's timetable, not the demon's."

"I pray you are right," Vitelli said. "Come. I've ordered the chapel closed for the day. But there are people in Vatican City State who outrank me. If they find out what we're up to, they will try to stop us. Not because they are part of Drakul's cabal. But because what we propose is unheard of, and will be met with much skepticism."

"Thank you for putting your trust in me," Garcia said.

"If this fails, you and I will have much to answer for. Both our lives in the Church will be over. Where is Cardinal Drakul?"

Morgan motioned for them to move the sedated Drakul from the van to an empty gurney. He fought the urge to kill him on the spot. *Sick bastard. You don't deserve any mercy. But I need you alive.*

"Even a split second of consciousness could be fatal to us. We must hurry."

Vitelli led the way to the Sistine Chapel, shuffling along at an old man's pace. "Father Garcia explained we don't dare risk overloading Cardinal Drakul's system with sedatives and stopping his heart. We need him alive, hosting Lilith, when he burns."

Morgan pushed Linda's gurney. Garcia pushed Margarita's. Morgan wanted to rush the Cardinal along, but knew better. The Swiss Guard never left Vitelli's side, staring straight ahead and slowing their gait to match his.

"If this works," Vitelli said to Garcia. "you will be famous. No one since Christ has destroyed a demon."

"It was really Father Sebastian and his descendants who found the lost or removed Biblical passages," Garcia said.

Vitelli bristled. "Removed? What are you implying?"

Garcia blanched. "Nothing sinister, or intentional, Your Eminence. But you know the translation of those ancient languages can be fraught with challenges, either because the languages don't have equivalent words, or multiple meanings in the original language, or our own inexperience with them. Even the best translations can miss something."

"I assure you our Vatican scholars miss nothing," Vitelli said.

Morgan tensed. *He's pissed. Calm him down, Javi. We need him.*

"Of course, Your Eminence," Garcia said. "But I wonder if any of them have been trying to solve the problem we're facing. Without that context, anybody would miss the subtle meaning."

"Perhaps. Or, perhaps you are mistaken. Perhaps the demon itself has put this thought in your head, and you are helping it execute its plan." Vitelli turned to Garcia. "Have you considered that possibility?"

Morgan gulped. *Don't lose your nerve now, Cardinal. This is our last hope.*

"I pray that is not the case." Garcia bowed. "God provides when we need it most. He is leading us to the solution, in response to Drakul's evil intentions."

"You shall refer to him as Cardinal Drakul," Vitelli said. "He has earned that despite his errant actions."

Garcia bowed. "My apologies, Your Eminence."

Morgan's stomach lurched. *Is he not convinced Drakul did it? What if he changes his mind?*

They completed their trek through the private museums brimming with priceless sculptures, paintings, and artifacts, and reached the entrance to the Sistine Chapel. A dozen Swiss Guards stood at attention around the entrance. Morgan expected to find at least that many inside.

The acting Commandant met them at the entrance. "Your Eminence, I must protest. These materials are not appropriate for the Chapel's delicate environment."

Morgan suppressed a laugh. *Wait 'til you see what we plan to do with them. You'll throw us all in the looney bin. Or the catacombs.*

"I understand and respect your concern, Commandant," Vitelli said. "But this is important Church business, authorized by the Pope, to be performed in his personal sanctuary."

Morgan looked at Garcia, who turned white. *I bet he's never heard a cardinal lie like that.*

"As you know," the Commandant said, "His Holiness is not available to confirm your statement. I find the timing troubling." He glared at Morgan. "And bringing a man suspected of killing my predecessor?"

"You know Dr. Morgan has been exonerated." Vitelli stepped forward to challenge the Commandant. "I want all Swiss Guards removed from the chapel. Even the ones upstairs and in the basement."

The Commandant gave Vitelli a confused expression. "That's highly irregular."

"Much like the conclave," Vitelli said, "we require absolute privacy. Your guards will stand watch at the entrance. Make sure we are not disturbed."

"Can we keep a firearm?" Morgan asked the Cardinal.

"No." With that, Vitelli led his entourage past the guards and into the Sistine Chapel. The Swiss Guards stationed inside followed orders and departed.

Morgan gaped at the ceiling. Biblical scenes from end to end, floor to ceiling. The ceiling itself, a mirage of indescribable beauty with its restored paint, because of the painstaking protections - no photography, no talking, no smoking - provided by the Swiss Guards. *The most famous paintings on the planet.* He shivered. *And we're about to ruin them. It's unbearable.*

On the far end of the rectangular building was the altar. Bags of sulfur and cans of gasoline were in the corner under a painting of "The Brazen Serpent," positioned next to "The Last Judgment."

"I smell rotten eggs," Taylor said. "Gross."

"Powdered sulfur," Riki said. "Straight from the ancient mines in Sicily from the Sicilian Gold Rush. Powdered sulfur doesn't give off much of an odor, but in a contained space like this, it adds up."

"I read about those mines in school," Taylor said. "Described as the nearest thing to Hell on Earth. Isn't sulfur poisonous?"

"Burning it creates hydrogen sulfide," Linda said, her voice a shadow of itself. "That's toxic and gives off a much stronger odor. And flammable. The gas will explode when it gets hot. We can't be anywhere near it after we light the fire."

"We'll be long gone," Morgan said. *Don't ask me the logistics about that. I have no clue how to both light the gasoline and get away. I may have to stay back.* He shivered. "Let's move Drakul onto the Altar and douse him." He and Garcia moved Drakul's gurney up the Altar steps and placed him over the gasoline and sulfur.

"Hold on," Vitelli said.

Morgan turned on Vitelli. "There's no time."

The cardinal grimaced. "Cardinal Drakul may have sinned, but does he deserve to be burned alive?"

"We have to do it *now*, before Lilith wakes up." Morgan ripped open a bag of sulfur and the stench increased. He dumped the yellow powder over Drakul's body. "Javi, open the gas cans."

The smell of gasoline merged with the sulfur to create a toxic cocktail. Morgan motioned for Garcia to back away. Morgan stayed put, directly at Drakul's body. He poured gasoline over the possessed cardinal, inadvertently splashing himself.

A horrific thought blasted Morgan. *I don't have a way to ignite this.* Morgan panicked. "Does anyone have a light?"

A common look of anxiety struck them all.

Lilith's voice broke through in Morgan's mind. *Too bad Vitelli slowed you down. It would have worked.*

Morgan gasped as Drakul sat up. His vertigo returned. He fought through it and reached for the second syringe in his pocket.

Too late, Lilith admonished.

CHAPTER 74

Lilith forced Drakul's remaining eye to open as his body sat upright on the gurney. The gasoline burned it, but she didn't mind. Her use of his body was almost done.

But she knew time was critical. The sedative would limit her, and her powers, until it wore off.

And the sulfur burned. Not on Drakul's skin, but in her soul. *Sulfur dangerous. Must get out of this body.*

Confident resolve replaced temporary panic. *I am Lilith. I am all powerful. I will kill them all.*

She focused on Morgan. *He's reaching for the sedative. Can't let him do that.* She sent him a private message, hoping to distract him. *If you make any move toward me, I will go directly into Taylor. Never to leave. We both know once I'm in there, you'll never get me out. And you won't have the nerve to torch her like you do the cardinal.*

Morgan met her gaze and froze. His face turned sheet white. His hand retreated from the pocket, empty.

That's right. If you follow my instructions, I will spare Taylor any pain. I won't kill her when I'm done with her. I'll turn her, and she'll live forever, ruling at my side.

Lilith laughed, thinking, *Actually, I'll torture and kill her, after I do the same to you.*

Lilith tested her ability to swap hosts. But the sedative still had too much influence. *Just another minute. Then I'm back to full strength, and they can't hurt me.*

CHAPTER 75

After releasing the syringe Morgan dropped the gas can and lunged for Drakul, but Drakul grasped Morgan's wrist. His unnaturally strong grip stymied Morgan.

This time, Lilith spoke out loud. "I warned you what would happen if you defied me."

The sulfur-gasoline combination burned Morgan's eyes. Drakul held his arm tight. He glanced at Taylor, half-expecting to see her eyes turning black. But her natural browns blinked at him from a terrified face. *Thank God she's not possessed yet. But the fumes! Lilith might not have to finish us off. The chemicals might do the job.*

Morgan sensed something else. Gasoline had leaked onto the floor. His feet were soaked. He imagined a horrifying death, with no recourse.

With his free hand, Drakul formed a claw in Taylor's direction.

Taylor's eyes bugged out.

"No!" Morgan tried to pry himself loose, but Drakul's demon-enhanced grip may as well have been a vise.

* * *

Taylor's voice collapsed on itself. *Help me, Dad!*

"Taylor!" Riki screamed. "Your face. What's happening?"

"Can't breathe," she choked.

Riki stepped between Drakul and Taylor. "Leave her alone!"

Taylor felt immediate relief. *It must need line-of-sight to attack.* But Riki grabbed his own neck and fell to his knees.

* * *

Garcia didn't know whom to save. He split the difference and lunged for Drakul.

* * *

Lilith cursed. *Too many of them.* She tried to jump into Taylor, but the sedative still constrained her.

Forget the boy. Forget Father Chancho. Kill the Arrogant Loser, and they'll all lose their will to fight.

She repositioned her claw at Morgan.

* * *

Morgan's windpipe collapsed. He gagged.

What are you doing, Arrogant Loser? Lilith's voice pounded in his head. *Do you want Taylor to die a horrible death?*

Morgan glanced toward Taylor, who had fallen to her knees. *She's okay. Kill Drakul.* Morgan turned and met the hostile glare of Drakul's black eyes. "We're saving that for you," he choked. "Night Hag."

Drakul's face turned crimson and the cardinal eased his grip.

With the moment of lapsed concentration on Lilith's part Morgan removed the syringe from his pocket with his free hand. It slipped in his slick fingers, but he caught it before it crashed to the floor. He tossed it toward the advancing Garcia.

* * *

Garcia caught the syringe inches from the ground. He would need only two long strides to reach Drakul. *Say goodnight, demon.* But he stumbled and fumbled the syringe. It fell, but didn't shatter. He dropped to his knees to retrieve it and removed the protective cap.

The Night Hag

* * *

Lilith had no choice but to divert her attention to Father Chancho. She launched an offensive at the priests's mind, sending him images of his failed exorcism and the subsequent death of his parishioner.

Father Chancho lunged toward Lilith, but Lilith's assault worked. Father Chancho stopped in his tracks, then stumbled back, holding his head.

Inject yourself! Lilith commanded.

Father Chancho placed the syringe against his own temple, a certain kill shot.

* * *

Morgan watched Javi place the syringe against the side of his head. "Javi, no!"

But Garcia's glazed expression told Morgan his friend was no longer in control.

Morgan still had one hand free and desperately looked for a way to strike at Drakul.

The sulfur. If it can contain the demons in Hell, it can stop Lilith. He scooped up a load of the yellow powder and threw it in Drakul's face. "Take that, Night Hag."

Drakul shrieked in a pre-pubescent girl's pitch. The grip on Morgan crushed his wrist. Morgan wilted at the excruciating pain and piercing sound.

The ground erupted, a good magnitude seven quake. The six windows on each side the chapel exploded, sending broken glass far and wide. Morgan shut his eyes and braced for the next salvo from Lilith.

But, instead of a renewed assault, the room calmed. The throbbing in Morgan's wrist sent shockwaves all the way up to his head. He squinted to see what was happening.

Drakul dug at his own eyes, trying to remove the caustic sulfur substance.

"Now, Javi!"

Garcia stepped up and injected the sedative into Drakul's neck.

Drakul's black eyes glazed over. Disbelief etched his face. "You will pay," Lilith mumbled, but the eyes gave her plight away. The sedative had taken control, and it would immobilize Drakul for at least a few minutes.

Morgan drooped against the gurney. "We did it. But we have to hurry. We can't risk Lilith waking up again."

"You did it," Garcia gasped.

Morgan turned to Taylor, still on her knees. "You okay?"

In between rapid-fire breaths, she managed, "I'm good. Finish it."

Morgan tested his wrist. "Javi, Lilith broke my wrist. I need you to start the fire."

"Richard, what about the gasoline and sulfur? You promised we'd be long gone."

"Yeah. I may have exaggerated. Take everyone back to the Entrance Wall. I'll stay and light it. I have to verify we destroyed Lilith."

Taylor ran up to Morgan. "Dad, no. It's too dangerous. The hydrogen sulfide will kill you."

Vitelli cleared his throat. "We have flares. You could toss one from the far end of the chapel."

"That should give me some protection, anyway," Morgan said.

Garcia escorted a shuffling Vitelli to the Entrance Wall on the far end of the Chapel. Taylor and Riki wheeled Linda and Margarita. Morgan limped along, reaching the midpoint before stopping to catch his breath and process the pain. *Hang in there. Just a few more minutes.* But he wondered if the pain would overrun him, and he'd be useless to finish the job.

"What about the Swiss Guard?" Linda asked. "They had to hear that."

As if on cue, there came a pounding on the door. "Cardinal Vitelli!" The Commandant's voice. "There was an earthquake. We heard glass shattering. Are you injured?"

"I'm fine." The Cardinal struggled to speak. "I need flares!"

"Flares?"

"Quickly."

Riki ran up to Morgan. "I will throw the flares. I am an expert at throwing. Two hand sideline tosses for football, mostly, but how hard can it be?"

"No. I have to be the one. To verify Lilith's been destroyed." Morgan looked at the broken windows. "The fumes can escape up there. I should be fine."

"How will you know Lilith's destroyed?" Linda asked.

Morgan looked to Garcia. "Javi? Will we know if this works?"

"Beats the hell out of me."

Riki chimed in. "It will be like the scene in *Raiders of the Lost Ark*. We will see Lilith's tormented spirit fly away."

"I hope you're right," Morgan said. "Better than a hole opening and sucking us all into Hell."

The entrance flew open and a half dozen armed Swiss Guards ran in, then froze at the sight and smell.

"What is the meaning of this?" Vitelli said. "I gave strict orders we were not to be disturbed."

The Commandant followed them in. He pointed his drawn weapon at Morgan's heart halfway across the Chapel. "I reached His Holiness. Cardinal, you lied about having permission to be here." He looked closer at Drakul. "My God. What have you done to Cardinal Drakul?"

Morgan swallowed. "Cardinal Drakul is gone. All that remains is a demon. The only way to destroy it is to light him on fire."

The Commandant raised his voice. "You make one move and my men will shoot. And, trust me, we don't miss."

Morgan put his operating hand up. "Look. I know how crazy this sounds. But trust Cardinal Vitelli."

Near the entrance, a Swiss Guard got too close to Margarita, and she launched herself upon onto him. She wrangled the pistol from the surprised guard. "Get back!" she screamed.

Margarita fired at Drakul's gurney. The bullet struck metal, creating a spark. The gasoline ignited, then exploded.

Morgan, closest to the chapel's center, took the brunt of the blast. It blew him to the Entrance Wall. The gasoline on his pants ignited. He screamed as the flames spread.

Garcia ripped a blanket off Margarita's gurney and dove on Morgan, smothering his legs. Two rolls abated the flames, and guards with fire extinguishers put out the rest.

"Are you burned?" Garcia asked Morgan.

Morgan took stock. The pain in his wrist was much worse than the pain from any burning on his legs. "Medium rare. Thanks." He sat up.

Fire surrounded Drakul's body. The sulfur melted around him. The smell of rotten eggs on steroids permeated the Chapel.

Oh, shit. I should have planned for this. "Everybody out!" Morgan ordered. "The burning sulfur is making hydrogen sulfide. It'll blow when it gets too hot. You need to evacuate Vatican City."

The Commandant sized the situation and blew a whistle. "Sound the alarm. Evacuate Vatican City." He pointed his weapon at Morgan. "Do you have any idea the trouble you've caused? Closing the Sistine Chapel. Evacuating Vatican City. Thousands of tourists disrupted. You're coming with me."

"I can't leave until I verify the demon's destroyed," Morgan said. He stood. "But you should leave."

A shrill alarm blasted across the Vatican. The Swiss Guards escorted everyone else outside. Smoke built up quickly, choking Morgan. *The ventilation can't handle the flow. We'll die if we don't get out now.*

Engulfed in flames, Drakul sat up. His eyes opened, but they weren't human. *Jesus. They're serpent eyes.* Drakul's melting face contorted in inhuman ways. From the flames, like a Phoenix, a serpent rose, writhing in pain.

The brazen serpent in the painting behind the body glowed, then caught fire. In *The Last Judgment*, Minos, in the group of the damned, also caught fire. His painted figure came to life and screamed.

"Mother Mary, what is this?" the Commandant said.

And then Drakul's screaming began. In Latin.

"He's alive," cried the Commandant. "We have to save him."

"No!" Morgan yelled. "It's not Drakul. It's a demon. And that gas will explode any second. You need to go now!"

Before the Commandant could move, Drakul called out to Morgan in a booming voice. "Arrogant Loser. You have not won. I am Lilith, and I am immortal." Drakul leaped off the gurney, still ablaze. The serpent swung above Drakul's body, attached to him at the back of his neck.

Jesus. Won't Lilith ever stop? Morgan's heart pounded, and blood rushed to his head.

Drakul took one step toward Morgan, then another. With each breath fire spouted from the serpent's mouth.

But the approach wavered. The flames rose higher, and Drakul's screams grew louder. The serpent toppled backwards into the pool of molten sulfur on the gurney. The flames turned red, then black. Milos and the brazen serpent vanished from the paintings as the serpent vaporized.

Morgan pulled on the Commandant with his good arm, ignoring the crushing pain in his wrist. "It's done. Let's go."

They scrambled out and closed the door, running as fast and as far from the Sistine Chapel as Morgan's limp could muster. They didn't stop until they reached St. Peter's Square. Thousands were being evacuated. Morgan knew they'd escaped just in time. He alternated between sucking in fresh air and coughing up bile.

Yellow smoke escaped from the Sistine Chapel chimney. "I bet that'll confuse the tourists," Morgan said to the Commandant.

The Commandant stared at the chapel. "My God. What have you done?"

The captured gas reached its flashpoint, and the Sistine Chapel rumbled. Fire and molten sulfur exploded from the windows. The sky turned yellow, and the stench magnified to intolerable.

But the building held, and Morgan was alive.

Taylor ran up to him, Riki at her heels.

He hugged her, ignoring the pain. "Thank God you're safe."

"You did it, Dad. You did the impossible."

"Javi made it possible." Morgan collapsed onto his knees. *I can't believe it's over. We killed a demon.*

Garcia and Linda joined them. They formed a circle on their knees. Nobody spoke. Morgan and Taylor held each other and cried while Garcia said prayers of gratitude to God.

CHAPTER 76

Morgan gulped from a bottle of water in the Vatican infirmary. His leg burns had been salved and bandaged, and his wrist immobilized. Taylor and Linda sat in the examination room with him. The others were next door. Vitelli and the Commandant joined them.

"The evacuation did its job," the Commandant said. "Just a few scrapes and bruises. Nothing remains of Drakul's body. And the Chapel will be in for another long restoration."

"Drakul can rot in Hell," Morgan said. He blushed. "I *am* truly sorry about the Chapel, though."

"If it were my decision I'd lock you up," the Commandant said. "But Cardinal Vitelli convinced the Pope to forgive you."

Catholic forgiveness comes in handy sometimes. I didn't even have to go to confession. "Thanks. I never meant to cause so much disruption."

"The structure was mostly unharmed," Vitelli said. "When we reopen, no one will know what went on in there. Just like the restoration of 1980. That one lasted fifteen years. We hope to do as well this time."

"How will you explain it?" Linda asked.

The Commandant chuckled. "The press is always here, so the explosion is already worldwide news. We told them we had a gas leak."

"And the yellow smoke?" Morgan asked.

This time Vitelli laughed. "A warning from God to alert us and save everyone. It will add to the legend of the place."

"I swear you and your cohorts to secrecy," the Commandant said. "If any word ever gets out about Cardinal Drakul, the demon, well, we know where to find you. You'd rather face the demon than an angry Vatican."

"Don't worry," Morgan said. "I'm curious. What did the Pope say about losing his private chapel?"

"His Holiness found it a good tradeoff," Vitelli said. "Destroying a demon, especially Lilith."

"Are we sure the demon is dead?" Taylor asked.

Morgan hugged her again. "I saw it die, honey. It's over."

Vitelli exhaled. "We have no way to verify. Except by faith." He took Taylor's hand. "I believe Father Garcia found the clues God left for him. I truly believe you destroyed the demon." He turned to Morgan. "The world is in your debt."

"I'll settle for a normal life for my daughter."

"Amen to that," Vitelli said.

* * *

Two uneventful days of convalescence passed in the infirmary. No demons. No vampires. No threats.

For Morgan, the only stress besides the constant wrist pain was watching Taylor and Riki dote over each other. *We go to the airport in fifteen minutes. She'll be sad to leave him.* He shook his head. *When did she grow up and become a young lady, anyway?*

Possessed. Almost turned into a vampire. Kidnapped. Threatened with the most unimaginable horrors. I guess that will cause anyone to grow up, or they won't survive.

* * *

Linda approached Morgan on the fringe of St. Peter's Square. "You ready?"

"It'll be nice to put this behind us."

"I have a thought. We should invite Riki to come along. He's never been to the States."

Morgan looked askance at Linda. "Did Taylor put you up to that?"

"She didn't have to. Look at them. They're in love."

"She's sixteen. She knows nothing about love."

Linda pinched him. "You were sixteen once. And I bet hopelessly in love. I know I was."

"And then we grew up. Right? Learned that love isn't all it's cracked up to be."

"Maybe love at that age is *everything* it's supposed to be. No stress of being a grownup. Just pure feelings for each other."

"Regardless, he's not coming."

Linda tilted up to his ear and whispered. "I already bought his ticket. But I thought I'd let you be the one to tell them. It will mean more to Taylor than you can imagine. You'll be rock star dad. And he'll be good for her. She has a lot to forget. He can be the perfect distraction to get her equilibrium back. She can show him America - or at least Salem."

"I thought I was the shrink."

Linda poked him. "I'm learning."

Morgan laughed. "You really invited Riki without asking?'

"Well, I *am* going to be her stepmom. Aren't I?"

Morgan stopped breathing. His palms grew sweaty. He looked into her eyes and saw a world of possibilities. "Why, yes, as a matter of fact, you are."

* * *

Margarita approached Morgan on the fringe of St. Peter's Square. "It is time for me to go. I'm taking Valverde's body back to the Bribri village."

"Now that the lamia threat is gone, what will you do?"

"Help Juan on the farm. Perhaps have another daughter. Perhaps return to the Bribri village. We'll need a new *Awá* to fight *Bé's* next assault. Juan would make an excellent shaman."

"I'm so sorry about your *Awá*."

Margarita smiled. "He and his descendants valiantly fought this demon for centuries. He achieved his primary purpose. Who could ask for more?"

Morgan hugged her. She tensed at his touch. "Be safe. Thanks for all you did for us."

Margarita separated herself. "I'm glad it worked out. For you and your daughter." She paused. "I still can't quite believe it is over."

Morgan nodded. *I know the feeling.*

* * *

Garcia's last piece of business at the Vatican was to check in on Vitelli.

Vitelli brightened up at the sight of him. "Father Garcia. How good of you to come."

Garcia bowed, kneeled, and kissed the cardinal's ring. "I'm glad you're feeling better. We put you and the Church through too much."

"I am fine. And you are going home to your flock."

"I hope I'm still allowed to run my church. I'll understand if the Church doesn't deem me worthy, after all I've done."

"All you've done? You gave us new hope. A new path forward. A way to deal with demons we never knew existed."

"Let's hope it never needs to be used again," Garcia said.

"Ridding us of demons? Why wouldn't we aspire for that?"

"Because it requires a wicked Rome. I pray we never see the likes of Cardinal Drakul again."

Vitelli gave Garcia a look that disturbed the priest. "We are working always toward a purer Rome."

CHAPTER 77

Salem, Oregon - Two Weeks Later

The grandfather clock in the living room struck 3a.m.. Wind shook the windows - sure signs of another stormy day. Sleep continued to evade Morgan. Too much throbbing in his wrist. Too many terrifying memories.

He peeked in Taylor's bedroom. Taylor tossed violently in her sleep. *I wonder how long she'll have these nightmares. She says she's okay, but can anybody really forget that physical and emotional trauma?*

Their yellow lab, Bear, lay on the bed with her. *At least Bear's calm around her. He knew when she was possessed.*

Morgan inhaled, trying to shed the apprehension that continued to plague him. He distracted himself by thinking of Linda and their impending wedding. Garcia, of course, would preside. It would be a private ceremony, with Taylor as bridesmaid, and Riki, who was asleep on the couch, as best man. No one else in Morgan's life mattered to him any longer. *No one else would understand.*

He would restart his practice after the wedding. Linda would teach part time at the college. Enough to pay the bills. But a honeymoon for the two of them was out of the question. Morgan wouldn't be leaving Taylor alone for quite some time.

Amidst the wind's wolflike howl, Morgan listened for demonic sounds. He told himself he had to stop staring into Taylor's eyes. *She has to know why you're doing that. It's not helping her forget.*

Lilith's gone. You saw it perish.

Bear sat up on high alert. He stared at the window as it rattled. He growled.

"What is it, boy?"

The growling increased. Bear fired a warning bark.

Taylor groaned and turned over.

Bear growled louder. He stared at Taylor.

"Bear? What are you doing? It's *just* Taylor."

Right?

ABOUT THE AUTHOR

STEVEN G. JACKSON is a professional storyteller who writes thrillers, horror, and comedy, and has a long list of published and produced novels, short stories, and stage plays. He often combines these genres in his stories. His workshops on the craft of writing are always popular. An avid horror fan, he has a world-class collection of vampire first editions. His Yellow Lab, Bear, is a mainstay in his novels, and acts as both muse and inspiration.

ACKNOWLEDGMENTS

I am grateful to my publishing team, including critique groups Pure Fiction League (whose members were dedicated to my success from the beginning); WriteOn! (whose members helped me in the critical end-game); beta reader (and gifted writer) Annette Lahr; content and copy editor Sandy Homicz (also a gifted writer), who sees every detail and knows precisely how to fix anything that is less than perfect; and Jeniffer Thompson and her phenomenal team at Monkey C Media. Thank you.

And, as always, I am grateful for my wife, Yann, who makes my dreams come true every day.

ALSO FROM
STEVEN G. JACKSON

Novels:

The Zeus Payload
The Lamia

Short Stories:

"Full Service" - *It's All in the Story*
"Life Dies, and Then You Suck" - *It's All in the Story*
"Noma" - *Culinary Delights*
"The Asylum for Rejected Characters" - *Masquerade*

Produced Stage Plays:

"The Johnson Case" - Lincoln Elementary
School Graduation Ceremony
"The Loan Officer" - Camino Real Playhouse - ShowOff!

"The Loan Officer 2" - Camino Real Playhouse - ShowOff!

"The Asylum for Rejected Characters" -
Camino Real Playhouse - ShowOff!

"Fade to Crazy" - Camino Real Playhouse - 24 Hour Creative

"The Master Playwright" - Camino Real
Playhouse - 24 Hour Creative

"Life Dies, and Then You Suck" - Camino
Real Playhouse - 24 Hour Creative

"All I Want for Christmas is You" - Pure Fiction League

"The Optimism of Youth" - Camino Real
Playhouse - 24 Hour Creative

"Psycho Therapist" - Camino Real Playhouse - 24 Hour Creative

"The No-Goodnik, The Bad, and The Ugly" -
Camino Real Playhouse - ShowOff!

"Pharmaceuticals for Dummies" - Camino
Real Playhouse - 24 Hour Creative

COMING SOON

The Lust Gambit (coming in 2021)

For a sneak peak of these books and more, visit
www.StevenGJackson.com